ChangelingPress.com

Arkham/Along Came A Demon Duet
A Bones MC Romance
Marteeka Karland

Arkham/Along Came A Demon Duet
A Bones MC Romance
Marteeka Karland

All rights reserved.
Copyright ©2021 Marteeka Karland

ISBN: 9798706309626

Publisher:
Changeling Press LLC
315 N. Centre St.
Martinsburg, WV 25404
ChangelingPress.com

Printed in the U.S.A.

Editor: Katriena Knights
Cover Artist: Marteeka Karland

The individual stories in this anthology have been previously released in E-Book format.

No part of this publication may be reproduced or shared by any electronic or mechanical means, including but not limited to reprinting, photocopying, or digital reproduction, without prior written permission from Changeling Press LLC.

This book contains sexually explicit scenes and adult language which some may find offensive and which is not appropriate for a young audience. Changeling Press books are for sale to adults, only, as defined by the laws of the country in which you made your purchase.

Table of Contents

Arkham (Bones MC 5) 4
   Chapter One 5
   Chapter Two 16
   Chapter Three 24
   Chapter Four 37
   Chapter Five 48
   Chapter Six 60
   Chapter Seven 68
   Chapter Eight 80
Along Came A Demon (Shadow Demons 1) 95
   Chapter One 96
   Chapter Two 112
   Chapter Three 132
   Chapter Four 148
   Chapter Five 165
   Chapter Six 184
   Chapter Seven 198
   Chapter Eight 211
   Chapter Nine 228
Marteeka Karland 244
Changeling Press E-Books 245

Arkham (Bones MC 5)
Marteeka Karland

Rain -- The gangs of the underground can be brutal. I know this well and have the scars to prove it. So when a team of rough looking men start nosing around the slums of Rockwell, I make it my business to know what they're up to. One in particular catches my eye. He's rough and scary looking, but his touch is gentle when it needs to be. He's older and more experienced in every way than me, but I'm still drawn to him. I'm not sure why, but I want him. And when I let him take me, I'll savor the experience until it's time to go.

Arkham -- The little pixie warrior is a conundrum if ever there was one. She's strong and capable but scarred inside and out. I can't fix what's broken inside her, but I can share her burdens and make her part of my circle. I'll take her with me, with Bones MC. She'll be protected there.

But who's gonna protect her from me?

Chapter One

"What the fuck are we still doin' here? We cleared this sector yesterday." Arkham wasn't usually one to complain, but this micromanaging shit was for the birds.

"You pay, we come play." Torpedo was the top man in the field on this mission. He and Arkham took point as they walked down the street. They weren't in Afghanistan or Tripoli, or Ukraine. They were in a moderately sized city in the good ole U. S. of A. called Rockwell. ExFil had been hired by a group of disgustingly rich hero wannabes to help locate a runaway. Kid had been missing for three days, and his mother, who was a member of the staff of said disgustingly rich hero wannabes, was more than frantic. They insisted the child was in this area of the city. How they knew that he didn't know, but orders were orders.

"How the fuck do these guys know that kid's in this part of town?" Goose had been vocal about his protests from the get-go. All of it because of the micromanaging. "We've searched high and low. The kid ain't here."

"It's not like we've got anything else to do. We're gettin' paid by the hour. They want us to look here, we look here." Shadow was the newest patched member of Bones and probably the most levelheaded and calm person Arkham knew. "We just flex some muscle if we see anything suspicious and be ready to bean someone if they need it."

"Yeah. Way wide latitude," Arkham grumbled. "I don't like this."

"Cain knows these guys personally," Torpedo said. "If he says go, we go. We follow orders."

"Ain't never been good at following orders." The back of Arkham's neck was tingling like a son of a bitch. Never a good sign. "'Specially not from no pretty-boy, badass wannabe."

"My understanding," Torpedo explained, "is that these guys are the real deal. Seems Cain served briefly with Azriel Ivanovich. He's part owner of Argent Tech."

"The company that makes all those pretty gadgets Data is always forcing us to use? I hate the bastard already." Arkham wasn't opposed to technology per se, he just hated being forced into it. "Most of that shit is just used to dumb down the real work. I mean, I can fuckin' shoot straight and follow a compass. And I don't need a fuckin' leash shoved up my ass in the form of one of those fancy GPS things he hardwired into our radios and phones. Hell, even our fuckin' bikes are tracked. Where's the end?"

"You'll have to take that up with Data and Cain." Torpedo shrugged, his body posture letting Arkham know Torpedo was just as vigilant as he was, even while carrying on the conversation. "I just make sure you use it."

"Next thing you know he'll be wantin' to tag us with some kind of chip under our skin."

"It's already being discussed."

Arkham stopped dead in his tracks. "I will bust a motherfucker up."

Torpedo looked over his shoulder, grinning. "Gotcha."

Everyone laughed.

"Motherfucker."

Though he continued the disgruntled conversation, Arkham was only half paying attention to his brothers. Their actual mission was extremely vague. All they seemed to do was patrol the poorest section of the city and give people mean looks. They'd questioned every single person they saw, but no one had seen the boy. Arkham had no idea if he believed any of them or not.

The streets were mostly dark at night. Though the streetlights were replaced almost daily, by the end of the day they'd all be broken out again. Drug deals routinely went down in rundown buildings in the process of being renovated, though the team from ExFil had stopped some of it during their search. Drug sales continued regardless. Arkham thought Bones more suited to this than ExFil, but their employer had insisted on the paramilitary version. While Bones was the rough and ready MC, ExFil was the more disciplined and civilian accepted military-like organization run by Cain. This city needed the military, not the outlaws. Conditions had seemed to improve somewhat, but there was still a long way to go. Oh, well. Not his turf. Not his problem.

"How the fuck did a place like Argent Tech end up in this shit hole? It's no bigger than Somerset and has way less to offer. Not to mention at least a third of the city is nothing more than slums. These people certainly don't benefit from the tech giant." Shadow had that part right.

"I agree, brother," Arkham said. "Not sure what our goal here is, but it seems like more of a policing effort than searching for a missing kid. I'm ready to tell 'em all to shove it up their ass."

"The point is for us to give Ivanovich and his associates the help they need in locatin' a missin' child. And they *are* tryin' to better the place."

"You're just trying to defend Cain's decision to take this job, Torpedo," Arkham groused. "You don't like it any more than we do. If they'd let us do this our way, we might have found the kid already. *That's* what's pissin' me off."

"Ain't sayin' you're right. Ain't sayin' you're wrong. But if you don't shut the fuck up about it, I will turn Suzie on your ass so quick it will make your head spin. Stunner might have let her use most of the red and green glitter on him, but I know where there's a whole fuckin' tub of pink glitter, and I'll point her in the right direction."

That got a laugh from everyone. Even Arkham snorted. "Harsh, brother," he grumbled.

They passed the next hour in silence. Still, that tingle between Arkham's shoulder blades persisted. They were being watched. Had been since they'd gotten off the Goddamned plane. "When I find that son of a bitch, Imma throw him a beatin'."

"What the fuck are you talkin' about?" Goose had turned and was facing away from them now, guarding their six as they slowed their trek down the sidewalk.

"Someone's been watchin' us since the second we got off the fuckin' plane." Arkham tried to watch his area, but he knew the threat was from above. Now that he'd mentioned it, he gave up all pretense of pretending not to be actively seeking their stalker. He raised his gun to the rooftops, putting his infrared goggles in place. Everyone followed his lead.

"I thought I was just being paranoid," Goose muttered.

"No." Arkham had learned long ago to listen when that sensation was trying to tell him something.

Just as they rounded the corner, Arkham spotted him. "Got the bastard," he muttered. "Two o'clock, theater roof. He's got a rifle scope, but I can't confirm a weapon."

"Copy that," Torpedo said. "Shadow, you and Arkham fall back. See if you can go up the back way and get him from behind. We'll patrol the alley to the west. If he follows us, should be easy pickin's for you guys."

"Radios on," Arkham ordered. "I'm not losing anyone to a rookie mistake."

"Got it," Shadow and Goose confirmed on top of each other.

"Up the east side. And don't kill him unless he deserves it."

"He already deserves it for giving me a headache, "Arkham said, readying his rifle. "Bastard has it coming." Torpedo didn't argue. Arkham was a hard ass, but he wouldn't make a kill unless it was warranted. They all knew it and didn't insult him by suggesting otherwise.

Shadow was the best partner he could have for a situation like this. The man's special talent was disappearing into the shadows. Hence his name. Arkham was good, but he let Shadow take the lead on this one. If Arkham was spotted, Shadow would already be in position to defend him. It hurt to admit the big man was better than Arkham at anything, but truth hurts sometimes. Only meant Arkham would be working on that particular skill set even harder.

It took them seven minutes to gain the roof and another one to lay eyes on the target. He was slender, small. A boy? Arkham stayed put for several minutes. Shadow followed his lead, not breaking cover before Arkham gave the word.

The kid followed the perimeter of the roof, never taking his eyes from the team below. If he knew they were light two men, the kid didn't seem overly concerned. He stopped right next to Arkham. He could have reached out and touched the boy. Two more steps, and he'd run into Arkham. Instead, he stopped, never taking his eye from the scope.

"You're all clear," the kid said. "They've made a circle around the theater. All four of them. If you're going to take them, now's the time."

Three things registered for Arkham. First, his team was about to be ambushed by an unknown number of hostiles. Second, the kid wasn't a boy. It was a girl. Third, she was deliberately deceiving whomever she was talking to.

The second she put the radio down, Arkham and Shadow sprang at her. She got off a little squeak before Arkham's hand covered her mouth tightly, preventing further sound from escaping while Shadow zip-tied her hands behind her back. She struggled against him, trying to twist out of his grasp, but the little thing wasn't more than five foot two and might have weighed ninety pounds. She didn't stand a chance against his superior strength, but it didn't stop her from trying.

Just when he thought he had her, she kicked out hard, catching him inside his knee. He grunted, pain exploding through his leg. Arkham fell, landing on his other knee, which did little to improve his mood, or his pain. The little witch turned to sprint away, but he snagged her by the ankle, tripping her. She went down hard. With her hands behind her back, she face-planted, unable to break her fall. Arkham couldn't help but wince. He didn't like being the cause of a woman getting hurt even if it was necessary from time to time.

"You're about to have company, Torpedo," Arkham bit out, his throat mic automatically activating. "Heads up. Shadow's got you covered from up here."

"Do you know what we've got coming?"

Arkham sat up, pulling her to him by her upper arms. He locked gazes with the girl. Wide, frightened eyes met his, her youthful features now marred with scrapes along one cheek. For some reason, her fear tugged at him as much as the abrasions on her face. He'd never cared what people thought about him or if he hurt someone he thought needed it. He was as hard as they came. But looking into this girl's eyes was like looking into the eyes of a frightened child. A child who had seen too much and expected the worst from him. He didn't want her to see him that way, but now wasn't the time to rectify the situation. "You better tell me straight on this, kid. What's coming?"

"Five guys with guns." Her answer was instant, no hesitation.

"Street thugs?"

"Yeah. All but one. He always lets the other four go in first. Says he's ex-military."

"Look for at least five armed hostiles. Unknown level of experience."

She tried to say more, but Arkham gagged her with a scarf. The girl didn't struggle any more, but crouched under the lip of the wall surrounding the roof, as if trying to hide, her knees pulled in to her chest.

Arkham positioned himself to the north of his team while Shadow was at the south. "We're at the ready, Torpedo. Holding fire until you give the word."

"We'll try the beanbags first," Torpedo informed them. "If that doesn't work, we'll be countin' on you and Shadow to pick them off from up there." There was a pause, and Torpedo added, "Don't shoot us."

"Well, now, that depends on whether or not you make an attempt to get us out of this shit duty." Arkham knew he'd get the last word in if he was patient enough.

"Bastard," Torpedo muttered. Apparently, Torpedo had been waiting for it, too.

Seconds later, four men came charging down the street. Shots rang out in the night, followed by the *thump thump* of the beanbags being deployed. Two of the four dropped, screaming in pain. One of the remaining two backed off, but the fourth still charged, firing off several rounds. Another *thump* sounded, and he dropped with his companions, one of whom was scurrying backward. Before another beanbag hit him in the shoulder hard enough to knock him flat.

Then, just like the girl said, the fifth hostile came around the corner. His shots were more accurate, but Torpedo and Goose took cover behind a car. Windows exploded, sending glass raining down on them, but neither broke cover until the shots stopped. Both men took aim from different sides of the car. Two *thunks* sounded nearly on top of each other, and the fifth guy hit the ground, his gun skidding across the pavement.

"Clean it up," Torpedo said. "Package them for transport."

"On it, Top," Goose acknowledged.

"I'll make sure Arkham has the girl secure up here, then join you," Shadow said. "He had a little trouble." The man gave Arkham a wink before asking, "You got this?"

"Just get the fuck out."

Shadow chuckled then took the fire escape down to the street.

Arkham waited a few heartbeats. He needed to study the girl, get a feel for what she was about. She just crouched by the wall, her knees to her chest, looking at him with an unblinking stare.

"You gonna scream if I take that off?" She hesitated a moment then sighed and shook her head. Arkham removed the gag slowly, expecting she'd give a shrill shriek at any moment. She didn't. She looked up at him from under her lashes, peeking up quickly before lowering her eyes back to the ground. "What's your name, girl?" When she didn't answer, he crouched down before her. "When I ask you a question, I expect an answer immediately. Now, what's your fuckin' name?" He wasn't in the habit of giving an order twice. No matter how much he disliked her fear, he wouldn't let it sway him. This girl had information he needed. It was best to let her know what was expected of her sooner rather than later.

"Rain," she mumbled.

"Rain what?"

She shrugged. "Just Rain."

"Why were you trying to ambush us?"

The girl looked up at him then, annoyance on her little pixie face. "I only told them to do it because I knew you and the other one were watching somewhere."

Arkham opened his mouth to say something then closed it again, shaking his head slightly. "I don't follow."

Rain actually rolled her eyes. "You guys have been all over this neighborhood for three days now looking for that kid. You never split up for more than a block and even then you're always watching each other. When you separated this time, I knew if I sent the boys in, they'd already be surrounded when they attacked. You guys are way better at this shit than them."

"You didn't answer my question, Rain." Arkham wasn't letting her get off the subject that easily. "Why were you trying to ambush us?"

"I'm the lookout," she said simply but gave him a guilty look, fleeting though it was. "I just watch out for the boys."

"You obviously weren't watching out for them tonight."

"It's not right for them to beat people up." She sighed. "OK, so maybe some people it's OK to beat up, but all you guys have done since you've been here is tried to make sure people were safe and to look for a kid."

Arkham tilted his head. This wasn't computing at all. As he studied her, Arkham found himself being more and more drawn to the young woman. And she was *very* young. Her eyes, however, told another story. This girl had seen much in her lifetime. Maybe not as much as Arkham had seen, but she was a warrior in her own right. Though obviously nervous, she held his gaze, not wavering. Those glittering amber eyes reminded him more of his brothers than any of the women Bones had picked up lately. Though each woman had her strengths, had endured more than her share of abuses and hard times, they were gentle at heart. Arkham had the feeling this woman was as battle hardened as he was.

"You know where the boy is?"

"No. But I've heard rumors someone's got him holed up. Waiting for those rich men to offer a ransom."

"I think you need to come with me, Rain. Our bosses will have questions."

She looked at him suspiciously. "Who's your bosses?"

"You'll find out. Come on." He pulled her up by her arm and shoved her toward the stairs. Arkham had a feeling it was going to be a long night.

Chapter Two

Rain knew this had been a bad idea. When the boys had decided to beat up the badass newcomers, she knew she couldn't sit by and let it happen. It had given her a fantastic idea, though. Watching these men had proved to be the best thing she'd done in a very long time. They called themselves "Bones" or "ExFil." Rain had no idea what either were, and didn't really care. She'd learned everything she could about the men and had come to the conclusion they could handle anything thrown at them.

They were just like the men people called the Shadow Demons. Those guys weren't men to mess around with. Neither were these newcomers. The difference was the men she was currently surrounded by were rougher around the edges. And they didn't have the exotic tech the Shadow Demons did. Another thing they had in common was they *helped. Everyone.* They didn't discriminate between rich and poor or white, black, brown, or any other color. Someone was in danger, they helped. And it wasn't a conscious action on their part most of the time. She'd seen them helping old ladies cross the street, for fuck's sake! All the while, their eyes roamed the streets looking for... something. This hadn't been the first attack on them, and it wouldn't be the last if they stayed, but they'd never permanently harmed or killed anyone they came across. Of course, every single time they'd been attacked it had been by the bad boys of the neighborhood. The drug dealers and pimps and their ragtag armies. Rain had to wonder if Bones would be so forgiving if really challenged.

When they reached the end of the block, two big Humvees rolled up to a stop. The big guy with a full, dark beard currently sitting behind the wheel of the lead vehicle rolled his window down. "You ladies need a lift?"

"Fuck you, Trucker."

"You always whine, Goose. Why do you always whine?"

"One of those little fuckers winged me," Goose muttered.

Rain saw them marching the boys to the second Humvee and shoving them all inside. They were tied much like she was, but they were all gagged as well. Every single one of them looked terrified. Even Jason, the badass wannabe. So much for Mister Military there. Apparently, he wasn't as experienced as he'd led everyone to believe.

"They're kids, Goose. If you can't win against kids, how did you even make it into Bones?"

They all had a little chuckle, but Goose was having none of it. "Those fuckin' kids were armed with automatics. I had a fuckin' potato shooter!"

"All right. Knock it off," the one she'd identified as the leader ordered. "We'll take 'em in. Let Shadow Demons decide what to do with 'em."

"You're with the Shadow Demons?" Rain couldn't help her outburst. The Shadow Demons had been all over the city in the past year. Some called them saviors. Others vigilantes. She thought they might just be what the city needed. At least, what their section of the city needed.

Everyone kept on about their business. The one who'd caught her urged her into the vehicle before shutting the door. No one even acknowledged she'd spoken.

Goose hopped in beside the driver. "Get gone, Trucker. The others will meet us there."

Rain heard motorcycles starting up in the distance. From a warehouse about a block away, three bikes emerged, taking the lead in their convoy. Bikers. Figured. It actually made sense. The guys were obviously military, but they had a kind of pack mentality she'd only seen in some of the gangs in Rockwell. They stuck together. Always. At least, that's the way they'd been since she'd been watching them. It also explained some of the tattoos they sported.

The ride was only about five minutes and took them to a dead-end alley. Except the wall moved and there was a cave. The Humvee rolled on without even slowing down.

"Holy shit! What is this?" she asked, her face pressed to the glass. No one answered. They kept moving for another few minutes before coming out of the tunnel into a massive open room at least two stories high.

The vehicle stopped, and Rain opened the door. Stepping out, she looked around her in wonder. "This is the coolest place I've ever seen!" There was tech all over the place. Computers everywhere with high-voltage wiring crisscrossing the floor. On one end was a giant metal circle standing vertical with all kinds of wires and cables. A guy wearing a welding helmet was working on one side of it, sparks flying from the welder wand. When she moved toward a table with various items laid out, one of them snagged her arm, pulling her back.

"Just stay put, little lady." It was the same guy who'd nabbed her in the first place. She took the opportunity to study him. Aside from being a big-ass motherfucker, he was probably the scariest looking person she'd ever seen. A thick beard covered the lower half of his face, but he was scarred all over. What part of his body wasn't scarred was covered in tattoos. A thin scar ran from his hairline, through his right eyebrow, and down his cheek to his jaw. His eyes were another thing. They were strange, dual colored. The right one was a rich amber while the left one was a vibrant blue. She wondered if the scar had anything to do with the strange coloring but doubted it since the injured eye was darker than the other and both seemed to focus on her intently. The one thing about the guy that scared her most were those eyes. Looking into them she could see they were dead. Void of any emotion. The eyes of a killer, cold-blooded or otherwise. He'd slit a man's throat without batting an eyelash.

He shrugged out of his military jacket and the vest underneath, tossing them to the floor. His neck popped several times as he rolled it on his shoulders.

"Whatcha got?" The leader of the second team she'd been watching stepped into their group. He was dressed in jeans, a white T-shirt and a black leather vest. A patch on the chest proclaimed him "president."

"Five dumbasses trying to be badasses," Goose answered. The man sounded more than a little miffed. "Fuckers winged me."

"Jesus, Goose," Trucker said, slamming his door after he hopped out. "Why are you still whining? Are you a pussy? Cause you know Bones don't allow pussies."

"They let you in, didn't they?"

"Yeah, but I ain't whining about getting a scratch. I bet you ain't even bleeding."

"Fuck you."

"You already said that." Trucker was laughing openly at Goose, and the other man just scowled. Rain had seen more than one such argument turn into a deadly brawl. These guys seemed to enjoy it. In fact, it seemed like part of their culture. One an outsider like her couldn't understand.

"Would you two knock it off?" the first guy said, looking annoyed but not angry. "Arkham?"

The man who'd captured her sighed, scrubbing his hand over his neck. "She was their lookout, Cain. But she expected us to take care of them."

Cain crossed his arms over his chest. "How so?"

"Called them in once we separated, knowing we'd always have eyes on each other. Told them we were all together, not that we'd split. They did exactly what she expected. Rushed the two on the ground in plain sight. Her thought was Shadow and I could protect our brothers before those idiots could harm Torpedo and Goose."

Cain gave Rain a good hard stare, seeming to be trying to see into her soul. "You sure about her? She might have been trying to make sure her gang had the best chance of killin' your team."

Arkham shrugged. "Maybe, but I don't think so."

"You trust her, then?" Cain raised an eyebrow, crossing his arms over his chest.

"No." Arkham's answer was immediate. Which pissed Rain off.

"Now, wait just a minute!"

"She mentioned the kid," Arkham added, ignoring her as if she hadn't said anything. "Said word was he was bein' held until an offer of a ransom was made. Might want to let Azriel know."

Torpedo swore. "Why the fuck won't anyone talk? She can't be the only one who's heard this."

Arkham shrugged. "Maybe I'm less intimidating than you. You know. Cause I'm so pretty."

"We're not doing very well in this. I don't understand why Ivanovich needs us. His men could get the same results we've gotten."

"We want you here because you have a way with the populous of the eastern sector."

A large man in an expensive-looking suit approached them. He had the look of a predator, but a refined one. One that blended in with the elite of the city. Any city.

"If you'd let us do this our way, we'd've found the kid already," Cain said. "It's time you told us exactly what we're doin'. I'm tired of fuckin' around here, Azriel."

"We have a tracking device on the child. All the children have them, with their parents' consent, for just this reason."

"We'll, I'd say your tracker isn't workin' very well. This is the first mention we've had of the kid."

"There's interference. I know you've checked the sewers and subway beneath the city in that area, but we're sure he's there somewhere."

"Maybe the tracker got removed. Maybe it was found and removed."

"It's working. We can see him moving from time to time. Probably when they take him to a new location. And the tracker also monitors his vital signs. If it were removed, the bio monitoring would tell us."

Rain knew there were severe undercurrents surrounding the men. She was reminded of some of the gangs in the city. It was a power struggle with them. Most did everything they could to recruit the young. Those they couldn't win over, they enslaved. Or killed. Eventually, no one dared turn them down when they came looking for service and tried to pick the least brutal gangs before they were drafted. Her included.

"The young woman knows something," Azriel said, nodding in her direction. "She's one of them."

"She's not," Arkham stated solidly. There was no doubt in his voice. No question he was right.

"You said yourself she set your team up," Azriel pressed. "It was just luck they didn't kill all of you."

"Those boys wouldn't know how to kill if you put a knife in their hand and the blade at someone's throat." Arkham seemed to scoff at the idea. Rain knew better.

"They might surprise you," she muttered. Instantly, all eyes were on her. She winced. Not a way to gain her freedom.

"Might as well explain." Cain scrubbed a hand over his face as if this were all a big hassle he preferred to avoid.

When she glanced nervously at Arkham, he stared back at her, the intensity of those dual-colored eyes unnerving. Lifting her chin, she looked away and shut her mouth stubbornly.

"I don't have time for this fuckin' shit," Cain muttered.

"I'll talk to her." She snapped her head around to look at Arkham again. He had a look of grim determination on his face. "No matter how long it takes." That look said he was looking forward to the interrogation.

"Now, wait just a Goddamned minute!"

Arkham ignored her and tossed her over his shoulder. With her hands still zip-tied behind her, there was nothing Rain could do other than kick a little. If she fell, she risked hurting herself worse than she had when she'd face-planted on the roof of the theater. Finally she just yelled at him, "Put me down!" Which did no good.

He swatted her ass. Hard.

When she stopped fussing, he grunted as if satisfied with her response. "Bastard," she muttered, but didn't struggle further. The sting of the swat startled her, but also made her insides tingle.

What the hell had just happened? Even now, his hand rested on the side of her ass he'd just spanked, rubbing through her jeans as if to soothe her. In reality, she knew he was copping a feel, but she found she really didn't mind, when she'd always rebuffed anyone who tried to touch her. Without fail. Now this man comes along, manhandling her at every opportunity, and she... *liked it*?

What the fuck?

Chapter Three

Each member of Bones had been given a suite of rooms to himself in the East wing of the mansion Shadow Demons called their home. As they'd found out when they got there, Shadow Demons weren't an MC club, but more of a group of insanely rich men trying to set up a network of protection for their community. While Arkham respected what they were doing, he disliked being volunteered to help when there was obviously something more going on than simple protection.

He carried Rain over his shoulder, her ass right next to his face. She'd wiggled more than once, and he'd swatted that ass more than once. Her age was still undetermined, so he had to keep a leash on his aggression. The fact was, he was becoming a little obsessed with her, and that wasn't good. All those black, glossy curls and those amber-colored eyes were bad enough, but her compact body and slight, womanly curves were wreaking havoc on his mind. Especially if she was as young as she looked.

The suite he'd chosen had only one wall of windows. Situated in the corner of the house, most of the room was surrounded the landscape. They'd built the fortress next to a mountain and made it part of the house. Just like Bones had done with their clubhouse. Arkham liked it because he could position himself easily out of the line of sight of those windows and not have to worry about someone watching his every move. Apparently, Shadow Demons felt the same way because they'd furnished the room to reflect that defensive posture. There had been very little Arkham had to do to be secure.

Now, he set his prisoner on her feet. She stumbled away a little before standing her ground.

When she looked up at him, Arkham could see she was furious. Which put really bad thoughts in his head.

"Fuck," he muttered, scrubbing a hand over his face. "Last name, girl. I want it."

"I told you. It's just Rain."

He gave her his best "do not fuck with me" look. She just lifted her chin and repeated. "My name's Rain. That's it."

"That your real name or your street name?"

"It's *my* name. The only name I've ever had."

"Your *family* name?"

For the first time since this started, she looked away, her lips thinning as she pressed them together. At first, Arkham thought she wouldn't answer. She didn't look stubborn so much as... ashamed?

"Ain't got no family."

"So, you have no family now. Who were --"

"You ain't listening!" she snapped, her face a furious mask. "I ain't never had no family! Never. My first memory is a bunch of us kids fightin' over food! I grew up on the streets with a gang of kids! Our only goal was to find something to eat and to stay away from adults! So, *my name...*" she raised her chin proudly, looking him straight in the eye, "is *Rain*. That's it!"

Arkham was silent, holding her gaze while he processed this. "Fuck," he muttered. "Just... *fuck*." He pulled out a knife from the small of his back. "Turn around."

She took a couple of steps back, crouching defensively, her hands still firmly behind her back. "The hell I will!"

"Would you fuckin' relax? I'm just going to cut the fuckin' zip tie."

Slowly, eyeing him with suspicion, she did as he asked. She kept looking over her shoulder at him, watching every move he made. Once he'd freed her, she moved farther away from him, trying to angle herself to make a run for the door.

"Even if you made it out the door, you wouldn't get far. They keep this place locked down better'n Fort Knox."

"What do you want from me? Am I a prisoner?"

Arkham started to deny she was a prisoner, then thought better of it. "Yeah. I suppose you're a prisoner for now. How long it stays that way depends on you." He let that sink in. When she didn't react, he continued. "I need to know about these gangs. The boy. Everything you know."

"They're a bunch of thugs," she muttered, crossing her arms around her body. She took a deep breath, then sighed, sitting down on the nearest chair as she did. When she finally let down her guard, she looked older than she had previously. Like the weight of all she'd experienced had finally caught up with her. "As to who has the kid, I honestly don't know. Some say it's the Shaws. Others the Chinese. I can't find out either way."

"You seem to have a pretty good handle on the things in your neighborhood."

She gave him a flat, cold look. Much like the look he saw when he looked in the mirror. "The slums are my home. When you live on the streets all your life, you learn that, if you don't know everything going on around you, you don't live very long. In this case, I do everything I can to avoid the pimps and the gangs."

"Yet you were aidin' one."

"I was serving my own interest. I offered to help them because I knew they were going after your team."

Arkham took a step toward her. "Our team specifically?"

"Yeah. Y'all can take care of yourselves, though. You took out part of the Shaws gang, too."

Arkham felt a grin tugging at his lips. This girl was priceless. "How old are you, Rain?"

The question seemed to throw her off guard. "What's it matter?"

"I'm not turnin' you in to social services so don't get no ideas."

She shrugged. "Don't really know exactly. I was always small, so people thought I was young, but I'm pretty sure I'm older than most of the kids I grew up with." When Arkham just raised his eyebrows, she blew one dark curl out of her eyes. "Best I can guess, I'm nineteen. Obviously, I could be wrong. I started counting when everyone thought I was six. Every summer on the Fourth of July, I count another year. So far, I've counted thirteen years."

"OK then." That seemed a mundane way of putting it, but Arkham thought that at least he didn't feel too much like a pervert anymore. If she was nineteen, she wasn't chronologically a child. Mentally, she had obviously grown up a very long time ago under tough circumstances.

God, this wasn't good. If he were anything other than the bastard he knew himself to be, he'd take her to Cain and turn her over to him. He'd stay the hell away from her before he did something he couldn't take back. Like make her his.

The thought came out of nowhere. Never in his adult life had Arkham contemplated keeping a woman. Naturally, he took his pleasure from willing women whenever he needed to, but they always knew the score. He wasn't the type of man one settled down with. Wouldn't know how to do it if he were so inclined.

Yeah. He needed to keep his distance.

"You hungry?"

Shrug.

"Rain, what did I tell you about answering my questions?"

"Fine," she snapped. "Yes. I'm hungry. I'm used to it so don't feel like you have to feed me. I can look after myself."

"We're in a fuckin' mansion, Rain. These guys have anything and everything and it don't cost you nothin'. Now, what do you want?"

Her eyes went wide for just that split second before she could get herself under control, schooling her expression. "They got a menu?"

"Yeah. Your brain." He was getting a little exasperated with her. "What the fuck do you want to eat, Rain?"

She lifted her chin as if to say, "Challenge accepted. Fucker."

"I want steak and eggs. Eggs over light, steak medium. Toast with butter and grape jelly. Then I want chocolate cake with cream cheese icing. A tall, ice-cold glass of milk to drink."

He nodded. "Go take a shower while you're waiting," he ordered.

She shrugged then found her way to the bathroom. Arkham called the number Azriel had given them for the kitchen. Once he'd called in her order, he made another call to their estate manager, Ruth McDonald. The older woman ran a tight ship, to say the least. She'd made it clear they were to call her if they needed anything. He didn't need anything, but Rain did.

She wore tattered blue jeans that looked a size or two too large and an oversized sweatshirt that had seen better days. While she smelled clean, her clothing was rough and stained in several places. Not to mention it was fucking cold out. The girl needed warm clothes and a good coat. And footwear. And gloves and a scarf, and…

Fuck it. He just ordered her a new wardrobe. Mrs. McDonald was upbeat about it, sounding excited and happy. Apparently, the woman loved this sort of thing. Which was good because Arkham was determined to get Rain everything she needed. When she asked Rain's size, Arkham was at a loss.

"Never mind. I'll have Giovanni check his cameras. He can give me measurements enough to get close."

Instead of voicing just how much that freaked him the fuck out, Arkham simply thanked the woman and hung up.

As he approached the bathroom, he heard Rain singing decidedly off key in the shower. With a shrug, Arkham broke the bathroom lock and found her clothes. She'd lain them neatly on the sink and had attempted to scrub the worst of the stains from the sweatshirt. The hair dryer lay beside it as if she prepared to use it both on her hair and her clothes. Arkham snagged the garments and left her one of his T-shirts and a pair of gym shorts. Both too big, but they would do until Mrs. McDonald could bring the stuff he'd ordered that afternoon. Satisfied she'd be appropriately pissed off, Arkham smirked and closed the door.

* * *

"Fuckin' bastard! Bring back my fuckin' clothes!"

Arkham nearly smiled in contentment. The sound of an exotic woman so supremely pissed off was like beautiful music.

"You have clothes," he called back. "I know because I left them right where your others were."

"Asshole!"

"Just put 'em on and get in here and eat while it's hot."

There was a pause. "Eat?"

"You said you wanted steak and eggs. Right?"

There was a moment of silence followed by a couple of thumps, a muttered "fuck" and the door to the bathroom being jerked opened. Rain hurried to the main room, her nose in the air as if following her it to the source of the food. The second she spotted the silver-domed tray, her eyes locked on it. She practically sprinted to the table and tore off the lid. Her lips parted in a gasp.

On the tray was the biggest slab of ribeye Arkham had ever seen along with what had to be a dozen eggs cooked just the way she asked. Several pieces of heavily buttered toast lay in a separate plate, and an unopened jar of some kind of imported grape jelly sat next to it. In large bucket of ice, two large glasses of milk sat chilling, just waiting for her to consume them at her leisure.

"Holy fuck," she whispered in awe. Then dug in.

In his lifetime, Arkham had been to places where people hadn't eaten anything in days other than soup made from grasses and various other types of foliage. Feeding those people had been one of the few things he'd ever done that had given him pride in being a soldier. A man. It had made him feel like he contributed to the life of someone else. Even those starving people had never made such a show of eating a meal as Rain did now.

She closed her eyes in bliss, chewing slowly as if to savor each bite. Juice from the steak and even yolk from the eggs ran down her chin unchecked. It was soon followed by butter and milk, but she didn't seem to notice. The sounds she made were just shy of orgasmic. Her utter enjoyment of the meal fascinated him to the point of distraction. He couldn't have taken his gaze from her if his life depended on it.

It took her forty-five minutes to finish the meal -- and she ate every fucking bite. As she drank the last of the milk, he noticed her looking around as if scouting for more.

"You can't possibly still be hungry."

She glanced at him sharply, as if she'd forgotten he was there. That assumption was confirmed when she hastily grabbed a napkin and wiped her mouth and chin, then looked down at his white T-shirt now stained with grease, eggs, butter, jelly, and milk.

"Shit," she muttered.

"Go clean up. I'll get you another T-shirt, then we need to get some sleep. You're going to need to be on your toes when Cain and Azriel question you."

"Am I in danger?"

He shrugged. "Only if you lie or if you were trying to kill my team."

"You know I wasn't." Her little indignant face looked furious, her chin jutting stubbornly.

"No, I don't know. But my gut says you weren't. That's enough for me, but not enough for Cain. Azriel... Who the fuck knows?"

With a sigh, Rain headed back to the bathroom, whipping her shirt off as she went. Though her back was to him, his gaze riveted to her form. That sleek back rippled with fine muscle, but the delicate skin over her back and shoulders was crisscrossed with scars both old and new. When she jumped, whipping her head around to look at him and wrapping her arms over her chest, Arkham realized he was growling.

"What the fuck is this?" he snapped. Arkham could hear the unadulterated fury in his voice but couldn't seem to get a rein on it. There was something dangerous inside him. Always had been. He'd known it since he was a child when he'd watched his younger brother die from leukemia and he'd been helpless to do anything more to help him. He'd known it when he'd slaughtered a platoon of enemy soldiers after they'd killed two men in his own platoon. Never had the deadly fury clawing to get out been as strong inside him as it was in this moment. Seeing marks of violence on this woman that spanned her lifetime threatened to push him over the edge into the realm of criminally insane.

"What?" Her gaze darted around the room, looking for danger. He knew because he did the same thing himself when off balance.

"Your back." He reached her, gripping her shoulders and sinking down to one knee. Without thought, he yanked her shorts down to her thighs, her startled yelp loud in the silence.

"What the fuck are you doing, you son of a bitch?" Her outrage was drowned out by the roaring in his ears. His vision tunneled so that he saw only her. Only the marks all over her lithe body.

He didn't say a word, but spun her around. She kicked out at him, lowering her arms from her chest to strike out with her fists, but Arkham blocked her easily before finally catching her wrists and forcing them behind her back. He held them firmly in place in one of his big hands despite her struggles. When she kicked out at him again, he blocked her leg again, still unable to form words.

Finally, she settled, and Arkham examined her body closely. He'd vaguely noticed scars on her arms, but he had scars too. Previously, he'd judged her a warrior so he'd given it little thought. All warriors had scars. Especially on their limbs where they'd defended themselves or caught an edge while striking. Some had scars on their chest where a blow got through, and even fewer had scars on their backs, though most of those were bullets. This girl had thin scars from knife slices and rounded burn scars all over her back. Probably where someone had put out cigarettes and cigars on her skin. A few on her torso and limbs, but mostly her back. She'd been tortured.

"What the fuckin' Goddamned fuck?"

"Let me go." Her voice was steady but angry.

"Not until you tell me what happened." And, more importantly, who he needed to kill.

"Price of growing up on the streets."

There was a long silence while the two of them locked gazes. Arkham swore she was fighting him, daring him to either blame her for not fighting harder or shrug her off. He could do neither. She'd confessed to being raised on the streets, in basically gangs of children, from the time she could remember. No doubt there were kids -- or adults -- bigger, stronger, and more experienced, who'd taken advantage of her or, as her body told him, tortured her for various reasons. Probably for their own sadistic pleasure. Did he really want her to tell him? Did he really want to know? If he did, could he handle it? The answer to both was a resounding "no." He didn't want her to relive it because he knew he couldn't handle it. And if he couldn't handle it, he damned sure couldn't expect her to handle it.

"Never again, Rain," he finally ground out. His voice was rough in his rage. He knew he sounded more animal than man in that moment. "You're never going back."

"It's over now," she said, no emotion in her voice or on her face. "I paid my dues and learned from my mistakes. I'm strong and intelligent. No one hurts me now. No one."

With that, she kicked out. When he blocked her -- as she'd obviously expected -- she spun around, breaking his hold on her and snapping her heel into the side of his jaw.

Arkham saw stars. It was also enough to dull the raging fury threatening to take hold on his mind. He lunged for her, but she kicked his arm, deadening his hand in the process. She'd known exactly what part of his arm to hit to create just that sensation. Arkham was sure of it. There was deadly cunning in her gaze as she fought him naked as the day she was born.

Instead of running when she had the advantage, she attacked, leaping into the air and bringing her fist down to connect with his jaw again. Only he managed to catch her fist in his other hand. Again, it seemed to be what she was expecting because she twisted her body around to land on his back, the arm he'd caught wrapped tightly around his throat, her legs squeezing his torso with all her considerable strength. Fortunately for him, her legs were too short to lock tightly enough to give her the leverage she needed to constrict his breathing.

He could have tossed her off. Could have really hurt her if he'd wanted. Instead, he just sat there, letting her do her best to strangle him. When she realized she wasn't doing any good but that he wasn't going to fight back, she relaxed her hold and climbed off him.

Once she had, Arkham stood and turned around slowly. She stood before him crouched and ready to spring should she need to, but made no move toward either him or the door.

"What do you want from me?" Her question was angry, demanding.

"I don't know," he answered honestly. "I do know I'm not sending you back to the slums. You'll either stay here with the Shadow Demons and the rest of their household, or you'll come back with Bones. Either way, you'll be safe. You can build a life for yourself."

"And how do you propose I do that?" she scoffed. "I'm smart but I ain't got no education. No skills other than fighting. I can barely read and only words I recognize. Some life I'd have. I'd be back on the streets within a month and worse off because everyone would know I'd tried and failed."

"Decision made then. You're comin' with Bones."

"Fuck you, Arkham!"

"No. Not yet anyway." He pointed to the bathroom. "Clean up. I'll get you another shirt." He bent and picked up her shorts, tossing them to her as she passed him. Again, she didn't cover herself. The only time she had was when she'd first realized there'd been a problem. He'd startled her, probably because she'd been growing comfortable with him. Now that she'd firmly placed him in the category of either enemy or crazy son of a bitch, she didn't cover herself. Arkham was certain it wasn't because she was trying to seduce him or that she was particularly comfortable with her nudity. No. It was because she was more concerned with being able to defend herself than she was about her modesty. Scrubbing a hand over the back of his neck and then his face, he stormed off to get her another shirt.

Chapter Four

Sleep wasn't Arkham's friend. Never had been. Now, with a young woman in his bed and him on the couch the damned stuff proved doubly elusive. She was an enigma he couldn't figure out but desperately wanted to. He'd always been over-the-top protective. It was what had gotten him in trouble in the Marines. He'd thought he was learning to control it when his young cousin, Pig, had gotten the shit beat out of him by Stunner, one of the youngest patched members of bones. The kid had deserved it, but he was still family. Arkham had stood over him after Stunner had been pulled off by Mama and Pops and thought only that the little fucker should have gotten more. Or, at least, Stunner should have drawn it out a little so Pig had suffered more. That protective instinct had lain dormant within him. Arkham had thought he'd finally defeated it. Now he knew better.

Sighing, he sat up on the couch just outside his room where Rain lay, presumably sound asleep. He hadn't positioned himself so much to keep her from running but to satisfy himself that she was safe. That no one could get to her without going through him. After debating with himself as to whether or not he would go check on her, he finally lost and walked to her door.

It was locked, as he'd expected it would be. Fortunately he had no problem picking the lock. Three minutes later, he opened the door and stepped inside. His eyes went unerringly to the bed. The *empty* bed. Rain was nowhere to be seen.

Taking a few deep breaths, Arkham fought down an unexpected and unfamiliar surge of panic. There were no windows in the room so she couldn't have escaped that way. She hadn't left the bedroom. He'd have known. That meant she had to be in the room somewhere.

He stood there until his heart rate slowed and he felt better in control of himself. Then he started a methodical search of the room. He found her under the bed in the far corner, curled up on several blankets and a pillow.

Arkham cleared his throat. Rain's eyes snapped open and she gasped in surprise.

When he said nothing more, she tugged her blanket higher and continued to stare at him. He jerked his chin at her, indicating she should get out from under the bed. She did nothing for a moment, then sighed and did as he asked, bringing her blankets with her.

"I feel safe with something at my back and when I'm out of direct sight."

"Understood." Arkham moved to the bed and pushed, shoving the big thing flush against the wall, solidly in the corner. Then he motioned for her to climb in. She did, reluctantly, protesting when he climbed in with her. Arkham ignored her, facing away from her but putting his back solidly against her. "We've got about three or four hours before Cain calls us. Get some sleep."

"What do you think you're doing?"

"Putting myself between you and the outside. Anyone wants to get you, they have to go through me. Was like that anyhow, but now you've got a more solid idea I mean what I say."

"Yeah? Who protects me from you?"

"I have a feelin' you can take care of yourself in that regard."

She rolled her eyes at him, but settled under her blanket with a sigh, then didn't move. For about thirty minutes, neither of them did. Then Rain inched closer to him. Arkham didn't dare breathe. Especially when she rolled over and tucked herself into his back. Her mouth was in the middle of his shoulder blades. He could feel her warm breath through his shirt. Her body pressed tightly against him as if for warmth.

"You cold?" His question was soft, near a whisper. She didn't answer but snuggled closer. Carefully, Arkham turned over. He wasn't sure what to do, but she mumbled in her sleep then turned over, putting her back to his chest. After several seconds, she mumbled again, patting around until she found her blanket then tugged it higher. Still, that didn't seem to satisfy her. Rain mumbled again, this time shivering as she pressed herself still further against him. He would have smiled except her ass found his groin and pressed itself tightly into his body. There was no way to prevent or diminish the growing erection pressing against her ass. She'd be pissed when she woke, but really, none of this was his fault.

Just when he thought she'd relax and drift back into a heavy sleep, she found his wrist with her tiny hand. With a contented sigh, she pulled his arm to settle around her body and didn't seem satisfied until he'd wrapped her up tight.

This was a bad idea. He knew it. If she were awake, she'd know it, too. It would all be his fault, and he couldn't argue with her because he was awake. But the second he settled himself tightly around her, her wrapped up in his arms, the woman didn't move a muscle other than to breathe. She settled her muttering and squirming and just... slept. Like the dead. How long had it been since she'd had a good night's sleep? Or afternoon, as the case may be.

They searched the slums at night; the other crew took the day. Every evening they met before Torpedo took the second team out. Every morning, they met before Cain took the first group out. This was the first time they'd had anything more to pass on that wouldn't fit into a five-minute conversation. Now, he knew there should have been a longer one before, but the presence of Rain had discouraged it. The remaining team had probably given Cain the run-down anyway. He just had to fill them all in on what Rain had told him. And about her past.

How the fuck was he going to do that without saying something Rain would be embarrassed about? While Bones would never judge someone for simply surviving, Arkham knew instinctively Rain would see her past differently than they all did.

She sighed in her sleep. Without thinking, Arkham tightened his hold on her, burying his nose in her hair close to her ear. "I've got you, honey," he murmured. "I've got you."

"Arkham?" Her voice was sleepy, like she wasn't fully awake.

"Yeah. Go back to sleep. No one's gonna hurt you."

"You swear?"

"On my life, honey."

There was silence for a while. Arkham thought she'd drifted off again, but she added, "No one's ever kept me safe before."

"I'll always keep you safe, Rain. Always."

With a soft sigh, she snuggled more firmly against him, pulled her knees up a little tighter, then said nothing else.

Arkham lay drifting in and out for the next three hours. When he finally woke enough to really take stock of his surroundings his body ached like a son of a bitch. Rain still lay against him, still as death except for her breathing.

Carefully, he extracted himself from around her. He wanted a shower before they met after Cain's patrol came in for the night. He needed to be ready to go back out, but that was going to be a problem. He didn't trust Rain not to run at the first opportunity.

He'd nearly made it to the shower when he heard Rain's sleepy voice. "Arkham?"

"I'm here, honey. Just taking a shower before patrolling. I'll leave the bathroom door open if you want."

When she gave no response, Arkham pushed the bathroom door open wide, letting the light flood into the bedroom and over the bed where she lay. He stepped out of his sweats and underwear, whipping his shirt off once finished. As he adjusted the water in the big, open shower, he heard her stirring. It made him a little uneasy, until glanced over his shoulder and saw her standing in the doorway.

She watched him as he stepped in the shower, not in a calculating way, but just looking at his body. She seemed more curious than afraid or shy. He gave a mental shrug. If she wanted to look him over, let her. He'd done much the same to her earlier.

In the shower, he turned his back on her, giving his body a quick wash while he checked for scrapes and cuts. The hot water and soap always found the small nicks and cuts he hadn't noticed but needed to clean. The moist heat on his aching muscles felt wonderful. Staying so still in such an unfamiliar position had done a number on his body. All the while, he was conscious of Rain standing there. He hadn't glanced over his shoulder or tried to catch a glimpse of her in the mirror across from the shower, but he'd bet his last dollar she was still there watching him.

The thought had just crossed his mind when he heard her entering the open shower, her foot splashing lightly in the water of the tiled floor. He raised an eyebrow as she fully entered.

"There some reason you're naked in the shower with me?"

She shrugged. "If I'd gotten in here with my clothes on I'd be without again. Better my clothes be dry when I go with you on patrol tonight."

That made him smile a little. "So you think you're going with me."

"If you meant what you said about me leaving here with Bones, then yes."

He continued to scrub himself, soap sudsing over his skin as he did. "Not sure what one has to do with the other. Or why you're in here with me instead of waiting your turn."

That brought her up short. "I, uh..." She cleared her throat, turning away. "Good question, I suppose. Just thought you might like some company."

She started to get out, but Arkham lunged for her, snagging her arm and pulling her back in. "Get wet," he said, gruffly. "I'll wash your back."

* * *

Why in the world Rain had put herself in this position she'd never know. She knew it was a bad idea from the start, but she'd slept in this man's arms for hours. He'd held her, comforted her when she dreamed, kept her warm. For the first time in her life, someone had her back. He'd watched over her. Protected her. At least, that's what he'd said he was doing. Given he hadn't tried to have sex with her, Rain believed him.

He'd seen her scars, had intimately focused on every single one of them, so she'd thought it would be OK for her to do the same to him. Apparently, she'd misunderstood the situation. She knew he was interested in her. The cock pressed into her ass most of the night confirmed that. Then a thought struck her.

"Do you have a woman?"

He whipped his head around, looking at her intently. "Why would you ask that?"

"You obviously want me." She nodded toward his cock, which was long, thick, and very distended. "I'm same as offering myself to you, and you want to kick me out. That usually means a man has a woman, though it generally doesn't matter."

"If I had a woman, Rain, you wouldn't be in here with me. I wouldn't have slept in your bed either, even to comfort you."

"Then..." She swallowed, looking away. "My scars bother you."

"Of course they bother me!" His vehemence made her wince. Every man she'd ever been with had said pretty much the same thing. Why would they want her when she was so scarred? So why did it hurt so much worse coming from Arkham?

"I see." She moved away from him. "You're right. I should have waited my turn."

"Stop, Rain," he commanded. "Get back over here and stand in front of me."

"I don't need your pity, Arkham. I'm good. Really."

"Yeah? Well, I'm not."

The second she was within arm's reach of him, Arkham pulled her against him and fused his mouth to hers. Rain was so startled she gasped, and he took advantage, plunging his tongue into her mouth when she did. The second he deepened the kiss, Rain's knees buckled. Thank God he was a strong man because Arkham simply took her weight, lifting her higher into his arms so her naked body was mashed against his.

Before she knew what she was doing, Rain had wound her arms around his neck, sinking her fingers into the thick wet hair at the back of his head. He tasted wild, unlike anything she'd ever experienced. Kissing had never been particularly pleasant for her, but this was one man she could easily become addicted to from his kiss alone.

He flicked her tongue, coaxing her to lap at him the same as he was her. His teeth nipped her lip slightly before he lapped away the sting. The expertness of his kiss made her realize she was certainly in over her head, but she couldn't seem to pull away, to take that one step back and consider the consequences of her actions. And she didn't mean physical consequences either. Sure, she needed to think about those, but all she could think about was how she needed to guard her heart. This man, a man she'd only known a very short time, had steamrolled into her life and made her feel safer and more secure than she had ever felt before. She didn't know him, but she found she trusted him completely. That was why she'd followed him into the shower to begin with. He'd left her bed, had left her alone, intending only to be gone a brief time, and she'd begrudged him that space. Now that she felt safe, she craved it.

Just as she admitted those feelings to herself, Arkham ended the kiss, following the passion with tenderness as he kissed her eyes, her nose, her chin.

"Tell me why you followed me in here, Rain."

"Isn't sex enough?"

"With you, sure. Always. But you could have initiated that before we went to sleep. You were adamant you didn't want sex before. I want to know why the turnaround."

"Does it really matter?"

"It does when it's not what you want. At least, not right now."

Rain tilted her head. "If I didn't want to fuck you, I wouldn't be here."

He chuckled, tightening his arms around her and burying his face in her neck. Even that slight contact with his lips on her skin was enough to make her shiver.

"You don't have to offer yourself to me to make me stay with you, honey. I'm not going anywhere."

She stilled. Was that really why she was coming on to him? "I like that you make me feel safe, but I never said I wanted you to stay with me. I've never sold myself for any reason, even protection."

"And you're not going to now. You haven't even known me for twelve hours. You don't trust me yet. Once you do, we'll see about how long and hard I can take you." He continued to kiss and nibble at the skin of her neck and ear, which was driving her crazy.

"What are you doing?" Her voice came out breathy, and she found herself tilting her head back to let him have better access. The sensations were overwhelming her with every second he continued to touch her.

"Wishing I'd earned your trust."

Again, his lips found hers, his hand burying in her hair this time. Rain's heart beat out of control, her body coming so alive she ached. He crushed her against him, urging her leg up to circle his hip. When she contacted his cock with her sex, Rain actually cried out.

"That's it, honey," he praised between kisses. "Feel how much it wants inside you."

"Arkham," she gasped. "Oh, God!"

"Do it, baby." His soft whisper was the Devil in her ear. "Do it…"

Pleasure erupted through her body, consumed her sanity. Rain screamed, grinding her clit over Arkham's dick as hard as she could. She let herself go, unable to focus on anything other than the pleasure. Her vision narrowed until there was only Arkham. Only his arms around her. Only his mouth nipping and kissing her neck and ear. Only his body she craved with everything in her.

When those wicked sensations faded and she became aware of the water pouring over them in a gentle cascade, Rain realized she'd gone limp. Arkham fully supported her with those strong arms, that magnificent body of his. He protected her without her asking or even being aware of what he'd done until it was over. His cock was a throbbing mass between them, still rubbing insistently over her clit with every breath she took.

Slowly, Arkham pulled back, meeting her gaze and holding it fast. He let her slide down his wet body until her feet rested firmly on the floor. Still, he held her securely. As she came back to herself, Rain rested her hands on his shoulders, her fingers curling into the muscles there.

"What about you?" She asked the question softly, looking up into his eyes. In that moment, Rain knew she'd do anything he asked. Wanted to give him the same pleasure he'd just given her.

"What about me?"

"You didn't come."

"No."

"I can --"

"No, Rain." He kissed her again, so much gentleness in his touch. "I've already done much more than I should have. Get dressed, and we'll go meet with Cain and Azriel. Mrs. McDonald left you some things by the door. Find something thin enough to wear under a vest and some heavy jeans and boots. You should have all that."

"You're letting me go with you?" Rain didn't know what to make of that. Was it some kind of joke or merely a way to keep an eye on her?

"If you still want to. Could be dangerous. Would be safer if you stayed here. I'm sure Azriel and his men have something you could do to help from here."

"Didn't expect that," she said, stepping away from him. She snagged a towel and wrapped it around her body, careful to stay out of the spray. The shower was fucking huge, so it wasn't a problem.

"For me to let you come with us?" He shrugged. "It's not final, yet. But you know the area better than us, and you can handle yourself in a fight. As long as you promise not to shoot me in the back, I'll make a case for you with Cain and Torpedo."

"Well, if I were going to kill you, I reckon I'd've done it last night."

He snorted. "Yeah. I'll take you with me. Someone's gotta keep an eye on you."

"Well, just know that while you're keepin' an eye on me, I'm doin' the same with you."

"That's what a good woman does."

Rain wasn't sure how to respond to that, so she just left to go get dressed.

Chapter Five

"Let me get this straight." Rain pinched the bridge of her nose. "You have a tracker on this kid, and you *still* can't find him?"

"Something like that. It's shielded." Azriel sighed, crossing his arms over his chest. The man seemed to be daring her to say something derogatory.

"Not all tech is infallible." A tall, muscular man joined them in the basement Azriel called a workshop. Both he and the newcomer were dressed in some kind of black, form-fitting body armor.

"This is Alexei Petrov, our... *president*, as it were." Azriel grinned and clapped the other man on the back, obviously comparing his group of obviously wealthy men with the battle-hardened, world-weary men of Bones MC.

He might have served with Azriel in the past, but Cain was less than amused now. "You guys ain't us, so don't try to be."

"No," Alexei agreed, giving Azriel a sidelong look. "We're not. We're considerably wealthier and even more highly weaponized." If Alexei meant that as a joke, no one was laughing.

"Heaven help me," Rain muttered. "I hope the fucking testosterone isn't catching."

The one they called Shadow, the one who'd been with Arkham on the roof of the theater, actually barked out his laughter. "I like this one, Arkham. You decide you don't want her, give her to me."

Arkham bared his teeth.

"We got another hit on Tobie." A man with a head full of neatly cropped ginger hair poked his head up from a panel of monitor displays. Rain had missed him until then.

"That's Giovanni, our tech man." Alexei introduced the man with a wave of his hand. "He and my wife, Merrily, are the team's computer geniuses. If there is anything digital out there to be had, rest assured those two can find it. Tobie is the missing child."

"He's been on and off the screen, but always in the same area until now." The man looked up at Alexei. "We found him on the edge of the city this time. Just beyond the edge of Hell's Playground. My guess is he's in something reinforced. Like a bunker."

"You're just now figuring this out?" Alexei looked at Giovanni, who shrugged.

"There isn't anything in that area. Or the other areas where we've seen the signal. I was beginning to think I was getting a ghost signal or something. Like residual from where he'd been."

"Let me see," Rain said, pushing her way through all the big men surrounding her to get to the monitor Giovanni was watching. There was a map of the city with several flashing dots. One was a bright green, the others fainter and white. "I'm assuming the bright green dot is where you've found him this time and the others are where he's shown up in the past?"

"That's right," Giovanni said, looking at her suspiciously.

"Well, then," she said brightly. "I know where he is and how they're moving him."

There was a beat of silence before Shadow nudged Arkham. "If she beats out the tech geniuses here, I may fight you for her."

Arkham elbowed the big man in the gut, stepping closer to Rain. She rolled her eyes then turned her attention back to the map.

"For years, some of the gangs have been working on a project to connect the whole city with a maze of underground tunnels. They use the sewers and subway tunnels, but have also made some of their own using the small network of cave systems beneath Rockwell. My guess is, the thick layer of granite in the tunnels makes your tracker harder to follow, not to mention you have to have sky to make a GPS tracker work."

"We don't use GPS," Giovanni said slowly, as if speaking to a child. "We use military-grade trackers. They can penetrate the earth."

"In a cave? Under a city?" She blew a curl out of her face in exasperation. "Look." She bent over the map, pointing to one of the dots. "This is a tunnel entrance." She moved her finger to another one. "This too. In fact, judging by where the blips are showing up, I'd say it's the Shaw gang who has the kid. They control all these points except this one." She put her finger on one spot away from all the others. "My guess is that's where they entered. Either they struck a deal with the Chinese, or they snuck in to deliberately throw you off their trail in case they were spotted. Either way, I guarantee you that tracker is not penetrating the tunnels. It's why they use them." When Giovanni opened his mouth to respond, Rain cut him off. "Didn't you just say no tech was foolproof?"

"Yup. Definitely fightin' you for her."

"I will bust your motherfuckin' head in."

"So," Cain said, ignoring the byplay. "You keep tabs on the kid, Giovanni. Let us know when he's moved and where he next shows up next. Rain…" He turned to her. "Do you know these tunnels? Can you get us through them?"

"Absolutely."

"I thought you didn't belong to any of these gangs?" Torpedo shouldered his way forward, giving her an angry look.

"I don't." She gave the big man a steady look, meeting his eyes boldly.

"Then how could you possibly know your way around in their world?"

"I grew up there," she said, doing her best not to flinch at the memory. "I know every single tunnel through there like the back of my hand. Even after I escaped, I went back to rescue others. Every time a new tunnel was dug, I made sure I explored it thoroughly. I cross the city using those tunnels regularly, and I've never once been caught."

Torpedo continued to stare at her distrustfully. Had Arkham not been right behind her, his big hand on her shoulder, Rain might have backed down, intimidated by yet another man.

"Watch yourself, brother," Arkham growled.

Torpedo turned his head to Cain. "What do you think?"

Cain didn't hesitate in answering. "If Arkham trusts her, I'm good."

"OK then." Torpedo nodded once sharply. "Let's get to work."

* * *

The tunnels were dank and damp. The odor of everything from sewage to garbage to the pungent smell of something cooking over a campfire seemed to blanket everything. There were places where their steps echoed loudly if they weren't careful, but mostly, sound was muffled and misdirected. Arkham could see how it would be very easy to get turned around and be lost in the vast network. He also could see the evidence of a forgotten population making a whole separate city beneath the city. Not only were there tunnels, but small "villages" of homeless or maybe people in charge of the controlling gang. They had to watch every single step they made, every breath they took, lest they be discovered.

"Stay quiet and out of the light." Rain spoke quietly, the throat mike Arkham had given her picking up her words for all of them. "If they get so much as a whiff we're down here they'll descend on us like a plague." He gave her an impatient look. As if she had to tell them something that rudimentary. She raised an eyebrow but otherwise ignored him.

It took the better part of an hour for Rain to get them close to their destination. She was likely right they were hiding the boy in the tunnels, because the closer she told them they were, the more heavily guarded the tunnels became. The team had to knock out several men and women who served as guards. They'd been restrained and gagged. A small storage area had served as a place to stash the guards instead of killing them. It didn't give them a lot of time -- it wouldn't be long before the guards were found -- but it would hopefully buy them enough time to get Tobie and get the hell out before they were spotted. Fighting in quarters this close would definitely get someone killed.

The further they went, the more agitated and restless Rain became. She wore a Kevlar vest over her shirt like they all did. The thing could get warm, but Arkham noticed her skin was drenched in sweat. She was having a visceral reaction to something. His mind seized on the scars she'd seen over her back and torso. She'd said she'd grown up in this world. He'd bet his life she knew these tunnels so well because she'd lived here. And been tortured here.

She never asked for a gun, probably because she knew Arkham wouldn't give her one. Instead, she carried a Louisville Slugger. Rain stopped, kneeling down, her weapon at the ready. Arkham thought she'd wipe her arm over her face to stop the sweat from trickling into her eyes, but she ignored it. Holding her hand up, she indicated everyone should stop. After a couple of minutes, two men emerged from a wooden door. The second the door opened, an ear-splitting scream came from within, anguished and frightened. The child, Tobie, was ten, according to Azriel. It was entirely possible that scream had come from him.

The last thing Arkham wanted to do was to give away their position until he had a better sense of the layout of the area. He was used to scouting everything so he knew what to expect. Now? He had no idea exactly how many hostiles there were or where they were concentrated. There seemed to be no pattern to their patrols. His gut said they were inexperienced, but he wasn't willing to put his team at risk based on his gut.

Rain wasn't so discerning.

With a battle yell, she charged, bat over her shoulder. Both men whipped around, one with a gun at the ready. Rain slammed the bat down on the gun with ferocious intensity. The next swing was at the guy's head. He blocked it but got his arm broken for the defensive gesture. The second man scurried back in the face of the Louisville Slugger and the woman not afraid to use it.

"Easy! Easy! I ain't fightin' you, Rain!" The man cowered against the wall, his hands up defensively.

"Damn fuckin' straight you ain't fightin' me, bastard! Where's the kid?"

"In there. We didn't do nothin' to him. Just scared him a little."

"He's a *kid*, you asshole!" Rain yelled at him, getting in the guy's face as he pressed himself tighter against the wall. Arkham lunged for her, but she batted her hand at him, shoving him away.

"Didn't you warn us not about drawin' attention to ourselves?" Arkham hissed, looking around them to make sure they weren't about to be ambushed.

"If we're attacked, I'll beat the living fuck outta anyone doin' the attacking." She didn't take her eyes off the young man she obviously knew and now had flat against the wall of the tunnel, the bat's end pressed tightly into his throat. "Besides, I'm betting Jimmy here knows where everyone is and how many are down here. How well they're armed. More importantly, who took the kid to begin with and where they can be found." She pressed the bat into his throat hard. The guy winced. "Don't you, you little fuck?"

"Yeah! Yeah! I can help you!"

Arkham had suspected there was fire in Rain, but this bordered on the darkness inside his own mind and body. She was spooked. Lashing out at an enemy unseen. Much as he didn't really give a fuck about the little punk, Jimmy, he didn't want Rain to really hurt the kid. If it needed doing, he'd be the one doing it. Or one of his brothers. Not his woman.

Fuck.

"Just tell me who took the kid and why." Torpedo stepped close to the man and urged Rain to back off. Arkham recognized immediately what he was doing. Rain must have too because she gave one more hard shove of the bat against his throat and backed off.

"You keep that crazy bitch away from me!" Jimmy was posturing now, pointing his finger at Rain, who bared her teeth at him. "She's crazy! Always was! Like a rabid dog! You better put her down before she bites one of you guys."

"Tell me what I want to know or I'll lock you in a room with her and that bat. Then you can fend for yourself." Torpedo grabbed him by the scruff of the neck and shook the little punk. "You gonna talk?"

"All I know is the boss wants money. Money to buy weapons."

"He got a supplier?"

Jimmy shrugged. "I ain't in his circle. I just know he keeps saying he's gettin' the motherlode. Weapons like we ain't never seen before. Not sure how one kid could be worth all that unless he's some rich dude's kid or somethin'."

Torpedo grabbed Jimmy's arm and spun him around. "Get the boy," he said to Arkham. "Let Azriel know they're made." With quick, jerky movements, Torpedo zip-tied the kid's wrists behind his back and shoved him to the floor, zip-tying his ankles. "One peep outta you before we're gone, and I'll personally come back here and put a bullet in your head. You get me?" Jimmy nodded, his eyes wide. He couldn't be much older than Rain.

Arkham knew that was the last news the Shadow Demons wanted to hear. If the underground crime world here had figured out they were more than the wealthy men who owned Argent Tech, it was only a matter of time before others did. Enemies would be coming for them.

"You know," Shadow said softly to Torpedo, "could be they know the Shadow Demons own Argent Tech. Could be betting they can trade the kid for what Argent Tech has."

"Argent Tech doesn't make weapons, Shadow. They develop the technologies that go into the weapons."

"Maybe they're just misinformed."

"You really believe that?"

"Well, shit."

"Yeah. Chances are, these gangs have made the Shadow Demons."

The journey out of the tunnels was largely uneventful. The kid, Tobie, was a real trooper. He never made a sound, though he was obviously terrified. He trembled continually, probably a result of shock. He was dirty and hungry. His lips looked dry and were beginning to crack at the corners. Considering he wasn't sweating when everyone else was, Arkham figured he was dehydrated as well.

Though it was the height of winter, some areas of the tunnels were sweltering. Those sections between the hot spots where heat from the subway trickled over, and the colder sections near exits were, naturally, more crowded since the temperature was comfortable.

Rain skillfully led them through the maze of tunnels and people without blowing their cover. It seemed to take forever getting out, and he knew she didn't take the same path out as they had in.

"You sure you trust her, brother?" Torpedo muted his mic, his voice a soft but menacing growl. "Seems like she's deliberately trying to confuse us."

"She's being cautious," he replied.

"Are you sure? Because it's not just us. We've got a kid to protect."

"Absolutely." Arkham made his response quickly. Decisively. Yes, there was a niggling doubt in his mind, but he wasn't going to acknowledge that to Torpedo. He would give Rain his full confidence unless she proved she wasn't trustworthy. Besides, he figured it had something to do with the stress she was under. And it was obviously post-traumatic stress.

He eased his way to the front so he could be close to Rain. She gripped that bat like a lifeline while she crouched and scouted out the next tunnel series. There were four different directions, and she seemed to be torn on which way to go.

"You OK?"

"Fine." Her response was clipped, and she didn't look at him, just studied the way ahead.

"Don't lie to me, Rain. Tell me what you need me to do."

She closed her eyes. "Just give me a minute. We need to go down that tunnel. It's only a few hundred yards, and we'll come out on the other side of the city from where we entered. You should be able to contact your people then and have them pick you up."

"Why did you go to the other side of the city? Why not just bring us back where we entered?"

"I didn't want to backtrack in case they started missing the people we took out. I didn't want to risk a fight with the child to protect. He's been through enough."

"You haven't talked to him. He seems fine to me."

"That's because you've never been a prisoner of these gangs," she snapped. "Trust me. He may not have a mark on him, but he's been through enough."

Arkham let the silence linger for a while, thinking she was ready to move on. She knew which way to go but seemed reluctant to move.

"Talk to me, Rain."

She shuddered before she could stop herself. "I can't seem to make myself move," she finally admitted.

"Even if there is a guard at the end of the tunnel there will be only one. Two at most. Your team can easily take them. The way is smooth walls. No offshoots or any way to sneak up on you. The only direction you need to worry about is straight ahead or straight behind."

"Understood. Let's go." Arkham grabbed her by the arm, but she whimpered and resisted him, pulling away. Her eyes were wild, and she was clearly terrified. "Rain, you're going to have to tell me what's going on."

"I can't go in there," she finally said in a whisper. "I can't make myself go down that tunnel."

"You're not alone, Rain. I've got your back."

She nodded several times. Arkham could see the pulse at her throat fluttering like mad.

"Everything OK up there?" Torpedo's voice came through Arkham's earpiece. The team was anxious to move. So was Arkham.

"Give me a minute." She was freaking out. Arkham had seen it more than once, experienced it himself. If she couldn't pull herself together, he'd have to carry her out. "Do you trust me, Rain?"

Her head whipped around, her large, round eyes meeting his. She opened her mouth but didn't seem to be able to respond to him.

"Pull it together," he hissed, gripping her shoulders when her gaze slid to the side away from him. "Look at me!" He waited until she met his gaze once more. "I'm not going to let anything happen to you. Lead us out. I'll be right by your side. Understand me?"

Finally, she nodded. Arkham watched as her face hardened. She took a deep breath, fighting as hard as he'd ever seen anyone fight.

"Straight shot," she muttered. "Straight shot, then I'm out."

"I'm right here." Arkham hooked his left hand into the top of her Kevlar vest, hoping it would reassure her. "You want a gun?" His team had decided against it because she was still an unknown, but he would do anything at this point to help her overcome this crippling fear.

She shook her head. "I'd never forgive myself if I killed someone who was innocent. I have a gun, I'm likely to pull the trigger at anything that moves."

Arkham respected her all the more for the admission. "Let's go," he said. "Get out. Get home."

"Get out. Get home," she repeated. Then moved them into the tunnel.

Chapter Six

The last two hundred yards of that tunnel were the longest of Rain's life. She'd been trapped in this very same tunnel three years earlier. Had fought until she'd finally been overwhelmed from both ends. She'd killed more than she thought she could, but they'd subdued her, and her life in hell began.

"Not much farther," she whispered. She wasn't sure if she was talking to Arkham or herself. His hand never once wavered from his hold at the back of her vest. His fingers were under her shirt against her skin. It was the only thing keeping her grounded. "Not much farther. I see the tunnel entrance…"

"Keep moving," Arkham said at her ear. "I'm right here."

Rain thought they might actually make it to the outside without incident. Then a beam of light flashed from the mouth of the tunnel. "Juarez? That you? Where you been, man?"

Rain froze. Arkham had to pull her back against the wall, putting himself between her and whoever was at the entrance.

"Juarez?"

Arkham eased forward, gun at the ready. Rain was trembling so hard she was afraid her knees were going to give out. Making herself move with Arkham was the hardest thing she'd ever done. She glanced behind her, expecting to see light coming from the other direction. There was a roaring in her ears, and she knew she was hyperventilating. One of Arkham's men passed her. The next thing she knew, the child they'd rescued was at her side, tentatively taking her hand. She looked down at him and she could see the same fear in his eyes she knew was in hers. Rain squeezed his hand. They were in this together.

The men behind her and Tobie kept pushing them forward. Rain had to bite her lip to keep from whimpering, but she was in the midst of a full-blown panic attack. Her vision tunneled so that all she could see was the light shining from the flashlight at the tunnel entrance. There were heavy footfalls and sounds of a struggle somewhere around her, but she couldn't process it. Someone pushed her down, and she and Tobie clung to each other as they sat with their backs to the wall.

Sometime later, Arkham urged her to her feet. "Come on, honey. Help's on the way. They've got Tobie's mother with them. Let's get out of these tunnels."

The second he led her into the cool January night, Rain took a huge breath. She gasped and immediately started coughing as the icy air hit her lungs, sending her into a spasm. Her stomach heaved, and she puked over and over into the bushes. Again, she took a deep breath. The icy air made her lungs spasm again, which sent her into a coughing fit, but it felt good to breathe the clean, cold air. She *could* breathe now. Her heart rate slowed down gradually and she felt safer, though she was still out in the open. Tobie still clung to her hand, not convinced they were safe.

Finally, Rain's knees gave out and she sank down onto the ground, pulling the little boy into her arms. She still clutched the bat, still looked around her wildly, expecting to find someone charging toward her or pointing a gun at her. Instead, she found Arkham, Torpedo, Shadow, and Goose surrounding her and Tobie, standing guard. They were inside an impenetrable circle of protection, the guards vicious in their duty. It was then she dropped the bat and comforted the little boy in her arms.

Rain lost track of time as they waited. She knew they were away from the tunnel but had no idea how far or exactly where. Once she'd stumbled out into the cold night she'd just let Arkham and his brothers lead her where they would. It was cold, but she hardly noticed. In fact, after being in the heat of the tunnels, the night felt good.

A Humvee pulled up, and Arkham conferred with the driver as the doors opened. Tobie's mother leapt out and sprinted for her son. Rain surrendered him but had no idea what to do next. She was exhausted. Looking up, she saw Arkham standing over her, looking at her, his expression blank. Then he sighed, stooping to pick her up in his arms, cradling her against his chest with his chin resting on top of her head.

He climbed into the vehicle with her, holding her the entire way. It wasn't until they reached his room that he finally set her on her feet and only once they were in the bathroom. He ran water for a bath then helped her out of her clothing. Surprisingly, he stripped right after her and put them both in the hot water. Positioning her in front of him between his legs, Arkham urged her to rest her head on his shoulder while he washed her, cleaning the sweat from her body gently and almost reverently.

"You were very brave today, Rain. I've never seen someone fight the way you did."

"I lost my head," she muttered, ashamed he'd witnessed her fear and recognized it for what it was.

"You won a hard-fought battle inside your mind, one you had no control over. You won."

"Only because you and the others were there. You didn't give me much choice."

"Rain, you were the one to lead us into that tunnel. You led us through the whole damned mess. You should have told me before we started. We might have found a better way."

She sat up a little, looking back at him over her shoulder. "And leave that little boy down there one second longer than he had to be? No. I couldn't allow that."

He grinned at her as if she'd just proven his point. "Told you you were brave."

Rain grunted at him, not feeling the least bit brave but wanting the comfort of his touch. She leaned back, letting him continue to wash and massage her body with those big, rough hands of his. It wasn't long before she fell into some kind of trance, just closing her eyes and letting him work her body into a puddle of goo.

For a long time she sat there, completely relaxed against Arkham's hard chest, his strong arms surrounding her, those wonderfully rough hands molding and shaping her body. The next thing she knew, Rain heard someone crying, then sobbing uncontrollably. She opened her eyes and sat up, looking around her, needing to go to whoever was in such distress. When Arkham pulled her back to him, turning her over so she was lying against him chest to chest, she realized the person in such distress was her. It was like a veil slowly being lifted and the moment solidifying from a murky haze.

"Shhh," he whispered. "I've got you, and no one will ever hurt you again. I'll kill anyone even tryin' to get near you."

She clung to Arkham like she'd never done at any time in her life with anyone else. Rain was the strong one, the one everyone else leaned on. She was the one who'd gone back into those tunnels and gotten boys and girls out even after she'd made it out herself. In all that time, she'd never had anyone to lean on. Now, Arkham was there. He was there, and he was hell on wheels. She knew he could back up his words if for no other reason than he had his brothers backing him up. These guys were the real deal. And so was Arkham.

"I'm sorry." Rain was deeply embarrassed to lose control like this. Never in her life had she broken down to such a degree. "I'm so sorry."

Arkham rubbed her back up and down, kissing her forehead as he continued his gentle massage. "You've got nothin' to be sorry for. You helped us save that kid. Only you could have taken us through that place."

"I never would have made it out --"

"You could have taken us back the way we came in. We'd have probably killed several, but you could have done it. Instead, you chose to take us out a way you knew would have fewer people and raise less attention. You saved more lives than just little Tobie's. Now, can you tell me about this? I can't make it go away, but I can be the one you share this with."

"There's not much to tell," she started. "I got caught. In that same tunnel. Four came from the front. Three from the back. I killed one of them. Fought off two more before the rest overwhelmed me. They kept me chained in those tunnels for three weeks before I was able to escape. During that time…" She swallowed, shuddering uncontrollably before continuing. "That's when I got most of those scars on my body. But the girls I went in to save got out. I knew the gang was on to us and sent the girls a different way."

"So, you deliberately put yourself in harm's way to save others?"

She shrugged. "I never thought about it that way. Those girls would've never survived down there. They'd been taken from their homes in the city. I was raised there. It was hard on me, but they'd have died."

"Looks like you nearly did, if the scars over your body are any indication."

It struck Rain then how unappealing she was to look at. Now, she'd taken the one thing she had -- her strength -- and thrown it away.

She turned over, standing in the tub before climbing out of the oversized thing and grabbing a towel. Somehow, standing there, knowing Arkham was watching her was worse torture than what she'd endured in that stupid tunnel and the weeks following her capture. Rain tried to turn her profile to him so he couldn't see so much, but she knew he'd never forget the one really good look he'd gotten of her. She was scarred. Ugly.

Again, tears coursed down her face, even more unforgivable this time because it was over a man. Rain could honestly say she had never even considered wanting a man, even for a temporary fling. Growing up in the environment she had, sex wasn't even an afterthought. It was a way for men to exert dominance over women. When she'd offered herself before, it was because she felt she owed Arkham for not letting his club harm her and because she'd wanted it to be on her own terms. If it was going to happen, it would be when she chose with the man she chose. Now, she found she honestly wanted the experience with Arkham. But not like this. Not as a pity fuck.

Without a word, Arkham stood behind her, stepping out of the tub himself. She made two steps toward the door when he grabbed her arm. "Stay, Rain." His voice was soft, not like the man she knew he could be. This man was gentle. It made matters worse because she knew he was a man who took what he wanted, yet he wasn't making a move on her.

"Let me go."

"If that's what you want," he said, not letting go of her arm. Instead, he pulled her to him, turning her so she had to face him.

Her gaze landed squarely on his muscled, hair-dusted chest. Of their own accord, her hands landed there, tracing the contours lovingly. He was just as scarred as she was, only from battle. His body was perfectly made, thick muscle and tantalizing sinew dancing with every movement. Tattoos covered places with a piece of what she knew was significant art from his time in the military or his brotherhood with Bones MC. In a word, he was *beautiful*.

Again, tears sprang to her eyes though she tried to blink them back. Very gently, Arkham framed her face with his hands, forcing her to look up at him. She saw anything but pity in his eyes. There was a hunger that went bone deep. A need she wasn't sure she could ever satisfy, mainly because she had no experience in pleasing a man.

"I know I'm ugly, Arkham," she began, but he cut her off by lowering his head to hers and taking her mouth in a kiss.

His kiss started out gentle, coaxing her to kiss him back. Once she did, when she lapped at his tongue, he deepened the kiss. Aggression and a deep, all-consuming lust poured from him. Rain knew she probably matched those same traits with her own kiss. Arkham was like no man she'd ever met in her life. He was dangerous and unpredictable, but he was a man with a fierce protective nature. She knew in her heart he meant it when he said he'd keep her safe. The question was, did he actually want her or was he doing this because he didn't want to hurt her feelings?

"Stop," she whispered. "Arkham, I…"

"You what? Don't want me? Because I won't believe that. You want me or you wouldn't have initiated sex in the shower."

"Not if you don't want me," she said. "I'm not any kind of catch. I come with baggage and all these scars."

"I have scars of my own. While each and every one of yours pains me, it also shows me your strength. You survived and became this wonderful, compassionate, courageous woman." He kissed her again, nipping her bottom lip. "I want you, baby. When I told you you were coming with Bones, that was code for you're coming with me."

Rain couldn't help the smile tugging at the corners of her lips. Arkham was a force she was unable to resist and didn't want to. She'd take what he gave her and do her best to not let her heart get involved.

Chapter Seven

When Arkham wrapped his arms around Rain, he knew he'd come home. She clung to him sweetly, kissing him back with as much passion as he felt for her. He straightened, lifting her off the floor, and Rain wrapped her legs around him. Making it to the bed was difficult, but she needed him gentle. He needed to explore her body, learn what she liked and what she loved. Rain wasn't yet convinced he meant to keep her, but before they left for Kentucky, she'd know he meant business.

Once they were on the bed, Arkham wedged himself between her thighs, rocking his hips to position his cock over her mound. He intended to tease her like he'd done in the shower before he took her. There was no question she'd had sex before, but Arkham was certain she had never done so because of her own need. It had probably always been in payment for something. He intended to show her another side of sex. One he hoped she'd become addicted to.

His full weight resting on her, Arkham pressed her into the mattress, kissing her over and over. Rain clutched at his shoulders, shaped them and his arms with her small, delicate hands. He let his fingers tangle in the length of her hair, tugging occasionally just to gain that little gasp from her when the pain bit into her scalp. He knew that little pain would intensify the pleasure. Sure enough, the third time he flexed his fingers she cried out and wrapped her legs around him once again, lifting herself to make contact with her clit over his dick. That was his cue to back off.

He kissed her face from her forehead over both temples and cheeks to her chin. When she arched her neck to give him better access, Arkham took advantage. Her hands flew to his head, her fingers tunneling through his hair to hang on.

Arkham used his beard to trail over her skin, trying to stimulate her as much as he could. Soon, he had her writhing beneath him before he even got to her breasts. Once he took the peak of one into his mouth and sucked gently, Rain was a screaming mass of nerves.

Her responses were so real and raw Arkham was humbled to be the man to unleash all that passion. On the heels of that thought came the ruthless one that he would be the *only* man to have her passion. Rain was his, and he'd damn well *never* let her go.

Rain had a compact body, small and slight but sculpted with fine muscle. Her breasts were small, and Arkham hungrily enveloped one in his mouth, sucking and flicking her nipple as he groaned and growled around it. Before he realized what he was doing, Arkham found himself grinding his cock into the sheets of the bed in time to Rain's movement against his belly where she pressed her clit against him.

Control was a tenuous thing. Arkham held on to his by sheer force of will. As Rain squirmed her little body beneath him, Arkham knew she was unable to find her own control, and he didn't want her to. He wanted her lost in the moment and that was exactly what he got.

After lavishing attention on her other breast, Arkham moved to her belly, dipping his tongue into her navel and nipping the flesh just below. By now, Rain had her legs spread wide, her knees bent and pulled up so he had free access to her.

Arkham hovered just over her sex, drawing out the moment. Rain's eyes were glazed over, wide and wild. She repeatedly thrust her hips up to him, wanting what came next but not voicing what she needed.

"Talk to me, baby," he encouraged. Arkham wanted her engaged, an active participant. He wanted her to know who was doing this to her and wanted her to give him direction.

"Why did you stop?" she gasped out.

"Tell me what you want me to do." Arkham hardly recognized his own voice. He was actually shaking, he was so engrossed in Rain. "Tell me, baby."

"Arkham, I don't know what I want! I just... I just want you to keep doing what you're doing!"

"Do you want my mouth on your pretty little cunt?"

"Oh, God!" She whimpered, and her body broke out in a sweat, shuddering under him. "Please do that!"

With a growl, Arkham latched on to her pussy, licking her clit and lapping up the juice that spilled from her body. Holding her legs open, Arkham lapped and sucked to his heart's content. For long, long minutes, he lost himself in her cries and the evidence her body provided that she loved what he was doing. No woman had ever tasted sweeter. No woman had ever responded so honestly and unabashedly. The effect was intoxicating to Arkham. It was as if his whole life he'd been waiting for this one woman. She was too young for him, but there was no way he was giving her up.

Finally, she tugged his hair, pulling him up her body so she could kiss him once again. Her arms wound around him, her legs. She constantly whimpered and cried out. Her body was drenched in sweat. Arkham was in awe of the sight she made, of the feel of her lithe body beneath his.

Arkham pulled away, reaching for the nightstand, but Rain was having none of it. She wanted him inside her that second. "Arkham," she gasped.

"I've got you, honey. Just give me a minute."

"No! Arkham!" Rain pulled him to her with her legs, crossing her ankles and locking him to her. "Now!"

"Baby, I'm just trying to protect you. I swear I'm not leaving."

"Unh!" She reached between them to find his cock and guided him into her. She and Arkham both cried out.

"Fuck!" Arkham threw back his head as he sank into her as far as he could go. Rain pulled him to her, clawing at his shoulders until his full weight was on her. She kept his body close, clinging to him, moving with him as he surged into her. The sensations were strange but so fucking good! She was consumed by him and the sensations he effortlessly created within her.

It wasn't long before pleasure overwhelmed her. Her body spiraled out of control, building to a weeping crescendo of intensity so profound she knew she'd be forever changed. Never would she be able to think about this act of sex without remembering Arkham and how he'd so generously and wonderfully introduced her to how it could be between a man and a woman.

She screamed, unable to voice what was happening to her. Tears spilled from her eyes as she came in wave after wave of blistering pleasure. Seconds later, Arkham's big body shuddered above her. He threw back his head and shouted his completion and came deep inside her. It was then she realized what he'd been trying to do before. He'd wanted to use a condom and she'd refused to let him. For her part, she wasn't sorry. She honestly didn't want it any other way. What she'd experienced in his arms was complete with his seed inside her, no matter how irresponsible.

When he collapsed on top of her, breathing as heavily as she was, she stroked his back over and over, never wanting the moment to pass.

"Are you OK?" His voice was husky from his shouts. "I tried to protect you, but when you took me inside you…"

"I'm not sorry," she said, honestly. "Everything about this was perfect." She was still crying and tried to pull herself together. "That was the most beautiful thing," she whispered. "So beautiful."

"*You're* beautiful," he said with so much feeling Rain found she believed him. He actually did find her beautiful despite her scars.

"I'm not very experienced at this," she confessed. "I don't know how to please you, but I'm willing to learn if you'll teach me."

Arkham chuckled, rolling them to their sides but still holding her close. "I have no doubt you'll be a star pupil."

With a groan, he pulled out of her and kissed her forehead. "I'll be right back," he whispered. He disappeared into the bathroom and brought back a wet washcloth. He cleaned her then tossed the cloth back into the bathroom before climbing back into bed with her and pulling her into his arms.

One hand stroked her back lazily, lulling her into a kind of catharsis. All the anger and paralyzing fear she'd felt before they'd made love vanished with his gentle caresses. The lovemaking had pushed them away, but in the aftermath, his touch alone kept everything at bay, giving her time to make peace with herself. No matter what happened from here on out, Rain knew she'd never be the same. As she lay there in Arkham's arms, she realized that this change wasn't a bad thing.

* * *

The ride back to Kentucky and the Bones compound was long. By the halfway point -- three hours in -- Rain was second-guessing herself in a major way. Sure, the sex had been great, and she and Arkham seemed to have bonded, but there were so many dynamics she was unsure about. She hoped that, once they stopped and she could be at his side again, he'd alleviate her fears just by being near her. Rain certainly had no intention of confessing her insecurities to him.

All the men but Trucker had ridden their bikes. Arkham had put her in the chase vehicle with Trucker, telling her it was too cold for her to ride. Trucker had proved a pleasant companion, but he didn't talk about anything personal. Like Arkham. Rain got the impression the men had known each other a very long time, but he refused to talk about Arkham in a personal manner except to tell her he'd never allowed a woman to stay with him more than a few nights. If that. It didn't give her much confidence. In fact, she was starting to rethink the whole situation.

They didn't stop the whole six hours, just kept rolling. Several times she looked out one of the side windows of the RV and spotted Arkham. He never looked at her. She supposed he needed to concentrate on the road, especially with as cold as it had to be riding that stupid bike in January, but it still stung. She felt like he was pulling away from her and there was nothing she could do about it. Several times, she watched the men interacting with each other. She was sure they were talking but it was a circle she wasn't included in.

"Not long now, girl," Trucker called to her over his shoulder. "Half an hour."

"Good to know."

It wasn't. If things turned out badly, what was she going to do? She had no way to support herself or even to get back home. She was stuck here with a man nearly twice her age with more experience in *everything*. There was nothing she could contribute to his life. He was the warrior. He was the lover. She was... a body.

By the time they pulled into the parking lot of the clubhouse, Rain had worked herself up into a fit of nerves. She put on her coat and stepped out of the RV. The men pulled their bikes into a huge garage on the side of the building before shaking hands and slapping each other on the back in congratulations for a job well done.

They hadn't eliminated the gang problem in Rockwell, but they'd found the missing child and clued the Shadow Demons in to the fact that the city was figuring out who and what they were. At least, the underbelly of the city was. Gangs could do damage with that kind of knowledge, a fact the Demons found out when the child had been taken.

Rain waited for a minute, but Arkham didn't come for her. He lingered in the garage for some unknown reason. Finally, cold and tired, Rain gave up waiting and just went into the clubhouse.

Their compound looked like an overly large hotel. A resort maybe. Flanked with fruit trees and what looked like a space for a very large garden, she wondered how lush and green the place would be in the spring and summer. Would she be around to see it?

"Rain." Torpedo met her inside. He and Cain had been the first ones inside. She supposed the others secured their bikes or whatever and the president and vice president were left to do as they pleased.

She smiled awkwardly in greeting. "Thanks for letting me tag along."

"I hope you'll like it here. I know the women will be happy to have you here. I think they sometimes feel outnumbered by the patch chasers."

God, she had to learn a whole new vocabulary. "What will I be doing here? I mean, I have to earn my keep."

"We'll figure out where you best fit in in a few days. I'm sure you'll want to get your bearings."

"Where's Arkham?" She couldn't resist asking after him for another second.

"Uh, I'm not sure," Torpedo said, crossing his hands over his chest and looking anywhere but at her. "I think he had some things to do."

"Oh. Well, is there someplace I could dump my stuff?" She didn't have much, other than what Mrs. McDonald had brought her, but she needed to stash her bag someplace.

"Yeah." He motioned to a wizened woman behind the bar with a man about the same age at her side. "Mama will show you where to go." Torpedo waited until Mama approached them. Even at her age, the woman was stunningly beautiful with chestnut hair streaked liberally with silver. She had clear grey eyes that seemed to look into Rain's soul. "Mama and Pops over there aren't members of Bones, but are very important to our club," Torpedo said by way of introduction. "She can introduce you to the women once you're settled. If you need anything, you can go to Mama until you learn your way around."

"Such a beautiful young woman," Mama said with a warm, welcoming smile.

Rain blushed, her mouth dropping open. "I -- uh, thanks."

"Come on," she said, circling Rain's shoulders with one surprisingly strong arm. "This place is huge. Like a big hotel."

They walked down the hall and up one flight of stairs. Mama took her about halfway down the hall and opened a door, handing her a key. "This is your own space. Decorate it however you want. You clean after yourself and help with the housework. Once you figure out where you fit in, you just see what needs to be done and do it. Everyone kind of finds things they like, and it becomes their special thing, you know?"

"What's your thing?" Rain's chest was tightening. First, Arkham had other things to do than make sure she settled in here, now she was shown a room that wasn't Arkham's for her stay.

"Pops and I try to be a guiding influence on Bones. I was a doctor in a past life so I help patch them up when things don't exactly go their way in the field. Pops..." She trailed off, her eyes looking haunted for the briefest moment. "Pops is Pops." She smiled faintly. For a brief moment, Rain thought Mama looked much older than she first appeared. There was definitely a story there that Mama wasn't going to share.

"What kinds of things will I be doing? What if I don't find anything I fit in doing? I don't really have any specialized training." Other than what she'd picked up on the streets. Given how she'd reacted in the tunnels, Arkham wouldn't let her learn how to fight so she could go with him on rides or whatever MCs did. Besides, she already knew they were more than a bunch of guys running together on motorcycles. They had combat training. All of them. That much was clear.

She shrugged. "Depends, I guess. Mostly, the women cook and clean. A few of them... Well, this club does stuff outside the law sometimes. When they go looking for... companionship, keeping it inside the club is preferable, especially when they're running something questionable. Some of the girls are here for that purpose. They give the men a good time with no strings attached. But they still help with the housework and cooking. Everyone but me, Magenta, Luna, Darcy, and Angel."

Rain tilted her head, confused. "The four of them don't help with the upkeep of the place? 'Cause they have other jobs?"

"Somewhat. But mostly because they're ol' ladies of patched members. The men don't like to have their wives in with the rest of the club women. They're just too possessive. They don't want there to be any misunderstandings with other club members or prospects."

"I see." Rain did. And it felt like a punch to the gut. She wanted to cry. Instead, she gave Mama a bright, grateful smile. "Thanks for showing me up here."

"Come back down once you get unpacked. Supper should be ready in half an hour or so. You can join us and get to know everyone." Mama seemed like a genuinely nice person. There was a little something in her eyes that made Rain think she'd been through a lot but had found her happiness.

"Thanks. I might do that."

After Mama left, Rain locked the door and looked around. There was a large bed, a desk, a table, and a kitchen in two rooms. One bathroom. Like a hotel suite. The place really was like a resort or something. Instead of feeling relieved she was someplace safe, or happy she was finally in a permanent home if she chose to stay, Rain felt the weight of the world settling on her shoulders.

Arkham was just like every other man she'd ever met. He'd gotten what he wanted, and he was leaving her. Rain could handle that. It would hurt, but she could handle it. What she couldn't handle was seeing him with another woman. That would shatter her heart.

Rain walked to the window feeling more lost and confused and hurt than she could ever remember feeling in her life. Even her torture at the hands of the Shaw gang hadn't hurt like this. They'd never touched her inside. Arkham had captured her heart, her imagination. She hadn't even acknowledged to herself everything he represented to her. A home. A family. Someone to always stand in front of her when danger came. Now... She didn't know what she was going to do.

When she reached the window and looked out, her heart leapt to see Arkham hurrying out of the garage where they'd parked their bikes. Unbidden, a smile found her lips, and she pressed her palms to the glass as if she could reach out and touch him. Was he headed back to the house? To her?

Then a woman hurried out of the garage and handed him his jacket. As if he'd left it behind in his haste to exit. Was she adjusting her clothes? A slim African American, she was tall. Nearly as tall as Arkham. She sported long braids that fell past her ass in a thick mass pulled back with a tie. Several long strands had escaped the tie and fell around her face. Arkham took the jacket, unfolded it carefully and looked at the back of it. He nodded, seeming satisfied with something before folding it once again and holding it against his chest. The scene was enough to make Rain's knees weak, but when Arkham took the woman in his free arm and hugged her tightly, something inside Rain shattered.

She collapsed to the floor underneath the window, her legs just not supporting her any longer. She could hear herself moaning but couldn't seem to stop. The tears couldn't be stopped either. There was now a gaping hole in her chest where her heart had been, and Rain knew she had no one to blame but herself. She'd allowed herself to believe a man as extraordinary as Arkham could want her for his own. Hell, he might still want her, but he obviously didn't intend to be hers as well, and that was something Rain couldn't tolerate.

Taking a shuddering breath, Rain stumbled to her feet and went to the bathroom to wash her face. She had to pull herself together if she was going to get out of here. It was time to run.

Chapter Eight

Arkham still couldn't believe he was doing this. When Cheetah had given him the jacket he'd asked to have made for Rain, something inside him had swelled, leaving a full feeing in his chest, an excitement he'd never felt before. Rain was going to be his ol' lady. She'd wear his property patch on her back, and she'd be with him forever. He expected to feel a sense of dread. No woman had ever had a claim on him, and he hadn't expected one ever would. But Rain had taken his heart, and it was hers irrevocably. Now, he just had to explain things to her. Not only had he brought her with him away from her home and the danger there, he was *never* letting her go. She was his. He was hers.

He stepped inside the house and was immediately greeted by his brothers with shouts and claps on the back. Trucker was gleefully telling everyone about the woman who'd captured his brother's heart. He made Arkham out to be a mushy pushover and Rain to be a little pixie Amazon, but Arkham was OK with it. As far as he was concerned, Rain was one of the bravest people he'd ever met.

"Where is she?" Arkham looked around the room, searching for his woman. His heart seemed to swell with each beat. Just the making the decision seemed to have altered him in a profound way.

"I left her in her room," Mama answered. "I'm a little confused though. You said nothing about keeping this girl for your own. I'd have taken her to your room if I'd known."

Arkham held up the jacket for Mama to see. He couldn't help his grin at the satisfaction of letting others see it. "It's a surprise for her. She knows I intend to keep her with me, but I just decided on the way home I wanted it to be a permanent arrangement."

Mama grinned. "Well then. I suggest you go collect your woman and introduce her properly, young man. She thinks she's just another club girl around here, and none of us knew the difference."

"Oh, shit," he muttered. "Which room?"

"Middle of the hall on the left. Overlooking the bike garage." She tossed him a key. No doubt it was to Rain's room.

"Thanks, Mama."

Arkham jogged down the hall and trotted up the stairs. He knew exactly which room Mama had put Rain in and started calling her name as he neared.

"Rain!" He knocked on her door with a knuckle. "Rain, come out. I've got something for you."

No answer.

"Rain?"

When she still didn't answer, Arkham unlocked the door and let himself in. Her bag was on the bed, open, and her things seemed to be all there, but her coat was not.

With a sinking feeling in the pit of his stomach, Arkham went to the window and looked out. Below he saw parking lot where the RV was still parked and the garage where they kept the bikes in winter. He also saw the spot where Cheetah had given him the jacket she'd just finished with his property patch sewn lovingly on the back.

And where he'd embraced the woman in thanks.

"Rain!" He roared her name, his world tunneling toward one goal. Finding Rain before he lost his fucking mind. The door to the bathroom was open, but she wasn't there. He hadn't seen her in the hall so that meant she'd probably left not too long after he'd exited the garage. That had been about fifteen minutes.

"Fuck!"

Taking out his phone, he texted Torpedo. She couldn't have gotten far because she didn't have a car. No one had reported a car or bike leaving so he was confident he had a good chance of finding her quickly, but it still made his gut churn. Rain was hurting. Because he hadn't bothered to inform his club exactly what she was to him, it was his fault.

His phone rang.

"Everyone's on the move. What do you want us to do when we find her?"

"Let me know immediately. Follow her but don't approach her unless she tries to get into a car or something. I don't want to make this any worse than it already is."

"What'd you do?" Torpedo sounded angry. Likely, he suspected Arkham had acted like an ass. Torpedo was the vice president, but he sometimes had to function as the voice of reason when the members forgot they were human and not unthinking animals. Usually where women they desperately cared about were concerned.

"Didn't inform Mama Rain was to be taken to my room and not put in a common room like the other club girls."

There was silence. "OK. That's not good, but not devastating. What else?"

"Why do you assume I did something stupid?"

"Did you?"

Arkham wanted to answer in the negative, but he didn't lie to his brothers, no matter how hard. "Maybe. I gave Cheetah a hug when she brought me the jacket she'd sewn for Rain with my property patch on it. I can't be sure, but I'm betting Rain saw that. I haven't seen her since we got back from Rockwell."

"OK. Again, that's bad but not a deal breaker. What else?"

"Nothing else. Other than she's young and inexperienced in sexual matters. I don't mean physically. Mentally. I'm sure she knows the difference between sex and love and I'm afraid she may think we shared the former."

"Did you tell her you loved her?"

"Well, not in so many words. No."

"Idiot," Torpedo muttered.

"It's only been a few days. It kinda snuck up on me." Arkham scrubbed his hand over his face. "You know, someday you're going to be the one in this situation, and I hope I'm still here to watch."

"Let's just get your woman back so you can straighten all this out, brother." Arkham could hear the amusement in Torpedo's voice. His brothers would help him find Rain. They would help him bring her home. Then Arkham would bind her to him forever. It was as good as done.

* * *

It was cold outside. Perhaps that's why Rain couldn't seem to get moving. It certainly wasn't because she was hesitant to leave Arkham. If she wasn't good enough for him to be with her and no one else, then she didn't want him. Hell, she couldn't imagine being with another man the way she was with Arkham! How could he want to be with another woman?

Except she *did* want him. She *ached* with wanting him. Every step away from Arkham was like a knife to her heart. In the short time she'd known him, Rain had come to depend on him. And, goddammit, she just plain *liked* him! He was larger than life. A force to be reckoned with. He'd taken charge in the tunnel and hadn't condemned her when she'd become too incapacitated to continue. More importantly, he'd gotten her and the child out, protecting them both with a fierceness matched only by his brothers. Yet, they hadn't been needlessly cruel or deadly. When they'd given their report to Azriel, Torpedo had acknowledged leaving most everyone alive. He'd told the other man, "This isn't our territory to judge. You know the people much better than we do. This was a rescue mission. Not an execution party." Surprisingly, Azriel had agreed. Shadow Demons had no wish for anyone to be killed needlessly. They'd be dealt with individually. Not as a group. That conversation had shed more light on both groups of men than anything she'd witnessed before.

Rain made it as far as the road leading to the compound before she sat in a little thicket of trees, out of sight from anyone. She just couldn't make herself go any farther. Not yet. Rain doubted Arkham would look for her. It would probably relieve him to know he didn't have to take responsibility for her anymore. And why the fuck was she sitting there feeling sorry for herself? If she was the woman Arkham deserved, she'd be up there fighting for her man. Instead, she sat in the snow and cold, tears streaking down her face like a teenager with a hopeless crush. Which, she kind of was, she supposed.

"Fucker," she muttered.

"You wanna tell me what the fuck you're doin' out here in the fuckin' cold instead of waiting for me at the clubhouse?"

Arkham!

Even as her heart leapt, Rain wanted to scream in frustration. "Ain't none of your goddamned business."

"It's every bit my goddamned business, Rain! Fuck!" He reached inside her little hiding place and plucked her out by the back of her jacket and shirt. She nearly squealed like a little girl. "Just where the fuckin' hell do you think you're goin'?"

She stuck her chin up. "Away."

"Away where?"

"Don't matter. I'm leavin'. I don't like it here."

"Stubborn, pigheaded little runt," he muttered before scooping her up and tossing her over his shoulder.

"Put me down!" Rain screamed and beat against his broad back with her fists, kicking out wildly. Of course, he took the opportunity to swat her ass none too gently.

"Stop squirmin'!"

"Bastard!"

"Runt!"

"Oooh!"

Knowing there was no way she was getting away from him if he didn't want her to, she did as he told her, bracing herself with her hands on his back. "Just know that I will get down from here, Arkham. When I do, I'm gonna kick you in the balls and I'll be long gone before you get off the ground."

"You can try, honey."

The worst part was he didn't sound put out. He sounded almost amused.

"You better not be laughin' at me."

He cleared his throat as three of his brothers fell into step around them. "Wouldn't dream of it."

"Liar," she muttered.

They marched on in silence until they reached the steps of the compound. Arkham set her on her feet then. With the blood rushing to her head, she was a little dizzy but stood her ground with only a little sway.

Arkham spun her around to face him, steadying her by the shoulders. He met her eyes in a fierce stare. Without saying a word, he reached out to Torpedo, who handed him a jacket. Arkham raised an eyebrow as he turned the jacket around so she could read the patch on the back.

"PROPERTY OF… ARKHAM."

The stitching was in bold silver lettering lined in gold on a top and bottom rocker. In the middle was the Bones MC patch.

"Turn around," he said gruffly.

"Why?"

"Because I'm puttin' this jacket on you and you're gonna wear it."

"Property of? Really, Arkham?"

He snorted, though his brothers didn't, a fact Rain was acutely aware of. "It means I'm makin' you my ol' lady."

"Do I get a say in this?"

Now there were a few snorts from his brothers. "Sure. You get to say yes."

"What does being your ol' lady mean? 'Cause I ain't hangin' around if you're gonna be with other women."

Arkham sighed, but slung the jacket around her shoulders, urging her to put her arms in the sleeves before he answered her. "It means you're mine and I'm yours. No one else for either of us." Rain was so startled, all she could do was stand there with her mouth open. Tears formed in her eyes, but she blinked them back. "You saw me and Cheetah, didn't you?"

Rain stuck her chin up defiantly. "I did."

"Cheetah sewed the patch for me. I asked her to do it when we left Rockwell. She worked on it nonstop so she could have it done when we got home so I could give it to you." He shrugged. "Cheetah's what you might call a hugger. I was very grateful to her, so yeah. I hugged her. I don't want her. Not as my woman. Not even for an occasional fuck." He took a step closer so she had to crane her neck to look at him. "I only want you, Rain."

Rain couldn't help herself. The impact of his words was like a physical caress. Her knees went rubbery, and she probably would have just sat down right there if Arkham hadn't caught her. He pulled her tightly into his arms and buried his face in her hair. It was only then she realized his body was trembling against hers, and she felt a dampness against her neck where his face was next to hers. He was crying? And, goddammit, she was crying, too.

* * *

There had never been a time in his life when emotion had overwhelmed Arkham. Not when he'd lost brothers in Afghanistan. Not when his parents had died. Not when he'd lost any number of people in his life who were important to him. Knowing he'd hurt Rain enough for her to run from him nearly gutted him. Having her back safely in his arms, willingly clinging to him, was no less painful. His heart felt too big for his chest, but so vulnerable he wanted to clutch it tightly to him so no one could take it away. In a way, he supposed that was what he was doing, because he held Rain's bare body to him as tightly as he could. Rain was his heart. His world.

He'd carried Rain back to his room on the first floor. Once inside, he'd set about stripping her and himself. She'd helped, though she had been a little hesitant at first.

"I know this is movin' fast, baby, but I'm not givin' you up without a fight. If that means I keep you here naked with my body inside yours for days, that's what I'm gonna do."

"Hum," she said, nipping his chest sharply. "Don't threaten me with a good time. You might just get what you ask for."

"Fuck..."

Rain wrapped her slender arms around his neck and pulled her to him for a kiss. She licked at his mouth, nipping the bottom lip even as she stroked his tongue with hers. If he lived to be a hundred, Arkham knew he'd never get enough of this sweet woman. She gave him back something he'd thought he'd lost long ago. If he'd ever had it to begin with. Where Rain was concerned, Arkham had compassion and love like he'd never known existed in the world. And he had no way of telling her without sounding like a complete idiot.

Arkham moved them to the bed, but Rain wiggled out of his arms. At first he was confused, but she pushed him back until he realized she wanted him on the bed. He sat on the edge, and she knelt before him.

She looked up at him as she positioned herself between his thighs. "I've been wanting to do this since I walked in on you in the shower."

"Well, shit. If I'd known that..."

She giggled as she grasped his cock in one small hand. "It would have been for the wrong reasons then." Her eyes still danced merrily, but her words were serious. "I wanted you, but I also thought it would be a way to keep in your good graces."

"Now?"

Her smile was brilliant. "Now, I want to see just how crazy I can make you before you fuck me senseless."

"Goddamn, woman!"

Rain took him between her lips, sucking on the head of his cock with delicate pressure. He was certain it was the first time she'd done this. Not because what she was doing was inadequate. Quite the opposite. She didn't have a smooth skill about her touch, but a curious enthusiasm that more than made up for any inexperience.

Her hand continued to circle the base, but didn't move. Just held him still for her. She seemed to be getting used to the taste and feel of him, as if she wanted to learn everything about this part of him.

After a while, she began to take on the task with more seriousness. She slid her mouth over him as far as she could go, taking almost half of him. Arkham knew he was thick and long, and there was no way she could take all of him on her first attempt. Several times, he felt the back of her throat, but she never let up. Just continued to slide her lips over him again and again until she was whimpering around him. His shaft was wet with her saliva and his body with his own sweat.

Soon, he found himself gritting his teeth with the effort not to come. He had no idea exactly what she was doing to him, but it was like nothing he'd ever experienced. He brushed aside her hair so he could watch as his cock disappeared into her mouth inch by inch.

"Fucking Goddamn," he muttered. "Fuck!" His body shuddered uncontrollably. And still she enveloped his dick over and over again, humming around it with each stroke as if it were her favorite treat. She dug her fingers into his thigh with one hand while she started pumping his cock with the other. With each drop of pre-come he released, her tongue greedily swiped it up until he was sure she had figured out how to get those little drops from him intentionally.

When he could take no more, when he was sure he was going to come in her mouth, he fisted her hair in one hand and pulled her off him. She resisted, only giving up his cock when her mouth lost its suction with a little pop. Still she tried to reclaim her prize, her mouth open as she reached for his cock. That sight alone nearly made him spill.

"You're so Goddamned sexy," he growled. "And you're all mine."

He spun her around and pulled her to him so she straddled his legs, her back to his chest. His cock bounced between her legs, striking her clit with each movement. When she reached for him, he caught her wrist before taking both of her arms and crossing them over her chest until she grasped her shoulders. With one arm locking hers in place, he wrapped the other around her waist before finding her pussy with his cock and surging forward as he brought her down on him.

She screamed, letting her head fall back to lie against his shoulder even as she arched her back and ground herself against him. Arkham was struck at the difference in their sizes, the texture of their bodies. He was a large man. The sight wasn't particularly new to him when fucking a woman, but for some reason, this time it was extremely erotic. Her body seemed silky smooth against his hair-roughened one. Even her scars, though each one pained him, seemed more delicate than his own. Her muscles were lithe and lean where his were bulky and large. She was a conundrum of femininity and powerful warrior.

Just as he thought he had himself back under control, Rain thrashed her head and bucked her hips. Her cunt squeezed him like a vise, and he realized she was coming. Arkham slid his hand to her pussy and found her clit and pressed down. The effect was immediate. Rain bucked her body, continuing to scream. Her orgasm was powerful. Arkham knew because her little cunt had a stranglehold on his dick. The contractions were powerful, threatening to trigger his own release before he was ready. He growled, the sound menacing even to himself as he tried to regain some semblance of control.

"Little witch," he growled in her ear. "Trying to make me come?"

"Yes," she moaned. "Deep inside me, Arkham. I want to feel your hot cum inside my pussy!"

"Such a needy little thing." Arkham continued to fuck her, picking up a rhythm now but needing something more.

He stood with her in his arms. When he was at his full height, his body buried in hers, he had to lift her off the floor because of their height difference. She cried out and bent her knees to hook her feet behind him, digging into his thighs. Arkham couldn't resist a couple of shallow pumps with her in this position. It wasn't comfortable or possible for very long, but the very idea he could handle her, could fuck her in any way he chose was a heady turn on.

Finally, he crawled up onto the bed with her, blanketing her body with his and scooting her fully onto the mattress. He planted a hand in the middle of her back and began to fuck her with hard, sure strokes. Rain's arms were trapped between her and the mattress. With the added pressure of his hand between her shoulders, she was pretty much immobile.

Arkham wrapped his arms around her, his weight on her fully as he continued to fuck her aggressively. She was hot and slick and oh, so very tight. His woman.

She hooked her heels over his thighs, urging him to continue the only way she could move. The pressure was subtle, but she pulled him to her with every thrust, her cries now bordering on the insane. Her hips twisted and pressed up against him, and Arkham was sure she was grinding her clit into the sheets for friction.

"Do you want to come?" His voice was husky, gruff. This woman was driving him insane. His need for her was driving him insane. She seemed to crave the same wild, abandoned sex he did, so he continued.

"Yes! Oh, God! Arkham! Fuck me harder so I come so fucking hard!"

He did, slamming into her body with all his considerable strength. Her cries were loud, each one driving him further and further down a road to sexual insanity.

"Gonna come in you, woman. Gonna fill you with the fuckin' stuff!"

"Do it!" Rain whipped her head around and found his gaze over her shoulder. She bared her teeth at him. "When I come, I want you to come too. Fill me up with it! Come in my little pussy so fucking hard, Arkham!"

Her scream was shrill, her body covered in sweat now. Arkham pushed himself to his knees and gripped her hips, and he pounded her with his dick. Long, hard, fast strokes that slapped their skin together loudly until finally, he gave his own roar. He grasped her hips and ass hard and held her tightly against him, his cock buried deep as he came in a cataclysmic convulsion. The orgasm went on and on, spurts of cum gushing inside her, making her forever his. He'd come inside her before, but this was different somehow. This was them both knowing he'd made her his in front of his club. His brothers. She'd accepted him. There was no going back, and he didn't want to.

"Fucking hell, Rain," he whispered brokenly as he rolled them to their sides. He was still buried deep and had no plans of removing himself from the haven of her body.

"Arkham." Her voice was husky from her screams, her body relaxed against his. "I..." She swallowed, turning her head away from him, frustration etched on her face. She didn't know what to say to him? After what they'd just shared?

"If you're thinkin' of leavin' me again, don't." Arkham pulled her even tighter against him, giving a thrust with his semi-hard cock. "I don't put my claim on many people. You I've claimed. I can't live without you in my world, Rain. Understand me, I *won't*."

She looked up at him sharply, searching his face for something. "What are you saying, Arkham?"

This was it. Torpedo had asked him if he'd told Rain what she meant to him. Now was the time for him to do so. "I love you, Rain. I didn't really think I was capable of the emotion, but I know it's there because something's wrong inside me when I think about you leaving. You fill places in my soul I had no idea were empty." He leaned up and took her mouth gently. "Stay with me, baby. I swear you won't regret it."

"You... love me?" Unexpectedly, tears formed and spilled from her eyes. Arkham started to panic. Tears were the last thing he wanted to give her.

"I do, baby. Don't cry. I can't... I don't know what to do with your tears. The only person I can kill to make them go away is myself, and that would leave you unprotected." He was serious, panic beginning to seize him. What if she didn't love him back? What if she still wanted to leave?

Then, thankfully, she laughed. The tears still came, but he realized it was one of those silly female things. She laughed because she was happy.

"Don't be ridiculous. I don't want to leave you. I never did." She pulled him back to her to kiss him once before continuing. "No one's ever told me they love me before. And I've never said it either. I'm not even sure what love is, but if there is such a thing, I know that I love you."

Arkham let out a breath he hadn't realized he'd been holding. "Stay with me. I'll make you happy. When you're ready, we can get married."

She frowned. "I thought that's what we did when you gave me that jacket?"

He barked out a laugh. "As far as I'm concerned, we did. To make it legal, though, there is paperwork."

"Isn't there always," she muttered. Then she smiled. "I'll do whatever you think is best. You've earned my trust, so just tell me what to do. 'Cause I ain't got a clue."

"How about you just love me? Everything else will take care of itself."

"Sounds like the perfect plan to me."

Along Came A Demon (Shadow Demons 1)
Marteeka Karland

Billionaire Alexei Petrov is part of an elite group, *The Shadow Demons,* vigilantes hell-bent on protecting their city, working in the shadows, hunting down those who would prey on the most vulnerable in the city of Rockwell. Which is how he finds the most desirable women he's ever seen.

Merrily fled with her daughter with death on her heels. She has no idea what her father has done, but he's managed to throw her and little Bellarose into the middle of a mob war. Scared and hunted, Merrily gets caught in the crossfire of what looks like a gang war, but it's something far more sinister. A desperate flight lands her in the arms of Alexei Petrov. The man is everything she knows she can never have, but she wants him with every fiber of her being.

Even tucked safely away in the home of the richest, most powerful man in the city, Merrily's past finally catches up with her. Bellarose's father has come calling, and hell is hot on his heels. Fleeing seems like her only option, but Alex is just as dangerous as anything headed her way. And far too seductive and possessive for her peace of mind. Though she knows he will only break her heart, Merrily can't resist the lust that burns between them. Merrily knows she's up for the challenge. Welcomes it. But just who are these demons in the night, and why does she welcome this one's embrace?

Chapter One

The thing about homeless shelters was they were exactly what the name described and nothing more. Shelter. For the homeless. There was nothing remotely safe about them. Merrily Dane couldn't remember the last time she'd had a decent night's sleep. Between the creepy pervert who was supposed to be on the other side of the room away from the young mothers and children, and the drug addicts -- who weren't supposed to be there in the first place -- making deals at all hours of the night, she was turning into a paranoid insomniac.

She tightened her hold around her daughter, Bellarose, and whispered next to her ear, "I love you, pumpkin." Merrily hated being in this situation, but until she could get on her feet again, she didn't have much choice. Getting back on her feet wasn't going to be easy without an identity.

"I love you back, Mommy." Somehow, the child seemed to know she needed to keep her voice down. She'd learned quickly in the time they'd been on the run. It broke Merrily's heart nearly as much as it made her angry.

"Hey, Mommy?" Rose continued to whisper.

"Yeah, baby."

"When we get to our forever home, can I have a black cat, and a white cat, too?"

"Sure, baby. I'll do my best." Merrily's heart was breaking. Rose asked for the same thing every night. They'd left her black-and-white tuxedo cat when they'd been forced to leave and the girl had been heartbroken. Hell, Merrily had been heartbroken. Fortunately, the lady next door had agreed to look after the animal while Rose and Merrily were on "vacation." Mrs. Burton had offered to take the cat several times in the past so Merrily didn't feel like she'd imposed too much on the older woman. Instead of a fun-loving outing, however, she and Rose were stuck in a homeless shelter trying to make their way out of the reach of whatever gangster her father had crossed.

The barracks layout of this shelter wasn't exactly conducive to privacy or quiet, but it was all she'd been able to find with an available bed in this city. This time of year, the shelters were maxed out. Luckily, she'd found a spot in the corner so she could put her daughter on the inside of the bed and herself between Rose and everyone else. It was a small, bunk-style bed barely big enough for one person, but Merrily was small and her daughter was only four. She figured she needed to find something better in the morning because this place was seriously creeping her out. Then again, it was probably the only shelter that didn't require an ID and she couldn't afford to be on the grid.

Which brought Merrily to her greatest worry. Despite the shady characters surrounding her, despite not knowing where their next meal was coming from, despite the shelter being one step away from being out on the streets alone with a four-year-old, Merrily was terrified her father's "employers" were finally on her trail. It was nothing overt, just a feeling of being watched.

Bellarose shivered and Merrily brought the threadbare blanket higher to make sure the child was covered completely. She hated turning her back to the room -- especially since she knew she needed to keep an eye on everyone and everything -- but she knew she was too slight of build to be much good in a fight and the only protection her daughter had was Merrily's own body. She tried to shift the arm pillowing Rose's head to get circulation going again.

Life sucked sometimes. She and her beloved daughter were cold. In a homeless shelter full of shady people. Terrified out of their minds. Being hunted. She could practically feel the hunters breathing down her neck. She had to get out of this city. The only reason she'd stopped here was because it was as far as her money would take her and the only city with a bus station in the area.

After a couple of hours worrying about what her next move needed to be, she finally drifted off, wondering how the hell she was going to get herself out of this mess.

* * *

"If you keep Hell Bitch waiting, it will just be that much worse." Azriel wasn't actually referring to a person. He referred to the white cat that had adopted the Shadow Demons as her humans. She completely ignored the black cat currently dozing in Azriel's lap. The white cat's gaze focused completely on Alexei Petrov, and Hell Bitch's ears were laid back in that way cats have of showing their complete displeasure with someone.

Alexei Petrov glanced down at the feline warily. The beast might look innocent sitting there all prim and proper-like with her tail curled around her paws, but she was even more of a demon than any man in their organization. Alexei and his crew were justice when justice was overlooked or beaten down. Called vigilantes by some. Heroes by others. Personally, Alex thought all of them fought their individual demons so the name Shadow Demons fit in more ways than one.

"Don't let the pussy make you a pussy, boss." Giovanni Romano was *the* tech guy in a group of tech guys. If there was a gadget he didn't have or know how to get, no one had ever been able to name it. Not only could he obtain anything they wanted or needed, he made himself an expert with it in a few hours, thanks to his photographic memory and genius IQ. If he still didn't have what he needed -- or wanted -- the bastard simply made it. He was invaluable in their endeavors, but he was a bit of a smart ass.

Alexei flipped him off as he bent down to scoop up Hell Bitch, as they affectionately called the demon cat. She abruptly flattened her ears, bared her teeth, and scratched the shit out of him. When he dropped her, she turned and sauntered over to her food bowl and sat down, again looking straight at Alex.

"Bitch," he muttered under his breath. The cat growled softly, her dual-colored eyes narrowing. "Just for that you get the dry food." He poured a scoopful into her bowl. Hell Bitch reached over and upended the bowl as if to say *get me the fucking Royal Canin, bitch boy.*

Alex raised an eyebrow, glancing at Gio, who was studiously looking everywhere but at him. Then Alex stomped to the cabinet and grabbed Hell Bitch's favorite flavor from a stockpile of canned cat food. He opened it and the cat's whole face relaxed as if in bliss. Again, she sat all prim and proper with her tail wrapped around her feet until Alex had gotten every morsel out of the can.

"Have at it," he grumbled. When Azriel snickered, Alexei smacked the back of his head as he walked by. "Next time," he told Azriel, "feed her before six. I'm not the only one with access to the fucking cat food."

"She thinks it's your job to feed her in the evening," Azriel commented, raising a hand in surrender. "You know she won't eat unless *you* put her food out."

"Fucker," he muttered as he stalked through the room to the shower. It had been a long fucking day and he just wanted to scrub himself from head to toe.

Before he could, however, Giovanni stiffened and sat up straight in his chair. Alex paused. "We got bad guys afoot?"

Giovanni's workstation consisted of a wall of monitors showing every corner of the problem sections of the city of Rockwell. The wealthy, more affluent sections monitored themselves, but the people in the sectors the Demons monitored were at the mercy of the city's underground crime bosses. This was where men like the Demons were needed. Places the police were afraid to go. As time-consuming as it was setting up tech to monitor these places, as well as the endless testing of gadgets and physical training, this was something Alex knew he had to do. It was what he had been born to do.

"Hell's Playground." Azriel sighed as he glanced over Gio's shoulder. "It's every fucking week with that place. If there's trouble, you can bet it will be there."

Alexei rubbed the back of his neck. Something felt… off. He knew it the second Giovanni moved. No alarm pinged. Nothing even looked amiss, but Alex had a sixth sense when it came to trouble, and trouble was definitely brewing tonight and he just knew it was in Hell's Playground. "Drug deal?"

"No…" Giovanni leaned forward, bringing in a couple of camera angles up close. Still, nothing looked out of place. Hell's Playground was the nickname of a homeless shelter in the very center of their problem area. People there preyed on the innocent simply looking for a place to spend the night out of the elements. It was a known drug house and prostitution ring, as well as a place to make connections in the underworld of Rockwell. The only reason the Shadow Demons hadn't shut the place down completely was because they were still forming their organization and connections. All of the locals knew to avoid the place, but occasionally, some unsuspecting out-of-towner wandered in and there was always trouble. Alex had the feeling tonight was one of those nights.

"I'm not seeing anything out of the ordinary," Azriel said, squinting at the monitor, Satan cradled snugly in his arms. He petted the cat absently. The animal closed his eyes, limp as a dishrag.

"Well, look harder," Gio said, slowly getting to his feet, leaning in toward the monitor. With a click and drag of the mouse, he sectioned off a small square and blew it up. In the corner of a room filled with drug dealers, drug addicts, prostitutes, pimps, rapists, and mob men... were two young girls curled on their sides in a tiny bunk. One looked to be about three or four while the other one looked to be in her late teens.

Alone. No protection.

"What the ever-loving fuck are those two kids doing in Hell's Playground?" Giovanni scratched Satan's head.

Alex had been stripping off his body armor. Now, he shrugged back into it as quickly as he could. "Don't give a fuck. They can't stay there."

As Alex and Giovanni prepared to leave, four men entered the room on the monitor. They quartered off the room, starting at the far end away from the two girls, but they were definitely pros looking for something in a methodical pattern.

"Boys," Azriel muttered. "I got a real bad feeling about this."

"Yeah," Alex answered, filling his belt with as many knives and as much ammunition as he could carry. Two guns sat on each hip. He checked the clips then the chambers before holstering them again and heading back to the garage. "It will take us six minutes to get there."

"You have less than three before this place goes all to hell. Those fuckers have Snake patches. Someone has ordered a hit and those kids are going to be right in the middle."

"Fuck! Take the bike, Az," he ordered as he snagged his own helmet. The headgear was wired with audio as well as computerized tactical layouts judging distance, lighting, wind shear, thermodynamics, targeting, and any number of other useful things.

"On your six." Azriel straddled the bike, strapping on his helmet.

"Not this time. I'm counting on you to get there as quickly as you can." Alex looked at Giovanni. "I think now is as good a time as any to test the portal."

"I'd argue with you, but I'm not stupid." Gio crossed the room to an eight-foot-tall circular mass of steel framework, wires, and duct tape. Because, you know, all high-tech gadgets used rolls and rolls of duct tape.

"You're not really going to go through that thing, are you?" Azriel asked, a horrified look on his face. "The last time we sent something through, it melted to a smoking pile of goo."

"Giovanni's made some tweaks, haven't you, Gio?"

"Lots of tweaks." Gio didn't bother looking up from a laptop he had attached to the contraption. When he finally met the gazes of the other two men, he added solemnly, "and *miles* of duct tape."

"Well, I'm not going through it." Azriel pulled on his helmet. "I'll meet you there. Gio gets to tell your mother he melted you into a pile of goo." He started up his bike, revving the engine twice before giving them a two-fingered salute and peeling out of the room, down the tunnel that would emerge in a back alley six blocks from Hell's Playground.

Alexei admitted it was all very Caped Crusaderesque, but, really. *If it ain't broke, don't fix it.* Besides, Gio could make *way* cooler toys. Not to mention there was more than one man's obscene wealth funding this outfit.

He pulled up the hood on his suit. The thing was tight and designed to protect his neck from whiplash as well as penetrative injuries. The full-face helmet went over the hood, the visor as much a computer monitor as a shield -- another invention of Giovanni's. The armor -- including the helmet -- became stronger with excessive force. Unfortunately, that also meant the material became more rigid for a split second while the energy bled away, or something. Alex had no idea how it worked and didn't really care. As long as it worked. In most cases the changes in how the suit moved weren't noticeable and sometimes prevented serious neck injuries. When it stopped a bullet, the result could be near-total rigidity. If you weren't careful, it could seriously screw with balance, or cause you to twist a knee. It never lasted long, though. And as long as the suit covered him from head to toe, he was damned near invincible. Though lightweight, it was bulkier than he'd like. Something for Giovanni to work on. In the meantime, he and his team would take what they could get.

There were still kinks to be worked out, but with practice and an acute awareness of his surroundings, any disadvantage could be mitigated. Alex was hoping it would hold true when he entered that fucking portal.

* * *

That feeling of being watched intensified. Merrily didn't want to frighten Bellarose, but she knew with every fiber of her being she had to get them to safety. She'd intentionally chosen the back corner because there were fewer people, but it now felt like she was trapped, miles away from the only exit.

Careful to wake Rose gently so she didn't startle the little girl, Merrily scooted off the bed and pulled her daughter into her arms. Together, they rolled under the bed, taking the skimpy blanket with them. For once, Merrily was glad they didn't have much more than the clothes on their backs. She knew whoever had been hunting them had finally found them. She needed to disappear in the dark. She could feel it in her very bones. Was she paranoid? Maybe. But if being paranoid and spending the rest of the night under the bed saved Rose's life, she'd take it.

"Get as close to the wall as you can, pumpkin," she whispered to Rose. Ever the little soldier, Rose did as she was told. "Keep hold of my shirt so I know where you are, okay?"

"I won't let go, Mommy." Her little voice was a mere whisper. Together, they huddled under the bed as deep into the corner as they could get. Merrily tried to conceal Rose with her body, acting as a shield between her daughter and whatever danger was hunting them. She could *feel* the danger like cold fingers tickling the back of her neck.

There had been a hum of quiet noise all night while deals went down from drugs to sex to God-only-knew-what, but now everything was eerily silent. Occasionally, they heard a frightened whimper or quiet moan of pain, but the hum of normal activity had completely ceased, and not for sleep.

Then she saw people moving. Four or five. All she could see from her position was feet, but they stepped quietly, slowly. As if searching every inch of their surroundings. They'd spread out, covering the width of the room, steadily moving over the whole place. She and Rose were small and huddled into the corner tightly, but Merrily knew there was no hope they'd be overlooked. No. This group was professional. Over the last three weeks she'd learned enough to know these guys weren't ham-handed thugs. They meant business.

A roar of wind blasted through the big room, sending trash, leaves, and dust flying all around. Bellarose gave a startled yelp but only tightened her hold on Merrily's shirt. Merrily felt her daughter's breath through the thin cotton, indicating her face was buried there. Bright light flooded the area on the opposite corner at the back of the room, putting Merrily and Rose on one point of a triangle with the men on the hunt inside the shelter and this new threat.

"Mommy?" Rose was quiet, but Merrily could hear the fear in her daughter's voice.

"I don't know, pumpkin. Just hang on to me, but no matter what happens, don't make a sound and don't come out from under this bed. Cover up with the blanket and be as still as a church mouse."

One little whimper escaped Rose before she subsided. Merrily could feel her trembling, but the child was silent.

Heavy footfalls came straight toward them. Fast. A figure in some kind of black uniform dropped down. He wore a black helmet with a dark visor that he'd flipped up revealing the bluest eyes Merrily had ever seen.

"Stay put until my partner gets here," the man said, his voice distorted as if filtered through a telephone he'd amplified. "Don't move or make a sound. I'll keep the danger focused on me. When my partner gets here, you go with him, no questions asked." It was an order, pure and simple. An order given by a man no one disobeyed. Then he was gone.

Fighting broke out across the room. A high-pitched whine and a mechanical whirring built steadily until Merrily had to cover her ears. Not knowing what else to do, she turned over to cover Rose's head in her hands, trying to buffer the awful noise.

The sharp scent of ozone filled the air. Then there was a loud snap and the wind ceased, as did the whining. The fighting continued, men grunting and yelling. People screamed all around her, running toward the other end of the hall. Merrily just held Rose, not daring to move or make a run for it. Staying put when there were multiple unknown threats seemed the wisest thing to do. They might assume she'd fled with everyone else and she could escape.

"That's right, you fucks!" that distorted male voice taunted. "Be afraid." He sounded furious, but it was definitely the same man who'd come to them.

Merrily shivered and wrapped her arms around Rose even tighter. If they made it out of this one, she promised herself she'd seek help. It might have to be from a church or some other place who didn't care to aid two souls needing to remain off the grid, but she couldn't risk Rose like this ever again. *If* they made it.

Rose whimpered so softly Merrily wanted to weep. No four-year-old should be able to control herself this way. Sounds of the fight carried from across the room but Merrily didn't dare move from their hiding spot under the bed.

"Hey!" There was a whispered voice just in front of them.

Merrily jumped, barely stifling a cry as she jerked her head up from where she'd buried it in Rose's hair only to bang it on the bed above her. She looked back over her shoulder and whimpered. Another figure in a dark helmet beckoned her, one gloved hand outstretched, reaching for her. "Come with me if you want to live." Probably because she was so terrified her brain was on full meltdown, but Merrily suddenly felt like she was in a scene from a *Terminator* movie.

His voice might have been soft, but it held an unmistakable note of authority. It was also just as distorted as the other man's, the one currently fighting against God only knew how many men.

"Mommy." Rose squirmed to get loose. Merrily had to loosen her hold for fear she'd hurt the child.

"We have to go now," he said, reaching for Merrily. She didn't make a move, but he managed to snag her clothes and pull.

"No!" Merrily let go of Rose to fight the man. She rolled, kicking out with her feet, but Rose was already scampering out from under the bed.

"Come on, Mommy," she urged, though Merrily made a grab for her. As usual, when Rose didn't want to be caught, she evaded Merrily easily. "Don't you recognize him?"

The guy whipped his head around to look at Rose, and Merrily's gut clenched. Though he didn't remove his helmet, Merrily had no doubt his gaze bore down on the little girl. She looked up at him, wonder and excitement on her face. "You know who I am?"

She nodded her head vigorously. "You're a Shadow Angel." She whispered the name reverently, like she might have said "Santa Claus." Rose hadn't been able to see the first man, but unfortunately this one gave her no fear.

Merrily whimpered, reaching for her daughter. Rose had it wrong. They weren't angels. At least, if the stories could be believed. They did horrible things to people. They'd only been in the city a couple of days, but she'd already been warned about vigilantes combing this city and the surrounding ones, not caring how much collateral damage they did, according to the tales. Even at home she'd heard about the Shadow Demons, though they had yet to make an appearance there. Apparently, by avoiding one danger, she'd brought Rose into the middle of another.

"*Angels*?" The guy sat back on his heels, letting Merrily go. "Who said we were angels?" The voice was still distorted and creepy, but Merrily thought he was more than a little taken aback. Like Rose had insulted his manhood or something.

"Yeah," she continued, undeterred, nodding her head vigorously. "You know. Like guardian angels."

The man just cocked his head as if he had no idea what to do with the child. Then an explosion had Merrily screaming and Rose leaping into her arms.

The man stood, motioning for them to stay behind him. "Follow me exactly," he said. He didn't wait to see if they obeyed him but trotted toward the exit. Merrily had no idea what the right move was, but the guy could have killed them and hadn't. So she followed him, her arms tight around Rose as she ran after their savior. In the other corner of the room, the fight raged on. What had started out as five against one had dwindled to two against one. As she ran, Merrily saw those last two try to run away, heading toward the same exit she and Rose were.

"Wait!" she called to the man Rose had named an angel. Instead of heeding her warning, the man darted into the fight, fists slamming into faces. Bone crunched loudly and screams sounded as the last two men fell. She was about to breathe a sigh of relief when four more men jumped into the fray. Merrily had no idea if they were with the first group or were drug dealers or pimps defending their territory, but they would have done well to have simply ducked and run like everyone else.

The "Angels" continued the fight, easily dispatching all of them with incredible speed and viciousness. When one of the men -- she had no idea which one -- pulled a gun and began shooting their downed victims, however, Merrily ran for the door, covering Rose's head as best she could so the little girl didn't see anything she shouldn't. She didn't stop once outside, either. She darted down the street into the cold night, darkness and fog swallowing them.

* * *

"I thought you said you had them." Alexei was frustrated and more than a little pissed Azriel hadn't stayed with the two females. He absently pressed his hand to the center of his chest, an unexpected ache building there.

"I did. They ran when you started shooting people. Imagine that!"

"Are you telling me I should have let them go? That was a hit team! A damned good one, too."

"Do you know who they were after?"

"No. I'd hoped to question one of them but the last one popped a suicide capsule. And you shot them too!" Alex had never been so frustrated in his life. With a brutal yell, he punched the wall. Plaster crumbled around his fist. "Now those girls are running scared with nowhere to go, no appropriate clothing, and probably very little money." Alexei wanted to punch something of substance. Preferably one of those hit men. The girls weren't his problem, but he couldn't shake the feeling they needed help.

"You said they had been hiding under the bed?" Azriel questioned.

"Yeah. They knew how to hide and that says they're on the run. Hell, even the little one didn't make a sound. As to the shooting, I had to shoot once you started."

"Then we better find them. Being out on the street isn't going to help matters for them."

"Well, if you'd stayed with them, we wouldn't have to look for them." Alex knew he was being a bastard, but these girls were the whole reason he'd jumped through that fucking portal. To say the ride was bumpy would be a vast understatement. Despite the special suit, he had been certain his body was, indeed, going to be reduced to a puddle of goo.

"Pardon the fuck outta me for giving a shit that you didn't see the four reinforcements sneaking up on you," Azriel snapped. "I didn't figure on the girls bolting."

"Relax, guys." Giovanni's voice came to them through their earpieces. "I've got them on camera and am turning out lights in their area. As I predicted to Satan, the older one is following the lighted areas. I'm guiding her down the tunnel. She just entered with the little one squirming to get down."

Alex sighed, much more relieved than he should be. "Fucking runaways, I'm betting." He knew he sounded snippy but he was trying to cover his relief.

Why he'd fixated on the two girls, he had no idea. But he'd be damned if he let anyone figure out he'd had a "feeling." Feelings were a liability in their world and he'd happily existed without them for many years. Besides, it fucked with his reputation. "What happened to the fucking portal? Sounded like it shorted out."

"Told you it was still a work in progress. Besides, it worked when you needed it to."

"I don't think they're runaways," Azriel commented as he put in a call for the cops. The team didn't bother cleaning up the mess and there was no need to police their ammo. The bullets dissolved thirty seconds after impact and wouldn't be around to be traced after the fact. "They're definitely on the run, but I don't think it's by choice."

They headed out the door to Azriel's waiting bike. With all the guns and rocket launchers, it was more like a tactical unit than a motorcycle, but it was way cooler. *And* it had camouflaging cameras mounted all around it, giving it the illusion of invisibility. Azriel hadn't bothered to use that option because they hadn't anticipated being there that long. Besides, anyone trying to jack their ride would be tazed by the bike itself.

"What makes you think that?"

"The little one called the other one 'Mommy.'"

"So, on the run from the father? Custody battle gone wrong?" Alex didn't like that thought one bit.

Azriel shrugged. "Maybe. We'll just have to ask her."

Giovanni spoke again. "Whatever you do, just remember to change your clothes before you get to the project room. They'll be waiting for you there. They can't make the connection between the two of you and the Shadow Demons."

Chapter Two

The tunnel was dim and spooky. Merrily realized she was that stupid bimbo in the slasher movies the second the sparse lighting behind them went out. Sure, she could turn around and run with Bellarose but that would be even stupider. Was that even a word? She was moments away from hysteria and could do nothing to calm herself.

Thankfully, Rose didn't seem affected in the least. She squirmed to get down, looking around them like it was a grand adventure. Maybe it was. Merrily just hoped it didn't end in disaster. The feeling they were being watched was almost overwhelming. The itching between her shoulder blades intensified until she was so jumpy a spider would have sent her screaming. OK, so a spider could make her scream anyway but that was beside the point.

Unperturbed, Rose skipped through the tunnel, uncaring about dangers. The kid was fearless.

"Mommy!" she yelled, running forward, farther down the tunnel. "My cats! Look!"

As she rounded the corner, Merrily saw the two cats her daughter was so excited about. They waited just inside the tunnel where it opened up into a larger room. It was dark so Merrily couldn't see much, but the cats were distinctive. One black. One white. The latter sat primly with its tail curled around its feet. The black one paced back and forth behind the white cat, stopping when it caught sight of Rose and Merrily.

The little girl gave an excited squeal and skidded to a stop on her knees. She scooped up the white cat, burying her face in its fur. She put it down only to give the black cat the same treatment. Both animals were limp as rag dolls in the little girl's arms.

"Rose, be careful. They might not like people."

"My cats, Mommy! I said I wanted a black cat and a white cat at my forever home! We're here!"

Merrily sighed. "Rose, honey, we can't live in a cave..." She trailed off when lights started coming all around them across the vast, open structure. The place had to be as large as a football field. Tables with computers and various tools were spread out over the entire area as if each space was its own project. Indeed, the whole thing looked like a huge laboratory.

"Whoa." Rose put the cat down and walked farther inside. Merrily caught her arm and halted her.

"Wait, baby. We have no idea where we are."

"You're in our project room." The male voice boomed throughout the room so loud Merrily covered her ears and Rose ducked behind her, following suit. "Sorry!" The same voice sounded, the volume normal this time, from about twenty feet away. "Forgot I had the mic on."

"That was *loud*! You scared my cats away!" Rose stomped out from behind Merrily with her hands on her hips, scolding the man. "Cats don't like loud noises, mister. You should be more careful."

"Cats," he said, looking blankly at Rose as he took a couple of steps toward them. Raising an eyebrow, he pointed at the two cats. The black one hid behind Rose, peeking out from the little girl's leg. The other one, however, arched its back and hissed at the man, growling low in its throat threateningly. "You mean Satan and Hell Bitch?"

Rose clapped her hands back over her ears. "That's a mean word!"

The man looked contrite. He had ginger hair and stubble on his face. His skin was fair, with a smattering of freckles. Now, he turned beet red. "I-I'm sorry." He looked from Rose to Merrily as if he didn't have a clue what to do, actually wringing his hands. "That's just what we've always called them since they came here."

"That's not their names," Rose insisted. "This is Smokey." She indicated the black cat, picking it up. The animal, again, was limp in her arms, not fighting in the least. "That's Snowball." The white cat turned to her and gave a solid *meow* before turning back to the man and casually hissing again before turning back to Rose.

"Well then," he said, seeming to get himself together. "I'm Giovanni Romano. You can call me Gio if you like."

"My name's Rose. That's my mommy."

Giovanni turned his gaze to Merrily. He took the several steps separating them and extended his hand in greeting. "Pleased to meet you, miss."

"Merrily Dane," she said quietly, not taking his hand. "Rose, stay close to me." She didn't dare take her gaze from the man. His unassuming manner was offsetting, but Merrily knew no one with access to stuff like this was harmless. "Where are we?"

"I told you. You're in our project room. This is where I put together… special equipment."

"And you're just telling me this to satisfy my curiosity?" Merrily's heart began to pound. Had she and Rose stumbled into something worse than whatever men were already after her?

"Well, I suppose I shouldn't, but, honestly, what else was I supposed to say?"

"I'm not stupid," she said, really scared now. "I know when people stumble into something like this, they usually don't stumble out alive."

"Oh, for heaven's sake." A male voice from behind them made Merrily jump. She whirled around and Giovanni was on her in an instant. He snagged her arms behind her with effortless ease, securing her hands with a zip tie. "Rose, run!" she screamed at her daughter, hoping the little girl could get away, knowing it was hopeless.

Merrily kicked out at the new man who was in front of her now. He caught her foot but didn't hurt her. Rose screamed and the cats scattered. Snowball launched itself at Giovanni. The man yelled, letting go of Merrily to remove the cat from his back. The animal was out for blood, clawing and scratching the man's back, face, and arms before jumping down and eyeing the newcomer as if he were its next meal.

"Azriel, get Hell Bitch out of here before I kick her like a fucking field goal!"

"Got my hands full with Satan, Alex. Fucker was never aggressive before! What the fuck?"

"You leave my mommy and Snowball alone!" Instead of running like Merrily had told her to, Rose attacked. Much like the cat, she struck out with her tiny fists on "Alex's" leg. "And don't you call Smokey mean names, mister!" she said to "Azriel."

"Would everyone just calm the fuck down?" Alex said, raising his hands in surrender. "Giovanni, untie her hands. Why'd you do that anyway?"

The man didn't answer but an instant later, she heard a *snip,* the tie was gone, and Merrily snagged Rose to her side. The child tried to get away but Merrily had a death grip on her. "Who are you? What do you want with us?" Merrily was about to lose her ever-loving shit. She'd never been so scared in her life. In the shelter, no one had actually touched her except for Rose's angels. These guys clearly meant business.

"We were only trying to help you," Alex said, his voice calm, his hands still raised. "You were in a very dangerous part of town, in the middle of what looked like a turf war. The two of you were in danger so we did our best to remove you from the situation."

The two newcomers were impeccably dressed in expensive-looking suits that were probably tailor made. They fit the two flawlessly. They were big men with broad shoulders, thick arms, and wide chests that tapered down to narrow waists. Alex, however, had something about him that both frightened and intrigued Merrily. He seemed to look into her soul whenever he met her gaze. He was slightly taller than Azriel, but it was difficult to say who was bigger. Alex was definitely the more intimidating.

Merrily stepped to the side so she could keep all three men in her line of sight. Giovanni scrubbed the back of his neck, his face still red as if with embarrassment. "I just turned off some lights, hoping you'd stick to the ones that were on. I led you down here and…"

"Then you assaulted me!"

"I'm sorry about that," he said, hanging his head like a naughty child. Merrily wasn't buying it. "I thought you were going to try to bolt again and didn't want to take the chance you'd head back into danger with the little one because you were afraid of us."

"So you made it worse? Jesus!" Merrily recognized she sounded hysterical, but under the circumstances, she thought she was entitled.

Rose twisted her arm away from Merrily and marched up to Alex, tugging on the sleeve of the suit jacket he wore. "Mister, you need to not talk so mean."

All eyes were instantly on the little girl. Merrily reached for her, but she just lifted her arms up to Alex as if she wanted to be picked up. The big man hesitated, then slowly bent and picked up the child, looking as uncomfortable as a man possibly could.

Merrily took a step toward her daughter, but something stopped her. The expression on Alex's face... It was equal parts fear, wonder, and oh-*hell*-no.

"Where's my room?" Rose demanded. Merrily was just as dumbfounded as Alex looked. As a rule, Rose was usually reserved, shy around strangers. Not this time.

"Your room." Alex looked like he wanted to hand her off to Merrily and run for the hills, but to his credit, he didn't let the little girl intimidate him. Much.

"Yes," she continued, completely unaware of the man's discomfort. "I told Mommy when we got to our forever home I wanted a black cat and a white cat. So, now I just need my own room."

"I -- uh..." He cleared his throat and glanced over at Azriel. The other man shrugged, trying to smother a smile. Merrily noticed and something in her relaxed. These men had no idea what to do with a child, but they weren't out to harm them. "Yes. Well." He glanced at Merrily, lifting his chin. A mask of arrogance once again covered his face, as if this were all normal. "If your mom will kindly come with us, I'll show you to your rooms."

"Wait," Merrily said, reaching for Alex's arm. Her hand made contact with his hand curled under Rose where he held the little girl over his hip, and she was unprepared for the shock. A shiver of awareness went through her. When she would have pulled back, he turned his hand slightly and caught her fingers. Looking up at him, she saw his brows were drawn together, a recognizable look of confusion on his handsome face. Merrily hadn't fully registered how good-looking Alex really was until that moment. The saying that kids were chick magnets when a guy held them was apparently true. With Rose snug in his arms and that adorable confused look on his face, the intimidation lessened. Somewhat. "What are you doing?" she managed the question with only a slightly breathy voice.

"Seeing to it you have a safe place to stay," he said matter-of-factly.

"We can't stay here."

He turned the full effect of his penetrating gaze on her. Just like that, he was as intimidating as ever. This was a man used to giving orders and having those orders obeyed without question. "Where, exactly, did you plan on going? You were in a piss-poor *homeless* shelter. Do you have someplace better you chose not to use instead?" Rose gasped and covered her ears, giving Alex a glare. To his credit the man glanced at the child and muttered, "Sorry." When Merrily lifted her chin defiantly but said nothing, he gave a curt nod. "That's what I thought. Come with me, please."

* * *

Alexei took them to the elevator and up to the third floor where the guest residences were. Here, the girls could have a comfortable, fully stocked suite with everything they'd need but personal items. Which Alex would see remedied immediately. The manor had eighty-seven rooms with seventeen suites, not counting his own residence. That occupied the entire fourth floor. Though his instincts screamed for him to keep his new charges as close to him as he could, Alex fought it. Instead, he gave them a two-bedroom suite on the floor below him.

"The cats should stay in the project room," Alex muttered as he led them down the long hall.

"They like it better with me," Rose told him. Her thin arms had encircled his neck and she sounded more sleepy than excited now. As if she'd heard his thoughts, the little girl yawned and laid her head on Alex's shoulder. The feeling was so foreign to him, he nearly stumbled. Instead, he found himself nuzzling her silky head before he could stop himself.

"This place is like a fancy hotel," Merrily muttered. "Does it come with room service?"

Alex got the feeling she meant it as a joke, but it came out nearly resentful, as if she expected it to be offered only to discover she couldn't ever afford it. "Absolutely," he replied without hesitation. "Any time of the day or night, anything you need. I'll explain it all when I introduce you to Mrs. McDonald."

"I was kidding," she said with a sigh. "We can't stay here."

"You can and you will. I won't discuss it further." He was saved from her continued protest when they reached the end of the hall and the double doors leading to the room he'd let them use. He opened one, then the other. Rose stirred in his arms and lifted her head.

"Are we staying here?"

"You are," Alex answered before Merrily could say anything. He set her on her feet. "This suite has two rooms. You get your pick, Rose."

She grinned, and Alex could see she wanted to be excited, but her eyelids were drooping. "Smokey. Snowball. Come on. Let's go to bed."

Alex glanced to the side and saw the two cats had followed them. He shook his head. The cats seemed to have adopted the little girl as much as she'd adopted them. All three went to the closest bedroom. He watched as the little girl kicked off her shoes and crawled up on the bed. The cats jumped up and settled on either side of her, "Snowball" curling up but watching Alex warily, protecting the child. He closed the door and pushed a button on the phone but didn't pick it up. Even this late, Ruth McDonald would have someone ready to answer a summons.

"Really, we can't stay." Merrily was wringing her hands, distressed.

"Give me a good reason why and I'll look for a different alternative. One where you and Rose are safe." It was nothing less than a reprimand, and she took it as such, flushing. Good. She knew he meant business.

"I --" Whatever she'd been about to say was cut off by the curt knock at the door.

"Ah. Good." Alex took the three steps to the double doors and opened both wide. "Mrs. McDonald. I apologize for the late call."

"No trouble at all, Mr. Petrov," she answered, a genuine smile on her face as she appraised Merrily. "I had no idea you had guests in this room or I'd have welcomed them myself." She looked back to Alex and he wanted to groan. He could already see the older woman making plans. Plans he absolutely would not participate in. Ever.

"Merrily," he said, reaching out for her hand. To his surprise, she took it with little hesitation. "This is Ruth McDonald. She's been with my family since I was a boy and knows this house better than I do. She's my estate administrator as well as a good family friend. If you have any needs, you may bring them to Mrs. McDonald."

"Pleased to meet you, ma'am." Merrily extending her hand to the older woman. "We won't be in your way and will be sure to leave the suite like we found it."

"You'll do no such thing!" Ruth looked outraged. "No guest in this house will ever do the cleaning. You make sure you mess the place up good or I'll get my feelings hurt." Merrily blinked and looked from him to Ruth, a lovely, bewildered expression on her face. "In any case, you'll need breakfast in the morning." She glanced past Merrily to the little girl already sleeping soundly on the bed in the next room. "What would the little one like?"

"Honestly, Mrs. McDonald, we'll be fine."

As he knew she would, Ruth lifted her chin, her lower lip quivering ever so slightly. "I assure you, the food in this house is excellent. If you're worried you'll be disappointed, I promise you, nothing could be further from the truth."

Apparently, Merrily took the hint. With a sigh, she gave Ruth a genuine smile. "Of course that's not the case. We'd love breakfast."

"Excellent," Ruth said, her face once again bright with her beautiful smile. "I'm betting silver-dollar pancakes for your girl and you..." She squinted at Merrily as if sizing her up. "Eggs Benedict with our special Hollandaise sauce. Do you prefer bacon or Canadian Bacon?"

"I've never had Eggs Benedict," she said in a small voice. Merrily had a wide-eyed, almost terrified look on her face. Clearly, she was uncomfortable. Though he hated that the older woman had come to the room herself in the middle of the night instead of sending one of the other employees, he was suddenly relieved she had. No one could put a person at ease like Ruth McDonald.

"Then you'll enjoy a new dish." She looked so pleased, even Alex grinned. Merrily did, too. The girl had a lovely, if shy, smile. He wondered what she'd look like if she were truly at ease. "What else can I get you?" Ruth looked around. "I don't see luggage. Was this trip not planned? I can get clothing if it's needed." This was why Alex loved Ruth so much. Beneath that innocent grandmother look she presented, the woman saw everything. She always had. When they were boys, he and his brothers and cousins could never get away with anything Ruth hadn't noticed. Their parents might not find them out, but Ruth always did. Now was no different.

"We'll manage," Merrily said.

"Nonsense," Ruth said, waving her away. "Clothing from top to bottom. There are plenty of toiletries in both bathrooms for tonight, but I'll make a list and get more for you tomorrow."

"Honestly, we won't be here that long. Rose and I will head out right after breakfast." Merrily said it as if it was really going to happen.

"Before you go, Mrs. McDonald," he said, looking straight at Merrily. The girl lowered her head, not meeting his gaze. "Is there some place you could fit Merrily into your staff? She'll need a few days' rest, but perhaps she'd be more comfortable if she felt she were earning her keep."

"I've always got something for anyone willing to work. The pay would be more than this room is worth. I'd have to compensate her the difference." Ruth pursed her lips as if working out the problem. "It would probably benefit you most, Mr. Petrov, if I paid her in cash. That way, if the situation is temporary, the paperwork will be kept to a minimum and would be one less thing for me. Should you decide to stay with us, my dear, we can work on a different arrangement."

"I appreciate all this, really, but I can't stay past tomorrow."

"Why don't I leave you two to work out the details? I'll just make sure everything is ready for tomorrow." She opened her arms to Merrily, crossing to her before pulling the younger woman into a hug. "It's lovely to meet you, my dear. Don't let him bully you, but you do what's best for that girl in there. Even if it means swallowing your pride a little." When she let go, the worry was plain to see. The woman was genuinely concerned for Merrily, who she probably considered her young charge. Without further comment, Ruth left them, shutting the door behind her.

They stood there for long moments, Merrily looking everywhere but at him. Finally, he reached for her hand. "Come with me." She hesitated but obeyed, placing her small, delicate hand in his.

As before, the second his skin touched hers, there was an acute awareness. Alex considered himself jaded. He was an attractive, wealthy man. He'd had pretty much any woman he'd wanted in his life. Never had he felt a pull like this toward a woman. It wasn't an overwhelming physical attraction, though she was pretty. There was just something about her that made him want to wrap her up in his arms and keep her safe.

Okay, maybe there was a bit of physical attraction, because just the touch of her hand in his made his cock twitch. Why, he didn't know. He just knew he wanted… something. Sex? Yeah. But it was more than that. Probably some small sliver of humanity in him trying to make a comeback. He'd seen her huddled under a bed trying her best to protect her daughter, and it had done something to him inside.

He ushered her to a plush couch in the living area and sat next to her, not letting go of her hand. "Now, tell me why you don't want to stay here."

She tried to pull her hand away but Alex was having none of it. Never before had he wanted a physical connection with someone like he did now.

Being an insanely rich man, he was used to getting what he wanted. This was no exception. She and her daughter staying here wouldn't be, either.

"It's my problem," she finally said. "Just leave it at that."

"Unacceptable." He raised an eyebrow. "Unless you give me a good reason why you should leave. And I should warn you, it would have to be a doozy."

She sighed. "Look. I've got some people after me. I have no idea who or exactly why, but it has something to do with my father. I don't want innocent people getting caught up in my problems."

"Explain."

Merrily turned her head, looking at the window where nothing but blackness stared back at her. During the day, there was a lovely view of the mountain lake. On calm days the snowy peaks reflected in the still water. On a clear night, when the moon was full at this exact time of night, the moon reflected on surface of the lake, giving another serene and lovely view. Now, the moon was obscured by cloud cover. With the lights on inside, there was nothing to see.

Finally, she spoke. "My father found me about three weeks ago. He came in the middle of the night and told us to get out of town and as far away as we could get. He warned me to keep us off the grid if possible. No debit cards. No cell phones. No digital footprint if I could keep from it. He babbled on about his employer being upset at him and said he might send someone after me and Bellarose to get back at him. He swore he hadn't done anything wrong, but really. People don't threaten to come after your family if you don't do something wrong. Right?"

"Not usually. Continue."

"I thought about kicking him out, chalking it up to him wanting something from us again, but he had pictures of my mother. What they'd done to her…" She shuddered, tugging her hand from his and standing to pace to the window. "She'd been alive in the first several images. By the time they'd finished the photos, she was long dead. The timestamps on the photos showed it had happened over several days." She lowered her voice to a near whisper. "It was horrible what they did to her." Merrily was silent for a while after that before taking a deep breath and facing him once more. "I just couldn't take a chance with Rose. So I ran."

"I take it your father wasn't part of your life growing up?" Alex asked as a way of easing her into talking about her family. He'd gather all the information he could, find out exactly what her father had done and who he'd pissed off, then he'd go hunting. It was what he did.

"He left when I was five. He still sent the occasional Christmas and birthday cards, but I think that was mostly so he could keep in touch with my mother. And before you ask, I have no idea if he did it for money or sex or both. I just know that by him keeping in contact with us, he endangered Rose, even though I hadn't lived with my mother since before Rose was born."

Alex looked at her long moments, and for the first time, really *saw* her. When he'd gotten his first look at her, he'd assumed she was a child herself. She was slight of build and much shorter than his own six-foot-five-inch frame. He'd taken it into stride when he'd figured out she was Rose's mother, but he knew she was still very young. "How old is Rose?"

"Four. Almost five."

"And how old are you?"

She flinched, turning away from him. "Put that together, did you?"

"I know you had to be pretty young when you had her."

"I just turned twenty-two." She put her chin up and met his gaze, fire in her eyes as if she dared him to belittle her for it.

"You said you hadn't lived with your mother since before Rose was born. Have you been on your own or do you have a partner?"

"Just me." The defiance in her gaze was almost palpable as she stared him down, daring him to say something negative.

Alex shrugged. "Good."

Her delicate lips parted, making Alex want to slip his tongue between them. "I don't understand. How is that a good thing?"

"It means I have one less person to worry about," he snapped. In reality, he was thinking he wouldn't have to kill the man for her. "Tell me about the father of your child. Could he be involved in this thing with your father?"

Merrily shook her head. "No. I haven't seen him since…" She trailed off, turning away again. "No."

"I need names," Alex said, trying to be gruff. *Needing* to be gruff when all he wanted to do was pull her into his arms. What was it about this particular woman that brought out his protective instincts when all he'd ever wanted to do was push away any women who got too close?

"I don't see how this matters."

"It matters because the more I know about you, the better I can contain and eliminate the threat to you and Rose."

She shook her head. "I appreciate it, but I can't let you be any more involved than you already are. I shouldn't be here. I will admit, however, this place just screams 'security-at-every-turn.' I'd be lying if I said that didn't make me feel safe for the first time in three weeks. Thank you."

"Names," he said again, not letting her off the hook.

"Fine," she snapped, losing her temper. He liked that little bit of fire. Liked it maybe too much. "My father's name is Steve Black. Rose's father is Daniel J. Maddison III. I doubt he even knows he has a daughter. His parents didn't approve of me or my pregnancy and paid my mother for me to have an abortion. I'm sure they'll want to sue or something if they find out about Rose."

"Let me worry about that."

"No," she said, balling her fists at her sides. "I can't let you worry about that because it's not your problem. Don't you get it?" To Alex's utter horror, tears formed in Merrily's vivid green eyes, making them look glassy. One spilled over and she dashed it away with a snappish movement. "Once you take this to Daniel, his father will get involved and, one way or another, Rose and I are the ones who will suffer." She glanced at the room where the little girl slept soundly with the two cats curled up beside her. "Rose doesn't know her father because Daniel chose not to be a part of our lives before she was born. I'm not going to start some custody battle with him now that I have no hope of winning. That little girl is all I have. I love her more than my next breath and I won't let Daniel or his parents into her life until she's old enough to defend herself."

"Defend herself physically? Did they hurt you?" Alex knew he probably looked murderous, but he couldn't help it. He was a highly intelligent man, but everything he'd experienced with her to this point made him look about as bright as a burnt-out light bulb. All this alpha going-protective-on-a-woman-he-barely-knew bullshit wasn't going to cut it. He had no idea if they'd abused Merrily in any way, but he knew that wasn't what she meant.

"No, though I'm pretty sure his mother wanted to. Daniel and I were wrong for each other from the beginning, but we were young. I knew he didn't love me. Deep down I knew. Like a fool, I gave him exactly what he wanted and wasn't smart enough to insist on protection for myself. Anything to make him happy."

The nerve of the guy! Alexei decided right there he'd kick the kid's ass on principle. "Okay. I have a starting point. You rest here. Tomorrow, you and Rose can explore the house and grounds. Please don't try to leave. Mrs. McDonald will introduce you to the staff and show you the daycare we have in-house. Rose will be taken care of while you work and you'll live here until I'm satisfied the danger to you and the girl is gone." He met her gaze steadily. When she turned away, he cupped her face, forcing her to look at him. "In the meantime, I want you to cooperate with Mrs. McDonald when she brings you and Rose clothing or anything else she says you need. Don't fight her." Another tear slipped down her cheek and Merrily tried to free herself from his grasp. Alex was merciless, putting his other hand on the other side of her face. "Don't look away from me, Merrily," he said softly. "Take a couple days to rest and recuperate from your ordeal. Let Ruth do what she does, and I'll take care of the rest. After that, if you still want to leave, I won't stop you. But perhaps you'll find you like it here."

Finally, she nodded slightly. Alex was so relieved he wanted to kiss her. Instead, he settled for memorizing her face. But when her lips parted, he found himself falling forward, until their lips were pressed together.

The shot of lust was immediate and hard. Alex had to fight a groan, but he heard Merrily's little whimper. Her hands clutched at the front of his shirt, bunching the expensive material. He had no idea if this was her way of holding him to her or if she simply held on for dear life, but Alex had -- *had* -- to kiss her.

Somehow, he found the presence of mind to separate from her long enough to look into her eyes, to see if she was afraid or, worse, disgusted with him. He halfway expected her to slap him. Lord knew he deserved it. He was offering her a safe haven. A job. A means to save herself and her daughter and get the hell out of Dodge if she wanted. Would she think he expected the use of her body in payment?

What he saw in her eyes was such a mixture of everything it made him growl. She was definitely interested in him as a man, but she was also terrified to turn him down. "Just one more kiss, Merrily," he whispered against her lips. "I'm not taking my payment from your body, but I have to kiss you again."

"Okay," she managed. Alex could feel the fine tremors going through her body. Her hands still clutched at his shirt, and he was thankful. At least she wasn't rejecting him outright. He knew she'd have no idea what to make of this. Hell, he didn't either. But the need... the hunger. All for her.

Never in his life had Alex experienced such a visceral reaction to a woman. It was all he could do to keep his kiss gentle. Especially when her hands adjusted her grip. She gripped the muscles of his chest, her fingers flexing and relaxing, kneading like a little kitten. Her return kiss was tentative, but she seemed to want to explore as much as he did.

When she whimpered beneath him again, he held her tight, one hand going behind her head, the other circling her back, giving her no way to get away from him. He deepened the kiss, slanting his mouth over hers with a little more force, letting her know how much he simply wanted to take her and damn the consequences.

Alex knew this was wrong. Knew he was taking advantage of a woman much younger and so much more inexperienced than he was in more ways than one. She would likely expect things from him after this. Truth be told, he'd give her anything she wanted if he knew he could have free use of her body.

That thought brought back his sanity when nothing else could. Would she expect money? Luxuries? Would she expect them to be in a "relationship" now? Why did that thought not give him the anxiety he'd always felt when a woman got clingy?

Ending the kiss slowly, Alex pulled back, needing to see every expression on her face. Her eyes were still closed, a look of complete and utter bliss on her face. Her cheeks were the lightest pink, her lips kiss-swollen, giving her an adorable pouty look. When her eyes fluttered open, they sparkled like deep, clear emeralds. She didn't look like a woman who had landed the "big fish." More like a woman who'd completely lost herself in the moment and enjoyed it for the intensity of the pleasure she received.

As he watched, reality slowly began to take hold of her. Instead of elation or any number of other emotions, he saw shame. Humiliation.

"Don't." His command was a sharp reprimand. "That was nothing more than a kiss between a man and a woman who are attracted to each other. Don't make it into something it wasn't."

"I can't stay here," she whispered. "Please. Just… just let us go."

Alex felt his face harden and couldn't stop it. "There's no way in hell I'm letting you leave. Not until I know you're safe." When she opened her mouth to protest, he silenced her with one more hard kiss. "Go to bed. Rest. Forget this ever happened and take the protection offered within this manor." He stood back abruptly, needing to be away from her before he did something really stupid. Like take haul her pretty little ass upstairs to his bed.

When she nodded once, he turned and left the room. God help him, he knew that wouldn't be the last time he'd kiss Merrily Dane.

Chapter Three

The next couple of weeks passed in a whirlwind for Merrily. She'd only seen Alex twice and he hadn't acknowledged her at all, furthering her belief that their kiss hadn't meant anything to him. She still couldn't figure out why he'd done it. He was a very closed-off man, his expression giving nothing away. She noticed, however, that he'd looked slightly confused after he'd kissed her. He was definitely judging her reactions very closely, but he didn't seem to know what to do about her. The only thing she was sure of was that he'd enjoyed kissing her, for whatever reason. She didn't think he intended on repeating the experience, but he'd enjoyed it.

Mrs. McDonald, surprisingly, treated Merrily as if she were part of Alex's family, insisting on having breakfast sent to their room in the morning and inviting her and Bellarose to dinner in the great dining hall with Alex and the others, though Alex was never there. Every time Merrily asked about work, the older woman would tell her she'd get back to her "in a day or two." She continued to send clothes and accessories and makeup and electronics and toys to Merrily and Rose. The little girl squealed in delight with everything sent to her, but, by far, her favorite things were the cats. The feeling seemed to be mutual. The three of them hardly separated.

As to Alex, Merrily didn't know what to think. She was glad she hadn't run into him because she had no idea how to act. Pretending nothing had happened would be the smart move, but she wasn't sure she could do that. She'd never been a good actress, and her feelings would likely be known by everyone around to witness.

Besides, he probably thought she considered he was fair game after they'd kissed. That she'd try to use that to a financial advantage in some way. Hadn't he told her not to make that kiss into something it wasn't? He might have meant it one way, but Merrily was in danger of making it into feelings neither of them had. She wanted him to want to kiss her. She sure wanted to kiss him. Not to lay any claim to his money, but for the pleasure of it.

To take her mind off Alex, she'd finally hounded Mrs. McDonald until she'd agreed to let her help serve the gala the men were hosting the following week. To her shock, she'd found that not only did Alex, Azriel, and Giovanni live and work here, but each of them had several brothers and cousins as well. Everyone would be in attendance.

"You know, you could go as a guest instead of a server," Mrs. McDonald had said as she supervised the tailoring of Merrily's uniform for the evening event with a scowl on her face. A knee-length, form-fitting black skirt, white blouse with a black vest, a red bow tie, black stockings, and black, two-inch-heeled pumps was the uniform for a gala of this sort. White gloves were also a must. Apparently, the gala was a pretty big deal.

"A guest?" Merrily's eyes widened. "Have you lost your mind?" She shook her head. "No way I'd fit in with this kind of crowd. Besides, I have to start earning my keep."

The older woman's face screwed up. "You should be going as a guest," she muttered. "A beautiful young woman like you should dress up and go to the ball on the arm of a handsome suitor."

"Well, instead of that, I'll take serving drinks or *hors d'oeuvres* gladly. I wouldn't know how to act or what to do. Can you imagine if I used the stupid salad fork to eat a crab or something?"

Mrs. McDonald laughed. "You could start a new trend. My boys are so rich, everyone would follow your lead."

"*They're* rich. Not me. As evidenced by my presence here. Why would you equate me with them, anyway?"

"Because you're the woman for my Alexei."

Merrily started, looking up sharply. "No. Mrs. McDonald --"

"How many times have I asked you to call me Ruth, young lady?"

"Fine. Ruth. Don't say things like that. He's way out of my league and I have no illusion he's not."

"He's different, is all. He was raised and lives in a different environment than you, but he can make you happy. You can make him happy."

"He's barely spoken to me since he decreed my forced imprisonment." She laughed. "I hardly think he's happy with me at all. In fact, I bet if I make a big enough mess at this party, I could get him to kick me out."

Now it was Ruth's turn to laugh. "Not likely. I've never seen him so protective of anyone. He's more a playboy than a fighter, but with you, I think he might just fight off Armageddon." She rested her finger on her chin as she spoke, now looking Merrily up and down with a critical eye. "Lovely, my dear." She beamed. "Now. I'll show you what to do and you'll be perfectly fine. Unless..." She looked hopeful. "You've changed your mind and want to go as a guest? I can have the most beautiful gown ready for you in a matter of days."

"I think this will be fine, Ruth."

She was soon to second-guess herself. Serving at an event of this caliber was no picnic. As Merrily found out, each server had their own pattern throughout the room so they covered the entire place without actually proceeding in a line. The patterns were designed to look random and Merrily could see it worked like magic, keeping the food and drinks distributed evenly. When a server was close to running out of whatever they had, they took a direct route back to the kitchen for another tray.

Merrily found all the staff to be kind and personable. Everyone helped her, teasing good-naturedly when she became frustrated, keeping her spirits up. They told funny stories about their first times at a gala event to make her smile. No one seemed to know about Ruth's suspicion that Alex was interested in her, thank goodness. Merrily didn't think she could handle it if they did.

Now, with the gala in full swing, she picked up her tray full of *hors d'oeuvres* and made her way around the room carefully. At first, she was so nervous she nearly forgot to stop when guests signaled or reached for her tray. About an hour into it, however, she had the hang of things. She smiled, kept her tray full, and rarely spoke.

One thing she learned quickly was that the hired help were pretty much treated as fixtures in the room. Like they were furniture. People said and did things she was fairly certain they would never want out in the open. One group of businessmen was discussing insider trading. Merrily might not have known what it all meant if not for an economics class she'd taken in high school for college credit. She'd done some research and knew the terms, if not how it was applied in reality. Another couple was discussing a court case they were part of. Specifically, how to bribe a witness into recanting his testimony so their client could go free. Two other men were busy touching and caressing a woman under the table. Merrily wasn't sure either man was aware what the other was doing and wanted to linger to see what happened when they found out. The woman was carrying on a conversation as if nothing was happening, but she had her hand in the crotch of one of them while she covered the movement by angling her body as she talked. Merrily supposed, if she were a bad person, she could make a large sum of money with the information alone. Just one more aspect of Alex's world she could never be a part of.

Merrily was so focused on everything going on around her, she almost missed the large group of people congregating together near the center of the room as she passed. They parted for a man coming in her direction. When he reached for her tray, she finally recognized that man as Alex. He was only a few feet from her for the first time in more than two weeks and she found she was starved for the sight of him.

What struck Merrily the most was the difference in his appearance. He was, of course, in an impeccable tuxedo that molded his large, muscular frame lovingly, obviously tailored to perfection. His broad shoulders tapered to his narrow hips. He'd been good looking before but now he was devastating. That was only part of it. His expression was completely closed off, giving away nothing of what he was thinking. It had been much the same way before, but his eyes had been at least somewhat expressive as he'd stared into hers. Now, they were cold. Calculating. As if he saw and heard as much as she had and was making a mental note on every single indiscretion and how to use it against the transgressor. He might look like he was there drinking and having a grand time without a care in the world, but Alex was working that room even harder than she was. The only difference was he intended to do something with the information he gleaned. Either that, or he was looking for something in particular.

Their eyes met and he held her gaze steadily. A tall, thin blonde draped herself over him, as if he was all hers. Merrily had no idea if they were together or not and that made her blush, turning away. What if she'd kissed another woman's man? She was many things, but she'd never overstep like that.

She tried to keep moving, finding the pattern she was supposed to follow again away from Alex, but people kept snagging food from her tray. With any luck, she'd run out soon.

"I don't understand why you don't use this fundraiser for the local animal shelter, Alex," the blonde pouted. She'd burrowed so close to his side she was practically fused there. "The city has enough homeless shelters. Besides, who wants that element in our city anyway?" She purred her stinging, insensitive comment, as if she were so much better than people like Rose and Merrily.

"There are always those in need, Victoria," Alex said with a shrug. "People are more willing to take in a stray cat than a person."

"Maybe so, but shouldn't they be getting jobs or something? I mean, handouts only mean more handouts." There were a few murmurs, but no one outright agreed or disagreed with her.

"Spoken like a person who paid more for her shoes than she did for her admission donation." Merrily didn't realize she'd said it out loud until all eyes settled on her.

Victoria looked down her nose at Merrily, giving her a disdainful, scornful look. "I'll have you know, I'm on the board of directors for the Housing the Homeless committee. I guarantee you I know more about the city's homeless shelters than you do, girl."

Merrily knew she should just duck her head and leave. Keep her mouth shut. To her horror, her mouth had other plans. "I know every shelter in this city, and all but one is currently filled to capacity on one of the coldest nights of the year. The only one with any room is one of the scariest places I've ever been in." Before she could get her wayward mouth under control, she added, "But I'm sure with your superior knowledge of homeless shelters, you know all about the drug dealers and pimps taking over during the night. Why, I bet your sleeping bag is down there right in the middle of the room where you can be available to anyone who wants to talk to you about it after you leave here." She tilted her head. "Do you even know where all the homeless shelters are? Because I can name every one and tell you which street they sit on and the landmarks surrounding them."

Again, no one seemed to know whether to outright disagree so they kept quiet, looking to Alex for guidance. Merrily wanted to sink into the floor and disappear. She was more foolish than her mother had ever thought she was.

Alex gave a slight smile. "Our little Mary over there has yet to learn her place in my home, but I'd say she was well on her way." He didn't say it with menace or even as a reprimand, but Victoria took it as such. The blonde woman sneered and looked down her nose at Merrily once again. "Once she does, her words will have greater meaning."

"My name is *not* Mary," Merrily said between clenched teeth.

Alex shrugged, but met her gaze directly. "No. It's not."

"I suggest you leave now, little girl," Victoria snapped, cuddling even closer to Alex as if seeing Merrily as a threat instead of a servant. Merrily thought she might as well be trying to climb inside his jacket. "I assure you, you won't be here long." The carnivorous smile said she'd be the reason Merrily left. Apparently, they really were together. Alex gave Victoria the side-eye, still not showing any discernible emotion. Maybe a little irritation, but Merrily had no idea if it was for her or Victoria.

"You could use a break," he said, waving his hand toward the kitchen. "Take fifteen minutes to yourself."

"Without pay," Victoria called. Merrily wanted to throw the tray at her and had to concentrate on turning around. If her body ran away as horribly as her mouth had, she'd be in a world of hurt.

"Alex!" A deep voice boomed from behind her and a burly man pushed past her, nearly knocking her down to make his way to Alex. To her horror she recognized the man. Daniel J. Maddison... *the second*. Rose's paternal grandfather.

Merrily felt the room closing in on her. She couldn't breathe. Alex had gotten her to tell him about Rose's father; now the very man who'd paid her mother for Merrily to get an abortion was in the same room with her. *Talking to Alex!*

Taking a couple of steps backward, Merrily turned, intending to flee back to the kitchens. Instead, she ran right into Rose's father, who was hot on the heels of his father. Daniel glanced down at her. Did a double take. His gaze roamed over her outfit and the empty tray in her hand. He smirked in a how-do-you-like-me-now kind of way, then dismissed her without a word.

Merrily was going to be sick. She was going to throw up right here if she didn't move. One of the other girls took her arm and guided her to the kitchen. Tears she hadn't realized were falling obscuring her vision, Merrily went with her blindly.

Once through the doors, the girl took her tray and called frantically, "Mrs. McDonald! Mrs. McDonald!"

A couple seconds later, Ruth was at her side, guiding her farther into the kitchen and through the back entrance. She pushed Merrily down to sit on the stairs before kneeling in front of her. "Tell me what you need, sweetheart," the older woman said, taking Merrily's face between her hands. "I saw what happened. Do you know the men talking to Alex?"

"I -- I need Rose. And to leave. Right now, before he comes for us."

"Who, honey? Who's coming after you?"

"Rose's father," she whispered. "Alex made me tell him about Daniel. Now he and his father are here. I have to get Rose out of here before something bad happens."

Ruth gave a little impatient sigh before pulling Merrily into her arms. "I promise you, Merrily, *no one* will take Rose away from you. Not Alex. Not this Daniel." She forced Merrily to look at her. "Do you understand me?"

She didn't, but nodded anyway. "Now. Go upstairs and wash the tears from your beautiful face. I'll take care of Alex." In that moment, Merrily hoped the older woman had that kind of sway over Alex even as she knew that, if Alex decided to give Rose to Daniel, there would be nothing anyone -- including Ruth -- could do about it.

* * *

"I want her off the floor." Alex was livid, but he managed to deliver the instructions in a mild tone. The explosion of anger that wanted outside his body was contained, if barely. He kept it together by sheer force of will. Victoria still clung to him like she had some kind of claim on him. So far, he'd let her because it benefited him, but that would change soon, and he would make sure she knew it, too.

"Girl needs to know her place," Victoria hissed, repeating his words, obviously trying to curry favor and get her way at the same time.

Alex didn't acknowledge her, wouldn't unless it was to deliver a scathing put down, and the woman wasn't worth breaking the bored facade he presented. Besides, he hadn't been talking to the grasping woman.

"I'll get Ruth to take care of her." Giovanni's voice came through Alex's earpiece.

"She'll run," Alex said, ignoring wherever Victoria was saying.

"Ruth won't let her. Now, head in the game, *boss*. He's practically on you."

Alex nearly winced at the reprimand, something that had never happened. It was enough that Alex knew the rest of the team would be debating even now whether or not to continue with this part of the mission and, if they decided to move forward, would be considering replacing Alex on point. It was the problem with leading a bunch of alphas. There was absolutely no room for mistakes.

"Alex!" Daniel J. Maddison II was a snake. He'd known that before Merrily had told him about her experiences with the family. His son, Danny, was even worse.

"Victoria told me it might be worth my while to show up tonight," the elder Maddison commented. "Have you had a change of heart about my proposed merger?"

As if.

Alex smiled slightly at the other man. "I'm afraid not, Dan. I've been contacted by some associates of yours and warned off that project. Pity, too. It took me a while, but I saw merit to what you were proposing. Our robotics program could have used a little reboot." Alex was fishing. They suspected Daniel Maddison's company of laundering money for someone, but hadn't figured it out yet. In fact, it wasn't until Merrily had told him of her situation that they'd had a break in an investigation that had lasted many months and met with more brick walls than it should have.

To his credit, Maddison only tilted his head slightly. "Really. I can't imagine --"

"No worries, Dan," he interrupted before the man could deny anything. "Anyone worth his salt in business has more than one avenue open to him. You start with the best one and work your way down." He extended his hand. "Enjoy your evening."

Behind him, Victoria sputtered. She was the bridge to Daniel Maddison, had been planted in Alex's circle to feed Dan information. Her job was to reel Alex in, gain his loyalty to her because of a sexual relationship. Alex had enjoyed his part in her game -- the woman knew her way around a man's body -- but he was finished with her now. No matter what happened tonight.

"Wait!" Maddison grabbed his arm. "Perhaps we could discuss this later. Tell me when, and I'll come to your office." He smiled congenially, but there was an underlying tension in him.

"Are you sure you want to do this, Dad?" Danny, the younger Maddison, said in a bored tone. "We can get any number of companies to invest in us. I gave you proposals on three just this morning."

"None of them have the clout of Argent Tech," Maddison said absently before addressing Alex again. "I assure you, Alex, this is a deal we can make work."

Alex smiled. "If it were only the two of us negotiating, I'm certain we could. But, like I said, someone in your circle doesn't want Argent and Maddison merging their robotics divisions." He shrugged. "I protect the larger company at all costs, Dan."

"I told you, we don't need him," Danny hissed at his father's shoulder. "I've got this, Dad."

"Look, Alex. I'm going to level with you. Your research and development is off the charts. You have the backing of the most credible, most widely utilized tech company in the world. Maddison Robotics is smaller and less funded but we hold our own because of superior advertising and the connections my father built over a generation. If we merge our resources, we could take over the robotics industry worldwide. Contracts with every major government."

Alex studied the man -- and his son -- as if considering what he was saying. In reality, he and his team *were* studying the other men. Just not for the reason they thought.

"Whatever is going on, either they're both in on it or Danny is good and pissed because he's trying to prove himself and his Daddy isn't taking chances with someone else's dirty money." Giovanni's voice was confident. "Infrared camera is lit up like a Christmas tree. Dan wants access to those books badly and is nervous as shit. Temperature's spiking."

"Say I look into this further. Ignore the warnings I've received. How do you envision this merger working?" This was the setup. It would never work with most people looking to launder money, but Maddison was desperate. This was what had taken so long to figure out. Maddison had a thief in his midst. And that thief had gone after the one thing Maddison couldn't deal with legally -- the money they were laundering.

"All you'd have to do is sit back and collect the profits. We'll sign any necessary non-disclosure forms on the tech, and your staff becomes our staff. Maddison becomes part of Argent Technology, but operates under the Maddison Robotics name."

"Hmm…" Alex mused, letting the man think he was considering it, working out the angles in his mind. "It would give you greater collateral to work with, but I'd want full access to the books. Like I said, I protect the larger company at any cost. Even if it means cutting loose part of it should the merger fail."

"You can always have access to the books," Dan said without hesitation.

"My team would need to look at your current financials. I can't go into something like this blind. I admit, however, that you are very well connected, especially in the military world. We have our own contacts, of course, but we have been beaten out by you on several bids."

"Of course," Dan assured him.

Danny didn't like it. "Are you saying our books aren't what they should be? We're the top robotics developer in the country. A company doesn't get that way by making mistakes in bookkeeping."

For the first time, Alex let his gaze slide to the younger man. He supposed he was handsome. A little prissy looking for Alex. Too soft. His skin was so smooth, Alex had to wonder if he'd had his facial hair lasered. He was convinced Merrily wouldn't be enticed by his money -- after all, she'd tried to refuse everything Alex had provided for her -- so she'd apparently found the man appealing in some fashion. Just looking at him made Alex want to mess up his too-perfect face.

"Daniel, I suggest you explain to your son *Business Merger 101: Always Know the Books*." He shifted his gaze back to the older man. "Call my office first thing tomorrow. We'll set up an appointment. Shouldn't take more than twenty-four hours to get through everything." He reached out his hand and Dan Maddison took it.

"I look forward to it," he said with a smile that looked as fake as Alex knew his was -- the look of a man who smelled blood in the water. He thought Alex was buying into his proposal. In reality, Alex simply wanted a legal means to inspect the company's financial records. Oh, there was no doubt they'd be doctored, but there was nothing anyone could hide from his numbers men. They'd find the discrepancies and do what they always did -- follow the money.

"That's a wrap," Giovanni said. "If Danny Junior there doesn't talk him out of it, we'll be good to go."

Alex strode off toward the kitchen, intending to find Merrily and explain what had just taken place. Well, as much as he could, anyway. "What about Steve Black?"

"He's currently sweating and begging Azriel not to cut off his testicles with a butter knife. He'll fold soon." Giovanni predicted. "I give him... fifteen more minutes. Tops."

"Good. I want these guys, Gio. Then I want the bastards paying them."

There was a pause. "Is it personal?"

"Without a doubt," he said, upholding his vow to be completely honest with his team. Their lives depended on it. It was the one thing where none of them ever compromised. "I'll defer to you as team leader, Gio. I can't be objective on this."

"Understood."

Alex pulled out the earpiece and removed the lapel pin that served as a microphone. As he walked, he handed both to one of the servers, who pocketed them without a word. They were used to intrigues at these events. Well, all of them except Merrily. He could only imagine what she was thinking.

"Where's Ruth?" he snapped as he walked into the staging area outside the kitchen.

"She took Merrily upstairs." The young woman who answered had been the one to help Merrily after she'd literally run into Danny Maddison. "I'm afraid she'll try to leave us, sir," she said, not having to specify who "she" was. Already the staff thought of Merrily as one of them. He had tried to keep tabs on her, but, truth was, he'd avoided her as much as possible. He was becoming obsessed with her and that wasn't a good thing. Not with his life the way it was.

He skirted the edge of the law only because he and his "family" were all insanely rich independently. Deep pockets were essential to success. As was focus. Currently, he couldn't seem to concentrate on anything other than Merrily and her young daughter. If ever there was someone who needed the Demon's special talents, it was those two. More, Alex wanted Merrily for himself. Having given up command for this project, he could freely admit it now. It wasn't going to go over well in the inner circle, but hopefully his gesture would be enough to convince everyone he still had their backs and was still in the game. If not…

He'd have to deal with that if it happened. Right now, he had to get to Merrily.

Chapter Four

Merrily had gone straight to her suite, intending to wake Rose and leave immediately. Ruth, however, followed her, not saying a word until she closed the door behind them. Gloria, the young woman Ruth had stay with Rose while Merrily worked, was sitting quietly on the couch, reading where she could clearly see Rose sleeping soundly. As expected, both cats were curled on the bed beside the little girl.

"You're not going to run, Merrily," Ruth said gently. "If it makes you feel better, lock yourself in Rose's bedroom with the girl tonight. But don't do anything until you have a chance to talk with Alex."

"I can't, Ruth," she said, sniffling. "I may be ignorant of this world, but one thing I'm absolutely certain of is that Alex gets what he wants. He'll force me to stay, whether by persuasion or captivity. If I don't leave now, I never will."

"You're still not going anywhere," Alex said softly. He stood in the doorway, his demeanor aloof. Merrily hadn't even heard him enter. His gaze burned possessively over her, the look in his eyes anything but the cool detachment she'd seen at the gala. He extended his hand to her. "Come with me, please."

"I'm not leaving my daughter."

"No one is going to take Bellarose from you," Alex said with a small shake of his head.

"Why should I believe you? You're the one who brought Daniel back into our lives! You can't tell me it's coincidence he showed up here right after I told you about him."

"No," he snapped. "It's not. I made sure the Maddisons were here. What I didn't intend to happen was for them to know you were here at all, but you insisted on working. Which is fine, but you'll never again do it in a way that puts you at such a disadvantage."

Merrily narrowed her eyes. "I don't understand."

"Did you notice that when Victoria started spouting her nonsense, not everyone agreed with her? What about when you pointed out how ignorant she really was? If you'd been there as a guest, *at my side*, you could have done some good instead of taking a dressing down from a woman who has no idea what she's talking about." Alex didn't sound angry per se. His eyes, however, told a different story.

"If you're angry about what I said to your girlfriend, I'm not taking it back. What I said was the truth."

"Don't expect you to. And she's not my girlfriend." He beckoned to her once more. "Now, come with me." When she didn't take his hand immediately, he gave an exasperated sigh. "Please."

Merrily shook her head, but Ruth urged her on. "Go with him, dear. I'll stay with Gloria and watch over little Rose."

Apparently that was the extent of Alex's patience. He snagged her hand and tugged, pulling her to him and out the door. Once in the corridor, Alex tightened his grip on her hand and marched down the hall to the stairs.

"Slow down," Merrily snapped. "I can't keep up in these heels."

Instead of doing as she demanded, he simply scooped her up into his arms and sped up, taking the stairs two at a time when they reached them. Merrily's heart raced as they hurried up the stairs. Once they reached the top, he opened the door to another suite. She assumed it was his but that made no sense.

"Where are you taking me?"

"My home."

"This whole place is your home."

"My private residence," he said impatiently. "After tonight, you and Rose will move up here. Anytime you have to be away from Rose, either Ruth or Gloria will be with her. Either here or in the suite you currently occupy."

"I -- I don't understand. You want me to... live here?"

"I want you to feel safe."

Merrily blushed. Her thoughts had gone straight to a place she never should have ventured. A man like Alex wouldn't look twice at a woman like her. Not that she wasn't pretty. Merrily wasn't insecure that way. What she had trouble with was his status in life. His wealth. She had nothing. Only Rose. He had everything. Anything he wanted. Why would he settle for her when he could have someone like Victoria?

"I'm fine in the room you gave me."

"You'll be better here," he said. He still hadn't put her down, but walked through to a bedroom before setting her down and shutting the door. When he turned back to her, he pulled her into his arms, whirling her around until she landed against the wall. His hand protected the back of her head, but he crowded her personal space, bracing his other hand on the side of her head, caging her in.

"What are you doing?" Her heart pounded, and it wasn't in alarm. She supposed she should be scared, but nothing about Alex frightened her like it should. Either she was stupid, or she wasn't as good a girl as she thought.

"Showing you your place in this house." His growl sent shivers through her body. "After tonight, there'll be no doubt where you belong or who you belong to."

The moment his lips touched hers, Merrily was lost. She had no idea why he was doing this, but he was definitely doing it. Merrily wasn't going to stop him.

Between kisses he told her, "You want to work? I have plenty of things for you to do in the city." Kiss. "I'll even give you your own funds for a foundation of your choosing. You can do whatever the fuck you want with it." Another kiss. "Build more shelters. Fix existing ones. All yours." He deepened his kiss, swirling his tongue with hers until her knees gave out. Alex simply lifted her, urging her to wrap her legs around his waist.

Then he stopped, using one hand to gently grip her chin so she had to look at him. "But I will *never* see you in such a vulnerable position as I did tonight."

"You could have said something," she squeaked out.

"No. I couldn't." Alex put his forehead against hers, taking a deep breath before meeting her eyes again. "We set up that meeting for a reason. Your father works for Maddison. He does the dirty work. Maddison is in business with some very scary people, and apparently your father took something that didn't belong to either of them."

"What?"

"He's a mule, among other things," Alex said as he walked them to the bed, settling his body between her thighs, rocking side to side. Merrily shivered, clenching his shoulders convulsively. This was so surreal! In her wildest dreams, Merrily couldn't have predicted this turn of events. She still didn't know what to make of it, but she knew she wanted this time.

No matter what happened in the morning or even in the next hour. She wanted Alex. "Maddison can't prove it, but he believes your father stole over five million dollars in unlaundered drug money. Now, Maddison is hoping he can retrieve as much of that money as he can before it's missed. To that end, he needs a way to funnel money into his associates' accounts to keep it secret."

"I don't understand."

"Maddison wants to merge his company with a portion of mine. He'll cook the books and siphon my money to supplement the loss until he can get it all evened out. In the meantime, he's putting the squeeze on everyone working for him. I made a deal with him tonight that means he will turn over his company's books for my team to comb through. He's already fixed them and will likely think they are airtight. Unfortunately for him, no one is better than us at things like this."

Merrily stared at him as he finally pushed up to strip off his shirt, and she lost her breath. Muscles. Scars that shouldn't be on a wealthy playboy. He had a rugged body. One she ached to learn. "Wait," she breathed. Meeting his gaze, she asked, "Why are you telling me this?"

"Because I'm many things, Merrily. I'm a dangerous man. I make no bones about it. I've hurt people and will again. I've *killed*. But the one thing I've done my best to hang on to is my integrity. I may not always tell the whole truth, I may hedge or be vague or give a partial truth, but I never outright lie." He met her gaze steadily. "And I never will give *you* anything but the absolute truth. If you want to know the answer to something, be damned sure you can handle that answer."

"What about Rose? Has Daniel figured out he has a daughter? Did you tell him?"

He shook his head, kneeling on the bed before lowering himself beside her. "Not that I know of. If he does, he found out tonight from someone other than me, and I don't think that's the case."

"What are you going to do with me?"

He gave her a wicked smile. "I already told you. I'm showing you where you belong."

"I'm not a whore, Mr. Petrov. If this is for me to buy my protection or my discretion about what you've told me about my father, know that I'd rather leave, and that I'd rather forget I have a father altogether."

For long, long moments, Alex stared at her. "You're mine, Merrily," he said, a fierce gleam in his eyes as he settled his weight on top of her, pressing her into the bed. "You have been since the first moment I saw you. You belong with me. Not as my mistress, but as my woman."

She shook her head a little desperately. "I don't understand you. How long do you plan on keeping me?"

"A very, very, *very* long time," he said, then kissed her again.

* * *

This was probably not the smartest thing Alex had ever done in his life, but, dammit, he had to secure Merrily for his own. Tonight. He'd worry about all the secrets tomorrow. The team wasn't going to like it, but they'd have to live with it. He meant what he'd told her; he absolutely would not lie to her. Not in any way. If he thought she might not like what he had to tell her, he'd give her the option, but there would be no secrets between them. He'd spent the past couple of weeks gathering information about her and her parents, so he had an idea of what to do, but now wasn't the time to talk about it.

As he kissed her, Alex wondered for the first time in his life if he could keep a woman with him and happy. It had never mattered before. Any woman with him knew the score. He might see them for a time and made sure they were taken care of, but Alex Petrov had no desire to marry or have a long-term relationship. Truth was, he couldn't. Not with the Shadow Demons. No matter. He'd figure it out.

Alex rolled them over so that Merrily lay sprawled over him. Locking her to him, his arms around her like a vise, Alex growled as he leaned up to kiss her again. She was tentative but kissed him back, moaning a little into his mouth. When he would have deepened the kiss, Merrily lifted her head, one hand going to his face to cup it.

"Stop," she whispered. "Just give me a minute."

No question she was spooked. Alex didn't really blame her, but he wasn't about to let her fears stop him. Not when everything in him was fighting to make her his. "Take all the time you need, my Merrily." He rested his hands on her thighs, rubbing up and down leisurely. "I'm not interested in making you do anything you don't want to do."

She took a deep breath. Alex could tell she was thinking about getting off him and regrouping. He was careful not to force her to stay put, though that was exactly what he wanted to do. Willing her to stay, he simply stared at her. Finally, she spoke.

"I'm not going to deny I want this. But I want you to understand, it's about the pleasure." As she spoke, her gaze shifted. Instead of meeting his gaze boldly, she looked at his bared chest. Alex knew what he looked like. Not only was he ruggedly built, he had many scars, something most men with his kind of money didn't have thanks to cosmetic surgery. Alex wore them proudly. To him, they were symbols of a lifetime of work. He couldn't really say sacrifice because he enjoyed what he did, thought it necessary. If Merrily wasn't strong enough to accept him as he was, then she'd prove him wrong when he was convinced she was the woman for him.

"Of course it's about pleasure, baby. As much pleasure as I can give you."

"I have no doubt you're a capable lover, Alex," she whispered. "I just need to know that I have a choice. You've said you won't lie to me. I'm extending the same courtesy to you. I need help. Not for myself, you understand. For Rose." Then she swept her gaze back up, meeting his eyes with her own. "I will do anything to keep her safe. She's my world. I'm just asking you... No. I'm *begging* you. Please don't make me do this for her protection." A tear slipped down her cheek, and Alex's gut clenched. The desire he felt for her wasn't lessened, but the need to put her mind at ease, to help her find a way to live with a man like him without feeling like she was prostituting herself was more than his need for her body. "I'll do it if that's your price. I'll do it, and it will be incredible for me whether it is for you or not. I'm just... I'm asking it not to be the price I have to pay. Because, again, to be honest, I want it so much I couldn't tell you no, and it would break my heart."

"This is your choice, Merrily," he said, lifting his hands to her cheeks, cupping her face gently. "If you choose to walk out of here right now, I'll likely spend the rest of the night in a cold shower, but you're free to leave. No repercussions. But I'm not going to even hint that I wouldn't try to persuade you back in here." He pulled her down, meeting her halfway to kiss her lips gently. "You and Rose will have anything you need. You'll be protected, have a safe home, and I will find who's hunting you. No matter what. If you do this, if you let me have you, it's for the pleasure."

"Only the pleasure?" She looked vulnerable, but so desirable Alex had to restrain himself from pouncing, taking the advantage he had now.

"If I didn't want you so badly, Merrily, I'd laugh. You're probably the only woman in the world who wouldn't try to use my need to her advantage."

"I know what it's like to need something very badly," she said, not pulling away from him but relaxing just a little. "I want you, too. Let's just enjoy the time we have. Two regular people with no worries or cares other than satisfying each other."

Alex couldn't help the grin. "That's the best suggestion I've ever heard."

* * *

Merrily hadn't had sex since before Bellarose's birth. She'd been too busy surviving to worry about relationships or even simple sex. Beside the fact that she'd had no babysitter, she would never bring a man into her life she didn't trust with her daughter. Building that trust took time, and she had never found a man she wanted to invest the effort into. Now…

Alex Petrov was anything but a safe man, but she sensed the underlying good there. He was fiercely protective of what he considered his, from property to family. Once he considered someone part of his unconventional brood, he protected them. She could see that in the way he treated Ruth and the way Ruth treated him. And the way the whole staff treated Ruth and each other. Hadn't it been one of the other servers who'd helped her off the floor, then called for Ruth?

Did she trust him with Bellarose? Yes. Solidly. Why, she had no idea, but there it was. She trusted Alex Petrov with the most important thing in her life. She firmly believed he would protect her little girl with his very life. She did not, however, trust him with her heart. Not because she thought he'd break it intentionally. The fact was, Alex was a playboy. One woman would never satisfy him. It wasn't his fault. It was his lifestyle. His mindset. He might think she could be enough for him, but she knew she could never be what he needed. For now, Merrily would enjoy sex for the first time in nearly five years with the most incredible man she'd ever seen. Tomorrow would take care of itself.

Impossibly strong arms wrapped tightly around her, accepting her surrender as he kissed her thoroughly. Tongue delving inside her mouth, he swooped in, the conquering hero to take her away on a tide of sensation. Merrily couldn't think about anything other than the flicking of her tongue against his. His scent was an intoxicating blend of leather and musk. Rough hands skimmed down her back, snagging on the delicate material of her blouse as he tugged it from the waist of her skirt. When those same calloused hands slid up her bare back under her clothing, Merrily moaned, arching into his touch. At the same time, he nipped her lower lip gently and she opened wider to him.

Had kissing a man ever felt like this? Merrily was fast drowning in sensation, her body coming alive like she could never remember it doing before. His groans, the way he kneaded and abraded her flesh with his big hands drove her nearly insane with need. Without realizing it, Merrily found herself grinding against him where she straddled his lap.

When she stopped abruptly, Alex chuckled against her lips. "Needy little thing," he growled. "I love it that you don't hold back. Tell me what you need. What you like."

"It all feels so good," she whimpered. Merrily was mortified she sounded so inexperienced. Shouldn't a man like him want a woman who knew what she was doing? Merrily might have a child, but she was far from the worldly woman he probably thought he was getting.

"Sit up on me," he commanded. "Take off your blouse."

Alex urged her to do as he said, lifting her off him when all she wanted to do was mash herself against him. Only the thought of her bare flesh being against his made her not resist him. With trembling fingers, she undid the pearly buttons, pulling off the bowtie at her throat. Alex snagged it, but didn't toss it aside, fastening it once again around her bare throat while she finished taking off her top and bra.

"My little Merrily." His voice was gruff. "All tied up in a bow."

When she was bare from the waist up, Alex's gaze roamed over her, a possessive gleam in his eyes. His hands slid from her thighs up her sides to cup the slight weight of her breasts. His thumbs brushed her nipples lightly. There was something about the way he looked at her. More than just lust or even possession. It was a soul-deep... yearning? Like he was looking at something he wanted with his whole being and knew it was just out of reach. What Merrily hoped he never figured out was that she'd be willing to go all in with him if that look was real, because she knew he could easily play her.

In slow, leisurely movements, he let his hands roam over her body, around her back, down to her ass, over her thighs and then hook under her skirt. Merrily took the hint and reached behind to unzip the garment. Alex slid his hands upward, taking the skirt over her head. That left her in panties and him in slacks.

"You're lovely, my Merrily," he said, his voice husky. Gruff. "I'm not sure there's a woman anywhere who can compare to you in beauty."

"There's no need for flattery," she whispered. "This is happening, as far as I'm concerned." Merrily managed a small smile while part of her desperately wanted to believe him. "I'm a sure thing."

"I never say anything I don't mean. Part of the not-lying bit." He pulled her to him then, rolling slowly so his big body sprawled over her much smaller one. His lips found hers again, and she didn't care anymore.

Alex wrapped his arms around her tightly as he kissed her. His tongue lapped and thrust wickedly, making her answer with her own. Whimpers and moans came from her without her meaning to let them out, but, really, she was helpless against this man holding her so possessively.

He rocked against her, mimicking the act she wanted so desperately. Pressing her thighs to either side of his hips, Merrily moaned as he took her mouth. The feel of his hard body pressed against her pushed her to a near-euphoric state. Was she so desperate for intimate contact she was imagining how good this felt? Or was it the man in question? She strongly suspected the latter because, even when she'd been an innocent, sex had never felt like this.

Her fingers clutched at the muscles of his back, digging in to hold him to her. The more he kissed her, the more desperate for him she became. Her world narrowed to the man in her arms, to his drugging kisses and touches. He skimmed his lips down her throat and she whimpered, her fingers threading through his hair. The sensation almost tickled, sending goose bumps over her entire body. When he reached the swell of her breast, she cried out, arching her back to him.

"I love how sensitive you are," he breathed against her skin before scraping his chin down to her nipple. "You'll respond to every single thing I do to you, won't you?"

Merrily couldn't answer. She wanted to, but her brain was scrambled with sensation, her mouth not able to force out even the affirmative she wanted to utter. Instead, she thrust her breast at him, needing the contact.

He again rolled them, to their sides this time, his hand resting possessively on her hip. Hooking his thumb at the waist of her panties, Alex tugged until she lifted her hips to assist him in pulling them off her. With a growl, he cupped her bare bottom, kneading and squeezing almost convulsively as he held her tightly against him.

"Alex," she whimpered, unable to suppress the need in her voice. She nuzzled his throat, rubbing her breasts over his chest. The feel of the dusting of crisp hair gently abrading her nipples was maddening, so much sensation she couldn't process it all. When he pulled her leg over his hip, Merrily hooked her foot over the curve of his ass, pulling him to her with a soft cry.

"My Merrily," he whispered. She felt him probing her entrance with his fingers before bringing them to his mouth, closing his eyes as if in bliss. "So fucking good…" He looked into her eyes as he licked his fingers clean. "You're so wet for me." Merrily held her breath as Alex shoved his clothes out of the way, positioned his cock and pressed into her. "Look at me, baby. Look into my eyes when I enter you."

With a shaky breath, she did. Intense blue eyes captured hers. He tightened his grip on her hip as the tip of his cock pressed through her tender folds. He was large. While Merrily wasn't a virgin, she had been celibate nearly five years. When Alex slid into her, the burn wasn't painful, but the pleasure was dulled.

"Stay with me, baby. Relax."

"I'm good," she said, but she was tense. With his arms wrapped so tightly around her, no way Alex missed it. Slowly, he withdrew before easing back inside her again, farther this time. And again. Once more, and he was seated all the way inside her, their bodies pressed together tightly. He held her for long moments before moving again. When he raised an eyebrow at her, Merrily smiled tentatively and nodded. "I'm good," she repeated.

Then Alex began to… *move.*

Up to this point, everything he'd done to her had been so pleasurable Merrily had a hard time wrapping her mind around it. But this… It was as if he'd opened up a whole new world of sensation she had no idea existed outside of fairytales. Perhaps he had. After all, it was easy to think of him as her Prince Charming. With a bite. Though Alex had been unfailingly kind to her, she could feel the latent power in his body. Feel the need to drive into her with a brutal force he tempered.

For how long? Did she even want him to hold back? Right now, she thought it best. Her body still struggled to adjust to him, but there was no way she could voice it. Every single stroke made her shudder. Her clit throbbed in time with her heart, on the very edge of the ultimate pleasure.

"That's it. Just relax. Let me have you." The words might have been whispered and tender, but it was a command nonetheless. God help her, but Merrily responded, letting her head fall back as she leaned into him. Alex found her bared neck with his lips, licking and sucking gently as he continued to thrust into her.

His hand gripped her ass possessively, urging her to move with him. She did. Her breaths came in little gasps, and she was lightheaded. Sweat beading on her skin soon had her shivering, though not with cold. Anticipation sizzled in the air around her, making her all the more needy.

"Alex," she gasped.

"Let it happen, love. Give me your orgasm. Can you do that?"

He asked so sweetly, as if it was all up to her, when Merrily knew he was demanding it from her as surely as if he'd ordered her to come.

"Yes," she whispered, then her body fragmented. Merrily shuddered, crying out sharply as the first wave hit her. His cock was so thick she could feel it throbbing inside her spasming flesh. He stilled his movement inside her as she rode out the pleasure, her orgasm seeming to linger. She knew she should be ashamed at her lack of experience because she came, and he hadn't even broken a sweat. Later. She'd worry about it later. Right now, she was overwhelmed -- delightfully so -- by how good sex could be.

When she finally stilled, Alex rolled once again, this time pinning her solidly beneath him. "Now," he growled, "It's my turn."

"Oh!" She cried out when he thrust into her with quick but shallow snaps of his hips. He threaded his fingers into her hair, angling her head for his kiss. Wicked flicks of his tongue drove her higher and higher. He moved more aggressively inside her, but with nowhere near the power she knew was in that magnificent body. He'd started to sweat, his jaw set in a grim line of determination.

"You need more," she whispered.

"You can't handle more. Not yet," he bit out. Again, it wasn't harsh. He was simply stating a fact. "I absolutely will *not* hurt you."

"I won't break, Alex. Do what you need to."

"I need to pound into you on your hands and knees. To take you like a raging animal." This time, he let the full range of his emotions show on his face. He snarled as he picked up the pace but was still careful with her. "I need to mark you, to hold you still so I can come in you until I'm spent. Most of all, I need to fuck you hard. Mercilessly." He shook his head. "You're not ready." Then he gave her a grin that was almost sinister. "But you will be."

Then he threw back his head and roared as his cock swelled inside her, releasing. He held her hips pinned beneath him. Just like he'd said. His hot seed spilled inside her and none of the outrage she knew she should have felt that she hadn't insisted on protection surfaced. Hell, she hadn't even voiced the concern! All she could think of was how right it felt. How good.

Alex finally collapsed over her, his breath coming in great heaves. His lips trailed gently over her neck up to her jaw then finally to her mouth. Languidly, he kissed her, praising her. When he rolled off her, he didn't separate from her, merely continued to kiss her, his arms around her tightly.

"My Merrily," he said against her lips, continuing to kiss and nip her gently. "What am I going to do with you?"

She had no answer for that. What could she say? She didn't put stock in men's pretty words. After all, she'd had a child who belonged to another man. A man who didn't want Rose or her.

"You don't have to do anything with me." She tried to keep her voice steady. Her gaze too. This was the most wonderful experience of her life, and she would enjoy it to the very last second. "Just hold me a few more minutes?"

"Definitely."

Chapter Five

"This better be fucking good," Alex snapped as he entered the underground project room. He'd left Merrily asleep in his bed, and he didn't want her to wake without him.

As usual, Giovanni ignored his bad humor. Sometimes, Alex wondered if the man truly comprehended emotions. He never seemed to really process them unless it was detrimental to the current job or had the potential to endanger someone.

"Our Merrily's *friends* turned Hell's Playground into a blazing inferno."

Alex looked at the large viewscreen that dominated the room as he crossed to Gio and Azriel. The shelter, and four other buildings nearby, blazed like a beacon in the night. Fire trucks and police surrounded it. Ambulances could be seen on the fringes but hadn't ventured too close. Either they'd already evacuated the injured, or there were none alive needing assistance.

"Any luck tracking them down?"

"The hit men? Yes." Gio's voice was as terse as always. "They come from a group in Colombia. Available to the highest bidder."

"But what about the snake patches?" Alex hated puzzles. He'd hoped this one would be pretty much cut and dried. "Invite" the leader of the Rattlesnakes to a meeting, get him to tell them who'd hired him for this job. The end. Instead, Giovanni was pulling this shit.

"Oh, the Rattlesnakes were involved, just not by themselves. They were likely the muscle. The men who burned the place down."

"Not very effective," Azriel commented, though he was still studying the screen intently. "Terror level high, though. You think the Colombia group just wanted to scare the crap out of people? What did they hope to accomplish by destroying the place if not that?" He seemed to be talking to himself more than the others.

"Unclear," Gio said. "Probably sending a message as well as destroying evidence of the other players."

"Which tells us they have no idea where she is," Alex said. He crossed his arms as he studied the viewscreen. "How many did we kill?"

"Seven total. All were part of the Rattlesnake hit team. There were a couple of punks from the neighborhood who got in the way, but you guys only shoved them around a bit. Both had concussions but maybe it knocked some sense into them."

"Possible they were part of the Colombian team?" Azriel always asked any question that came to his mind. Alex figured it helped him work through a problem from every angle. No one questioned where he was going or his line of thinking, they all just let him work. This was what he did.

"No. I identified every single one. All of them have lived here their whole lives. But I'd say your Colombian group will definitely want retaliation. These guys have a perfect termination record. It's why they're so highly sought after." Giovanni started typing with furious speed until a couple of grainy photos appeared on the screen along with a few reports from various law enforcement agencies.

"Perfect?" Alex raised an eyebrow.

"As in they never miss a hit," Gio continued. "They've been traced to at least thirty suspected contract killings over the years. Likely there are more, but they've gotten better at covering their tracks in the last couple of decades. The last thing anyone has been even remotely suspicious about happened nearly two years ago. Before that? Closer to twenty-five."

"Are you sure about this, Gio?" Azriel punched a few buttons over Giovanni's shoulder. Gio glared at him but didn't pull his gun so Alex didn't intervene. No one touched Giovanni's computers. On the screen, an image appeared. It was a grainy photo that looked to have been taken in the early to mid 1800's, by the clothing. He straightened.

"I've seen that picture before." Alex said, moving closer. "The Brotherhood?"

"That's what they're called," Gio confirmed. "Passed down from generation to generation."

"So a family of hit men?" Alex asked.

"No," Azriel stated. "No one in the order is married and all are celibate. They never risk having children."

"I imagine they're a very small group."

"They are, but very devoted. For most of them, it's nearly a religion."

"Yup," Giovanni said, leaning back as if this were nothing new. "In fact, as far as I can find, only one person has ever left their ranks and survived."

Confused, Alex glanced at Azriel to find the other man clenching his fists and jaw. "Something you want to share?"

"Only that you need to keep those two girls inside this estate at all times. Unless you don't care if they live or die." When Alex crossed his arms and glared at Azriel, the other man met his steely gaze with one of his own. "Don't go there, Alex. Not until I figure out where they are and exactly what their instructions are."

"A group like this doesn't make public statements like burning down half a city block. They want to remain in the shadows. Like us."

"Unless it's what they've been paid to do."

"A move like this could expose their operation," Alex argued, not buying it. "Are you sure this is their work?

"No," Azriel snapped. "I'm not. But Giovanni says it is so I'm going on that assumption since he's *never wrong*."

"Hey, easy," Alex said, raising his hands in surrender. "I'm only trying to get an idea of what we're up against."

"If the Brotherhood has been sent to kill those girls, then they are as good as dead."

"Not with us on the job," Alex said confidently. "No way they get past us."

Azriel gave a bitter laugh. "You have no idea who they are, or you'd understand how ridiculous that sounds."

Alex took a couple of steps toward Azriel, his anger rising as well as his irritation. "Then fucking explain it to me." He knew Azriel had a past. They all did. But this wasn't the time to hedge.

"That image is the only one that exists of them. Right after it was taken, their families were wiped out by their enemies. Before that, they were proud of what they did, which was pretty much the same as what we do. Bring justice to those thought untouchable. In those days, the people they went after were just as relentless as the Brotherhood has become now. You got in their way, they stepped on you."

"And now?"

Azriel sighed. The man looked as if the weight of the world were on his shoulders. "Now, they take jobs from people just as ruthless as those they were once sworn to destroy."

"You say it in an almost ritualistic manner," Alex commented. Azriel had a blank look on his face, as if he were so absorbed in remembering the past he couldn't be bothered with the present. "Finish it."

Azriel met Alex's gaze then. "I was one of them. I left when the job became... questionable."

"Because you have a conscience. You're one of us. End of story. Tell me about *them*."

"I left them barely a year before you found me. They teach their men to survive on the outside in a multitude of ways. I used what I knew about making money."

"Which has come in very handy for all of us."

"Yes," Azriel continued, "but I used my own funds and kept things on the down low in order to keep off their radar. It was only one skill they taught me. They are as ruthless in business as they are in combat. They rarely use anyone outside their family unless it's to launder or move the money. If we dig into Daniel Maddison's books, I'm guessing we're going to see a few subtle discrepancies. Things you wouldn't ordinarily notice. Might even miss if you *were* looking for them. Maddison is nothing if not thorough, and the Brotherhood accepts nothing less than perfection."

"So, we'll go under the assumption Maddison is working for them. What are the odds his son is involved?" Alex asked, needing every angle of the problem.

"If Maddison's smart, zero. His son is a liability. A huge one. Especially if anyone suspects he has a child. His father does."

"Do you think Merrily's father gave her and Rose up or do you think Maddison put the Brotherhood on her trail?"

"Toss up," Azriel said. "Maybe a bit of both."

"Azriel's right," Giovanni said quietly. "Maddison had his books delivered, just like you requested, Alex." He scrolled through several documents until he came to several he'd flagged. "Maddison Robotics is a shell company. It took me a while, but, as far as I can tell, they have no real product. They've partnered with several larger companies for short periods of time -- always on a short-term contract of no more than a year -- and always show company growth for both his company and the host company." He waved his hand as if he knew what the next question would be. "I haven't figured out the 'how' and don't really care because it's irrelevant. The important part is, they're laundering money through Maddison Robotics, using it as a parasite company, in such a way that any investigation would look like the host company was the one at fault. Whose money they're laundering, I have no idea. I found a few fledgling discrepancies that make me think someone was trying to skim. If Danny Boy knew his old man's business, he might have gotten greedy." Giovanni let them contemplate that one a moment. "If he were caught -- and I have no doubt even a mediocre money man could uncover what he was doing -- he might have turned on Merrily's dad. The mule is easy to blame and even easier to manipulate into helping steal. Steve could then have turned on Merrily, but that might be an attempt to throw both hounds off his tail. Which would be why he warned her." Giovanni handed Alex a manila envelope. "Before I forget."

"Get everyone looking for Merrily, and he slips quietly away." Alex had about reached his limit. This was normally the kind of thing he loved. Clear-cut bad guy with more bad guys to track down. Not so in this case. "Do you think Maddison knew Merrily was here?" He absently opened the envelope Gio had handed him and skimmed the documents, his mind taking it all in like a sponge. Interesting.

"Doubtful. Both men were too surprised when they ran into her, and Dan didn't even notice her. You know he had that whole meeting recorded. Once he reviews it, he'll know, so that cat's out of the bag."

"In that case," Alex said, "we'd better be ready. They know she's here now. If they have assassins with them, they'll definitely send them our way."

"Agreed," Azriel said. He stared at the computer screen at his desk. "I could try to open a dialogue with them. It's not going to hurt. They're coming after us anyway."

"Do they know you're here? Will they try to take care of your loose end?" Alex wasn't sure what he was hoping for. He definitely didn't want his friend in danger, but he didn't want Merrily in danger either. And she was far less equipped to take care of herself than Azriel. Besides, it wasn't like they were leaving him to fend for himself.

"I seriously doubt they ever lost track of me. I've simply not given them any problem before now," Azriel said. Without another word he sat down and started typing. Whatever he was doing, there was nothing Alex could do to help him. Yet. When the time came, however, he'd stand with his brother, and all three of them would stand in front of Merrily and Bellarose.

* * *

Merrily woke in a bed much too big for her. Events of the previous night swamped her, and she automatically turned to reach for Alex. The place where he'd rested beside her, held her so protectively in his arms, was cool. He'd been gone a while. With a sigh, she sat up. Her body was deliciously sore, reminding her of their long, long bouts of sex. He'd worn her out, blowing her mind more than once. The last time, she'd woken him, which he'd clearly loved if his reaction had been any indication. As gentle and careful as he'd been with her the first time, that last time had been hard and rough, riding the edge of too much. She'd loved every blistering second. It made his absence all the more disappointing.

With a sigh, she dressed in her uniform from the night before and headed back downstairs. With any luck, Rose would still be asleep and not see her walk of shame. It was just one more thing out of character for her. Merrily didn't hook up indiscriminately. Yet, here she was.

"Good morning." Ruth smiled when Merrily opened the door quietly. The older woman was busy in the kitchen with something that smelled heavenly. "I was afraid you'd sneak out before he got back." There was genuine amusement in Ruth's voice as she continued working on breakfast.

"I'm sorry I left you here all night. Did Gloria go home?"

"The girl lives in the east wing," Ruth said. "She left about fifteen minutes ago, though under protest. She'd gladly have stayed with little Rose all day."

"I hope I didn't impose on her time. I'm sure she has better things to do."

"Nonsense, dear. Don't you worry about a thing. Let us help you."

"While I play with a playboy?" Merrily wanted to laugh and cry at the same time. "Ruth, I have no idea what I'm doing. I should be here with Rose or working."

"You should be *living*, sweetheart. How long has it been since you took time to build a relationship? With a man *or* a woman? I don't necessarily mean romantic either. When was the last time you even had a girls' night out?" When Merrily didn't answer, Ruth shook her spoon at her. "That's what I thought. Enjoy being an adult. Enjoy being a beautiful, desirable woman. Most of all --" she crossed the small space between them and laid a hand on the side of Merrily's face, "-- let yourself be happy. If not with Alex, then with someone. But I think if you give him a chance, Alex will do everything in his power to make you happy."

Merrily wasn't so sure. "I'm not into subterfuge or pretending I'm something I'm not. We enjoyed ourselves last night, but that was all it was. He scratched an itch." Then she muttered, "Maybe he just likes slumming."

"Rubbish." Ruth laughed. "I've never seen a woman he followed after to make sure she didn't leave him. Usually, it's him trying every way he can to drive women away. You're special to him."

"I'm a novelty," she said with a sigh. "He'll tire of me soon enough." Before Ruth could refute that, Merrily continued, "In the meantime, I'm just playing it a day at a time. He promised he'd protect Rose whether or not we were… together. I'm going to take him at his word, and I won't run."

"Very well," Ruth said, letting it drop. "Now, go say good morning to little Rose. I'll finish breakfast, then get her off to school, and you can come by and see her after you rest. You know where the school is in the south wing."

"I can't possibly take a nap." Merrily sighed. "I have to go to work."

Ruth rapped Merrily's knuckles with her wooden spoon. Not hard, but enough to get her point across. "Nonsense! Not after last night. Alex will be most displeased if you're seen as anything less than he is. I won't have anyone on my staff mistaking your importance here."

Merrily wanted to groan. There was no sparring with Ruth as tired as she was. With a sigh, she let it go and went to wake Rose.

"Hey, pumpkin," she said, stroking the child's hair as she sat down. Snowball gave a halfhearted hiss and scooted out of the way, snuggling into Rose's pillow right beside her face. "Time to get up. Ruth has a delicious breakfast for you before school."

Rose's eyelids fluttered several times before she stretched and opened them completely. "Did she make silver-dollar pancakes again?" There was a hopeful note in the little girl's drowsy voice.

"I'm not sure. I guess you'll just have to get up and go find out."

"Ruth said I could go to school with the other kids here. She said we could all play together."

"I don't know about that either, pumpkin. But I know you're going to school, and that there will be other kids there. I'd assume at least some of the kids living here will be there." She grinned at her daughter. "I suppose if you and they happen to be in the same place and they just happen to be playing..." She shrugged. "Well, I guess you'd have to play with them. Right?"

Rose giggled and jumped up. Smokey gave a forlorn "meow." Rose picked the cat up and gave him a hug before putting him back down and running to the bathroom.

Merrily was surprised to find she was really tired. She did her best to converse with Rose as she ate, trying to share the child's enthusiasm over going to school and making new friends. All she wanted to do was crawl into bed -- by herself -- and sleep the rest of the morning.

Never in her life had she thought she'd ever be grateful she didn't have to take Rose to school, but she *was* grateful Ruth had volunteered. Grateful the school was inside the massive manor and not away from the safety it afforded. There was no doubt in her mind that as long as they stayed inside the house Rose would be safe. Why she had such confidence in Alex she didn't know. Maybe it was his blatant show of wealth, knowing that any number of people would be willing to make a try for him if his security wasn't what it should be. Maybe it was Ruth's unflappable confidence and belief in him. Maybe she just wanted -- *needed* -- to believe. Whatever it was, she found herself stumbling to the shower after Rose had kissed her goodbye and left with Ruth.

The shower was as intimidating as the rest of the place. A big, walk-in, glass enclosure with multiple sprayers left her a bit befuddled until she figured out how to use them. Then she just let the hot water pound over her body, working out the well-earned soreness of the night before. She rested her head on the glass, sighing in pleasure until she was nearly ready to collapse onto the tiled floor.

"You could have used the shower in my suite." Alex leaned against the open entryway, arms crossed over his muscled chest, gloriously naked. She'd seen him the night before, but not like this. Powerful arms and shoulders, muscled chest and rippled abs narrowing to his lean hips and equally impressive thighs. Several scars marred the beauty but only served to make him even sexier. She tried not to imagine scenarios for each mark, but failed miserably. Unbidden, she had an image of the Shadow Demon in the shelter who'd first spotted them. She could easily imagine this heavily muscled, scarred version of Alex in that role.

Though it was silly -- the man had already seen everything she had -- she draped a hand over her breasts and mashed herself against the wall in an effort to cover herself. "What are you doing?" She tried to sound stern, but even to herself she sounded breathless.

Hands up in a non-threatening gesture, he eased into the shower with her. The enclosure was large, enough so he could bathe on the opposite side and never get close to touching her. "Easy there, my Merrily. I'm not going to ravish you." He threw her a cocky grin. "At least not without your permission."

"You said I didn't have to sleep with you." There was a spike of panic. At least, she hoped it was panic. Otherwise, it was probably excitement and she couldn't let him see that. If he smelled blood in the water, Alex would press his advantage.

"You don't." Alex stepped under the cascading water to wet his hair, his hands slicking the silky strands back out of his face. Water sluiced over his gorgeous body, making her need to chase every single drop on his chest. *With her tongue.* "I just thought you might like to talk."

"What about? Did you find out who was hunting me and Rose?"

"Oh, yes. Really bad guys." The grin he gave her was nearly evil. She imagined how the devil himself would look, and Alex's face immediately came to mind. Fiercely handsome with a spike of danger, he could truly be a demon from hell sent to torment her.

"Are you going to... renegotiate my living arrangement?" Merrily didn't know if she could look herself in the mirror if he insisted on the use of her body in exchange for her and Rose's protection. It was bad enough she'd already slept with him.

"Merrily." His whole demeanor changed in an instant. Now, instead of mischievous and wicked, he was very serious. "Anything we do together, you do because you *want* to. Not because you feel you *have* to. I've never paid a woman for sex, and I don't intend to start now. Especially not with someone so vulnerable." He tilted his head then, an analytical look coming over his handsome face, as if something was just dawning on him. Like he was trying to fit her into a nice, neat package and wasn't quite able to. "Why is that, by the way?"

She blinked, thoroughly confused. "Why is what?"

"Found out some things about you. Interesting things. You're intelligent as fuck. Were offered full rides to several prestigious universities. Yet, you chose a small online college where you only finished half your coursework for a shit degree in Information Technology. Why not finish it? Hell, why didn't you take any of those scholarships? You were on track to be one hell of a computer geek. You could be rich instead of living paycheck to paycheck."

Fury shot through Merrily. "You know jack about my life, Mr. Petrov. Any decisions I made, I did for Bellarose." God, he confused her! She almost preferred the brooding, dangerous man over this side of him. Up to this point, he'd been doing the playboy persona with her, and she found she didn't like it. That wasn't the real Alex. It was almost as if he were trying on personalities to see which one got to her the most. He'd told her last night he'd hurt people, even killed people. Though she was frightened of that side of him, it seemed... genuine. This flippant side of him, the analytical asshole, didn't feel right. Like he was angry with her and taking out that anger by trying to belittle her but couldn't quite commit to the task.

"I'm aware of that," he continued. "You dropped out of high school, got your GED with the highest score in the state, scored perfect on your ACT, and the college entrance exams you took you blew out the top. It was enough you got the attention of the Lockheed Martin recruiters even before you'd taken the first college course. They offered to pay your way through school in exchange for a contract with them for ten years of employment. You're hyper intelligent. Why not --"

"What? Put my own wants and desires above what's best for Rose?" Forgetting how uncomfortable she was with her nudity around Alex, Merrily spun around, her fists clenched. God! The man could get to her so easily! Besides, this wasn't any of his business, no matter how much he was helping her. "I made a choice to have Rose. *Fought* to have her. I was probably too young to do it on my own, but I was determined to give my child the best home possible. My mother kicking me out of the house was the best thing that could have happened because she was the exact persona of what a mother should *never* be. So, if it meant I worked three jobs and sacrificed my dreams, then so be it. I'd gladly do it all over again. I'll continue doing it until she's old enough to take care of herself. Even then, I doubt I'll stop. *She's my daughter.*"

"So, at sixteen you did more for your child than some mothers ever do." Alex made it a statement, as if it were an observation instead of a question. It threw her off balance yet again.

"I don't know about that, but I used my intellect and my will to take care of her any way I could." Then she blinked, a sudden realization washing over her. "Wait. You dug into my background?"

Again, his attitude was flippant. "Sweetheart, anyone who steps onto these grounds -- even if it's the mailman -- is fully vetted. I know everything there is to know about every single member of my household and make no apologies for it. I also don't judge."

"Really? What do you call this conversation then? It's *none of your business* how I've lived my life. Nothing I did -- other than give birth to Rose -- could have led anyone to want to hurt us. This isn't my fault!"

"Relax there, little wildcat. I never thought it was. Of all of us, you're the only true innocent."

Merrily wanted to cry. She was so raw. Off kilter. Alex made her so, but it was more than that. "I've never been more terrified in my life than I have been these past few weeks. The only ease I've had came when I decided to stay here." She sat sideways on a marble bench, the spray hitting her back. Merrily pulled her knees up to her chest and wrapped her arms around them, giving Alex her side. It didn't do much to hide her nudity, but she could at least pretend he couldn't see her. "This place... you... I feel safe here. I feel like Rose is safe." She laid her head on her knees so she looked at Alex. Merrily knew she was weak for not standing up for herself more, but she was so tired and confused she didn't know what else to do. No matter she knew she should be afraid of Alex -- she wasn't. "Why do you interact like this with me? If there is something you want to know, why not just ask me? Have a normal conversation instead of cornering me in the shower?"

"I find that if I keep someone off balance, they tend to say more than they intended." He took a couple of steps toward her, a lion on the prowl. "Would you tell me the whole truth every time I asked you something if we just sat down and had a conversation?"

"I have nothing to hide, Alex. I would have kept my lack of education secret if I'd had a choice because I'm embarrassed by it. Especially in front of someone like you. I would never have been in your class of wealth, but I'd have been somebody. Maybe even somebody who could have attended one of your events eventually. Now…" She gestured to herself from head to toe. "You've stripped me bare. Was it really necessary to tear me apart like this?" To her complete and utter horror, her bottom lip trembled, and a tear slipped from one eye. Not having the energy or emotional endurance to fight it off, Merrily just let it happen.

Alex was at her side in an instant, lifting her from the bench and into his arms. Her body was flush against his, those brawny arms of his wrapped tightly around her. Her brooding, intense warrior was back now, looking straight into her soul like a demon searching for her greatest weakness. One big, rough palm spanned her back. Again, she was struck at the contrast in him. He was a wealthy playboy but didn't seem to be a stranger to hard work. His fit body, ragged scars, and calloused hands were testament to that.

"I don't want to tear you down, my Merrily." His voice was husky but gentle. When she ducked her head, he used one hand to gently force her to meet his gaze. "Quite the opposite. You're the bravest, most selfless person I believe I've ever met. When I said you were the only true innocent here, I meant it. Every single person here has a past. They are here for a multitude of reasons, but not one of them wouldn't be in some kind of trouble if they hadn't come to us. We gave them and their families a home and a greater purpose. Kept them out of danger and trouble. As a result, they are loyal to us. In return, we protect their families and give them a safe place to live without fear." He rested his chin on top of her head. Just like that, his personality had changed. Merrily had no idea which was the real Alexei. No idea if she even wanted to find out. But he intrigued her on a purely intellectual level. Sexual too, but she wasn't going there yet. This man had more than his share of secrets and abilities.

"I don't know what to do." Merrily knew she was talking more to herself because she sounded mournful. Not at all like she should be in the shower, naked, in the arms of one of the richest men in the world.

"Then let me tell you." Alex's arms tightened around her. Oddly, instead of feeling smothered, Merrily felt protected. Comforted. Why would he convey those feelings to her? No way was it simply because they'd had sex. This was a man who'd had more than his share of women. Was he like this with all of them? She doubted it. If so, he'd have women hanging all over him every step he made. While it was true there were probably several -- like Veronica -- who did, Merrily knew there couldn't be many. Otherwise he'd never be able to have a party like the last one without him having women making scenes, vying for his attention. "You're going to stay here. With me. You and little Rose. I have an idea of how you can help me and my brothers, but I have to know your skill level, and you have to make some hard decisions."

She looked up at him. That handsome face and those intense, blue eyes made her knees weak. It was a mistake in this game they played but she couldn't help herself. Swallowing to give herself at least a chance at sounding normal, Merrily jumped in with both feet. "What do you want me to do?"

"Giovanni is our tech guy. I want you to meet with him. Discuss your interests and see if he thinks you'd be a good fit for us."

"Doing what?"

He sighed, looking a bit sheepish. "I'll admit, I have no idea. All the stuff Gio does with the computers and equipment. He'll test you to see what you've got and make a recommendation. Even if he doesn't think you can handle it right now, with your background I'm sure he could teach you. In fact, he's the one who suggested we give you a try."

"This would let me earn my keep here?"

"And then some, my Merrily."

His voice changed whenever he called her "my Merrily." It was like a caress. She liked it. "Why do you call me that?" Her voice came out soft. Breathy. Their gazes locked, and she was nearly dizzy with want and need. "It's too... intimate. You shouldn't --"

"But I do. And I will continue."

Alex's gaze and voice were hypnotic, making Merrily fall into him. God, she wanted this! Wanted Alex and all his brutal good looks. His protectiveness. Not for his money. He made her feel alive. Special. Wanted. "Will you break my heart?"

In answer, he simply smiled at her and dipped his head to take her mouth.

Merrily really needed an answer to that, but once his mouth was on hers, his tongue lapping gently but persistently, she couldn't hold on to her reservations. Not with him kissing her like this. There was fire and intensity she'd forgotten could exist between two people. Or maybe it was just Alex, because she could never remember sex being like this. Not even when she'd embraced it gladly.

Alex's hand slid up to cradle the back of her head, tangling in her hair. She let him guide her where he wanted her because, really, she didn't have his kind of experience. If she was going to make sex good for him, she had to learn from what he taught her.

Arms tightening around her, Alex kissed and kissed her, his lips, tongue, and teeth driving her out of her mind. By the time he pulled back, Merrily was panting, willing to do anything he bid her.

Again, those impossibly blue eyes bored into hers, seeking answers to questions she didn't understand. Finally, he gave a growl as he lifted her, urging her legs around his waist. He stalked to the other side of the shower, sitting her on a marble ledge. Before she could wonder what he would do, he shoved her thighs farther apart and knelt before her, burying his face between her legs.

Chapter Six

Had sex with a woman ever been like this? No fucking way. Alex lost himself every time he touched her. No. It was more. He could simply look at her from across the room and he wanted her. He would have backed off if she'd resisted or expressed more than a passing concern he was making her a whore, but she hadn't. And the sweet way she responded to him told Alex she wanted him nearly as much as he wanted her.

He lapped at her tender flesh, the musky, honeyed liquid spilling from her like ambrosia. The more he took the more he wanted. Her cries filled the room, spurred him on, encouraging him to take more from her before he got down the business of fucking her.

And, God, he needed to fuck her! Even though he knew where to find her, he'd felt the loss all the way to his heart when he'd come back to his suite to find her gone. He barely knew her, but he knew she was what he needed. There was just something about the woman that called to him when no one else ever had. Losing himself in her body was like a dream come true for Alex.

When her cries became nearly constant, her fingers bunching in his hair almost painfully, Alex stood, pulling her from the ledge to spin her around. Reflexively, her hands went to the glass of the shower, her ass thrusting back at him in anticipation.

Alex wasted no time. He gripped her hip with one hand and guided his cock with the other until he sank into her sweet little pussy with a ragged groan. It took several precious seconds to get his raging body under control when all he wanted to do was pound into her. Though he'd taken her several times the night before, she still wasn't ready. Physically, she could take it, but emotionally, she'd never look at him the same way and would probably retreat. He never wanted to scare her. Alex knew she was too young and innocent for a man like him, but damn him, he wasn't letting her go.

Merrily arched her back, raising her ass and wiggling, moving on his cock as if she needed him as much as he needed her. "Alex," she whimpered, her body trembling around him. Alex slid his arm around her middle, his hand sliding up to her breast as he tugged her back against him. He pressed her against the glass and moved inside her slowly. Carefully.

"Oh!" Her cries were sweet music. She turned her head and met his gaze as he licked out his tongue to run it over her lips. "I -- I need…"

"I know, baby. Just let me have you. I'll give you everything you need. I swear."

Blood pounded in Alex's head. Deep inside Merrily, his cock felt full to bursting. His balls were so tight he had no idea how he'd last another second. He willed himself to slow down. He wanted this to last as long as possible, to take Merrily to ever-rising heights until they both plummeted.

"Alex, please!" Merrily pulled him to her for a searing kiss. Her other hand gripped his arm as he tightened it around her. "Please." Her little whimper was so sweet. "Please…"

He dipped his hand between her legs, his fingers brushing where they joined until he found her clit. With one flick of his finger, Merrily exploded. Her tight little pussy gripped his cock, milking him as if she wanted his very essence inside her. She cried out, her knees giving out. Alex held her up, still pounding inside her until he finally let himself go. With one last powerful thrust, he came, letting loose his own bellow to the ceiling.

For several moments, they simply stood there. Merrily was limp, leaning against him. He turned her around, his arms holding her tightly. She nuzzled his chest, brushing kisses over his skin. Her eyes were closed, and she had a soft look on her face. It was obvious he'd exhausted her the night before and now, but it was well earned for both of them.

Alex turned off the shower, then scooped her up, carrying her out into the bathroom. Fluffy, heated towels awaited them on a warmer in the corner. He wrapped one around her before giving himself a once-over, then took her into the bedroom. Putting in a call to Ruth, he had clothes brought to him. By the time he'd dressed, Merrily was curled on her side on top of the bed, her naked body limp in sleep. He smiled. Was there ever a more beautiful woman than his Merrily?

Carefully, trying not to wake her, Alex pulled her into his arms, urging her into one of his undershirts before carrying her up to his room. The woman simply sighed and laid her head on his shoulder, her breaths even as they feathered along his neck. Alex smiled. As soon as she'd rested, he'd take her back to the project room where Giovanni waited to test her. He had the feeling the next few days would be enlightening and very entertaining indeed.

* * *

"Son of a bitch, she's good," Giovanni muttered in awe, sweat pouring from his face. Alex tried not to react, but wasn't quite sure he suppressed his smirk. For the last week, Giovanni had put Merrily through a battery of tests to determine her proficiency with software, hardware, and programming. Giovanni had been more than a little condescending when they'd first started. The man truly had no idea how to behave in the company of people he didn't know. Merrily hadn't once pushed back, doing anything he asked of her without complaint or comment.

Currently, she was supposed to be trying to hack him. Gio had set up a controlled environment in a computer she was supposed to break into. He'd positioned her across the room so neither could see what the other was doing and put her to work. Two hours into it, Gio had stopped smirking and throwing little digs her way and started actively trying to keep her out. Five hours later, he'd started swearing under his breath. Both of them had fingers flying over the keys, but in contrast to Giovanni, Merrily had a serene visage, actually humming to herself as if thoroughly enjoying the experience.

"Ha," Gio exclaimed softly. "Thought you had me, didn't you..." He trailed off a second before the alarm on his real system started blaring an angry, urgent claxon.

"What the fuck?" Azriel pulled his gun, tracking around the room, looking for an intruder.

"Oh, come on!" Giovanni jumped up, knocking his chair over. He hastily hopped behind what he lovingly referred to as his "command center," which consisted of a wall of monitors and his workstation. All the monitors were flashing an angry red with the words "SECURITY BREACH" blazoned in big white, flashing letters. Giovanni looked around, confused. "Why is it doing that? It's not supposed to flash on the monitors *or* make such a racket. What the fuck?"

The monitor in the very center switched to a black screen with code in white lettering flying up it in a blur. "No, no, *no*! That's impossible!" Giovanni pressed a few buttons, his gaze focused squarely on the monitor until he finally dove under the desk and unplugged the whole thing. The silence was deafening, the monitors dark.

"Uh, what just happened?" Alex asked. He'd also pulled his gun, unsure of what to do but making damned sure he was ready if there was a need. It wasn't until that very moment he realized he'd sprinted across the room to cover Merrily. He'd done it without thought or telling Azriel what he was doing.

Giovanni crawled out from under the desk to collapse in his chair. Sweat streamed down his face, his red/orange hair a disheveled mess. His stunned expression met Alex when they locked gazes. "I got... hacked." The voice that had been filled with sarcasm and cutting comments was now shaken and more than a little awed. "I got hacked," he repeated. "*I... got hacked.*"

"All right there, buddy," Azriel said, helping Giovanni to stand. "I think this calls for a double malt. Right this way." He urged Gio to the bar in the corner of the room and poured him a shot before swigging from the bottle himself. Gio downed his with a gasp and held his glass out for more. Once filled, he downed the second one with less drama before wiping his mouth with his sleeve.

Once more, he looked at Azriel as if he were in a daze. "I got hacked."

"Yeah, I got that," Alex said. "But who..." He glanced at Merrily, who was leaning back in her chair, fingers laced together over her belly, that serene, innocent expression firmly in place. Too innocent. "Oh ho ho!" Laughter bubbled up out of nowhere as the full impact of what had just happened hit him. Amusement and *pride*. "Giovanni seems to have a small problem, Azriel," he announced, spinning Merrily around in the chair and scooping her up to toss over his shoulder. When she shrieked at him, he swatted her ass and stalked over to Giovanni and Azriel.

He set her on her feet and turned her to face Gio. "Something you want to say to the lady, Giovanni?"

The man looked about as shell-shocked as he'd ever seen a human look. Gio didn't even try to deny it had been Merrily who'd hacked him -- he just looked at her with a strange mixture of awe and fear. "I think she's the real Demon," he said quietly. Azriel and Alex guffawed. Never had Giovanni met his match in the tech department, but Merrily had obviously had it with his condescending attitude toward her.

"Don't worry, gentlemen," she said airily. "I only use my powers for good." She raised an eyebrow at Giovanni. "Even if someone truly deserves it. Well, on occasion, at least." How could the woman manage to look haughty and just the tiniest bit guilty at the same time?

"Okay," Gio said, pinching the bridge of his nose. "Maybe we need to start over." He lifted his head and met her gaze directly. "Exactly what can you do?" It wasn't so much a question as a demand.

She met his gaze with a steady one of her own. Alex might intimidate her -- even though he didn't want to -- but Giovanni... not so much. *"Anything I want to."*

Fuck. Alex's cock shot hard so fast he nearly doubled over. *This* was the woman he'd hoped was inside her. Confident. Cocky even. *Sexy. As. Fuck!*

Azriel gripped his shoulder, giving it a firm squeeze. "I'd say to take your woman upstairs before you lose your mind, but I'm not sure it would help."

"Hush," he hissed, wanting to see how this played out.

"No one can break into my system," Gio said. "No one."

"All evidence to the contrary," Merrily muttered. Then she wrapped her arms around her middle, all that confidence evaporating.

"Oh, hell no," Alex said, pulling her into his arms and glaring at Giovanni. "Don't you dare withdraw. You did something I thought was impossible, and you're not going to be ashamed of it." He pinched her chin and forced her head up. "I'm so proud of you I can't even describe… You just bested the best in the biz. Not only that, you did it right under his fucking nose."

"Oh, it's worse than that," Giovanni groused. "She did it while misdirecting me. She hacked two systems at the same time, and I never even suspected."

"There's nothing with a computer I can't do, given enough time," Merrily said, meeting Gio's eyes. She still had a wary look on her face, as if waiting for the other shoe to drop, but she fought to hold on to her confidence. Just like Alex told her to. Which, again, was like a punch to the gut. Lust, hot and swift, was going to overtake him if he wasn't careful. No telling what he'd do to the poor girl then, because no way he could go easy on her if she continued to be all bad-ass and stuff.

"Why didn't you use that skill to get yourself and Rose money and disappear off the grid? You could have been halfway to the moon by now and no one would have been the wiser." It was a valid question Giovanni asked. Alex wondered that himself. More than one company had tried to get an industrial spy on the inside of Argent Tech. No one had ever made it past Giovanni. "I don't know you, but I trust Alex. He would never bring a woman here who was batting for another team, but you can't deny the timing is a bit coincidental." When Merrily tried to push away from Alex, her body moving away from all of them, he tightened his grip to prevent her escape. "I'm not saying you'd do something with malicious intent," Giovanni hastily qualified. "I'm just saying that if they've threatened Rose or you to coerce your cooperation, now's the time to tell me so I can mitigate the damage."

"Unless the computer you have me using is significantly less secure than your command and control, there is no way what I did could cause any harm." Her voice was strong but shaky, her body stiff. "I hacked you. But it's contained to that computer." She pointed to the one Gio set up for her. "So, unless there is someone out there with your level of skill working behind me, at the exact moment I did this, you're safe." She ducked her head. "As to me and Rose, I meant it when I said I only use my powers for good. I don't know any criminals, so taking someone else's hard-earned money to help myself just feels wrong. I did my best to keep us off the grid, but I'm not into breaking into the city's cameras either, so I just tried to stay away from them." She shrugged. "I'm not opposed to putting a hurt on someone operating outside the law if necessary, but I won't use my talent for personal gain. I was protecting Rose as best as I could, and I can't say I'd be so selfless if she were truly in danger and I could prevent it by siphoning from someone who wouldn't miss it, but I wasn't there yet."

Gio nodded slowly. "And why would they send in a second person if they already had the ability? They'd simply be at a party we hosted and do their damage from there."

"And if they had someone that good, they wouldn't need to break into your system to get secrets. They'd simply make their own stuff."

All three men exchanged a look. It was now or never. "That's not entirely accurate," Alex said with a sigh. "Remember when I told you you'd have some hard choices to make? Now's the time."

"I don't understand." She glanced from one to the other, stopping on Alex. He was glad Merrily looked to him. He wanted her to always follow his lead when she was unsure.

"Before we explain, I have to know you can keep this to yourself," Alex said. "Consider this like Fight Club."

"And no one talks about Fight Club," she muttered. "Do I want to know this?"

Alex shrugged. "You'll have the opportunity to work with the most advanced technology on the planet. I can't promise you won't have to get your proverbial hands dirty, but I will swear on my life that we'll protect you from everything. Absolutely everything."

She held his gaze, not flinching away for several seconds. Then she asked, "Will I have to do anything to innocent people?"

"Never," Alex said without hesitation. "We operate outside the law most of the time, but we've never harmed innocents, nor do we intend to."

"Then count me in." She gave them all a small smile. "If you're very good, Giovanni, I *might* tell you what I did to get into your system."

A couple of hours later, Merrily looked like her head was spinning. Not only had Giovanni detailed some of their older escapades -- he wasn't letting her in until she was fully committed -- but she seemed to be stuck on the whole Shadow Demon thing.

"So, you guys are *actually* Rose's Shadow Angels?"

Giovanni looked aghast. "*Demons*! Shadow *Demons*! Who the fuck said we were angels? What the hell?"

"I know," Azriel said with a roll of his eyes. "Kick in the balls, ain't it? Kid shouldn't spread rumors like that. Messes with our rep."

"Well, she heard it from somewhere," Merrily said, leaning back and crossing her arms over her chest. "She didn't make it up. You've got more of a fan club than you thought, I'd say."

"Me and that girl gotta have a talk," Gio grumbled with no real rancor. Alex couldn't help but smile. Without trying, his little Merrily and her daughter were winning the loyalty of his brothers. "Angels." Giovanni continued to mutter. "There oughtta be a fuckin' law!"

"You'll have my back?" Merrily met Gio's gaze with a serious expression.

"We *all* will, Merrily. None of us are related by blood, but in this house, we're family. Every last man, woman, and child. No one knows the full extent of what we do, but they all know to protect the family, no matter what. That includes you now." He gave her a soft smile. "If you want us."

She sighed, shrugging as she said, "Doesn't appear as if I have much to lose and quite a bit to gain. If nothing else, playing with really cool toys will be an asset in future job ventures."

"Then we'll start with our plan to take down Daniel J. Maddison II and his son."

There was no missing the shiver that went through Merrily at the mention of his name. What was on her mind? Did she regret what she'd signed up for with her ex-lover?

"You going to be okay with this?" Alex had to ask. Had to know. A spike of jealousy jolted through him and he nearly growled his displeasure. "Because, if you're not, we need to know now."

"I'm good with it. I just get a creepy feeling when I think about him."

"Define 'creepy.'"

"There's something not right with him. And I mean Danny. Not his father. There was an oily glee about him that night at the gala I can't define. I was so upset I barely noticed it, but he thinks he's made it. And I don't mean that he's rich. His family always had money. That's why they didn't want me in his life, especially with a child. Yet, he gave me that superior look straight out of a Toby Keith music video. Like he was somebody."

"We'd been running the angle that Danny has been skimming his father and, therefore, whomever his father worked for." Alex looked to Azriel. "Any luck with your contact in the Brotherhood?"

"No. But I don't expect to hear back from them for three days."

"Three days. Exactly?"

"Yes. Part of their protocol. The party who messages first has to do the waiting." He lifted his cell phone and gave it a little wave. "I'll be glued to this thing until they contact me. I have three minutes to respond when they contact me."

"Then why be glued to it if you have to wait three days?"

"Because they might send it early. They know I know their protocols." He waved a hand dismissively. "It's all about mind games. They send it early, I have to know the second it comes in. That determines when my reply goes out to them."

"Too much for me, bro," Alex said, snagging Merrily's hand, needing to touch her. "What did our boys find in Maddison's ledgers?"

"Definitely laundering going on there. Also skimming, and from more than one party. I've told Maddison all is a go with the merger. We'll have a meeting in a couple of days with him, his wife and his son."

Merrily stiffened beside him. "What?"

Azriel shifted, drawing their attention. "We're putting this to rest one way or another, Merrily. When this is done, there will be no danger to you or Bellarose. That includes any claims to custody *or* visitation. If there is any visitation for anyone, it will be by your choice alone."

Merrily blinked rapidly, a stunned look on her face. "Why would you do that? My custody of Rose isn't your concern. You don't have to --"

Alex quieted her protest the only way he knew how. He kissed her, threading his fingers through her hair and taking her mouth until she melted against him. When he finally pulled away, he held her gaze.

"That family has no claim on your child. Rose might be Danny's biological child, but she's not his daughter. We're going to make sure that specter isn't hanging over your head. That son of a bitch is never going to see Rose unless you wish it."

Her eyes were bright with unshed tears. "You can really do that?"

"Absolutely," Azriel said. "You'll have a part to play with Alex."

"What do you need me to do?"

"Think of this as a production," Alex said. "Giovanni is the director. He calls the shots. He'll bring in each player on cue and keep an eye on the grounds for when our outside guests arrive." He pulled her closer, kissing her temple. "You'll be safe long before that, however."

"Outside guests?"

Alex exchanged looks with Gio and Azriel. "I told you about Dan's business dealings. You know he's in with some really bad people. We're not sure exactly sure who he's laundering for, but the people they hired to put the hurt on him are known to us. Azriel has put out a call to them. Feeling out the situation. We expect they will attempt to enter the grounds soon after Dan and his family arrive."

"What?" Alex held her tightly when she tried to pull away. "But, Rose --"

"Will be perfectly fine, honey. Everyone here will, including you. We've done this a time or two." He grinned down at her anxious face. "Granted, we usually take it away from our home, but this is the safest way. Until the threat to you and Rose is completely eliminated, I want us all close. We've even called in backup for this one. Everyone will arrive in the next few hours. They've already been briefed, so once they get here, we can move everyone else underground and send out the invite to Dan and his family."

"I'm scared," she said in a small voice, looking down at the floor. That was all Alex could take. He scooped her up and left, not saying another word to his brothers. There was nothing to say. Alex hadn't expressly told them how he felt about Merrily, but they knew. Just the fact he'd turned over lead to Giovanni told them volumes. They knew she was important to him. They would protect her -- and Rose -- with their lives.

God help anyone who threatened either of them.

Chapter Seven

By the time they got to Alex's suite, Merrily was trembling, not all of it from fear. Whatever happened over the next couple of days -- or hours -- she would handle because she did have faith in Alex. Whether or not they continued their relationship, Merrily was certain he would protect her and Rose, no matter the threat. Breaking into Giovanni's system had proven to her just how many resources these guys had.

Before she'd devoted all her time to having and raising Rose, she'd gone to camps for gifted high school students and seen for herself what all was out there. She'd been exposed to high-tech equipment, the latest developing software, and military-grade encryption, especially once they figured out her talents. None of that compared to what these guys had. That "project room," as they call it, was a geek's paradise. The computer system they'd had her working with was a wet dream. She doubted anyone outside government had anything remotely close to what they were rocking. These guys could do whatever they wanted. That included keeping a single mother and her small daughter safe. She'd believe in them because they'd proven themselves already. Especially Alex.

This time, Alex took an elevator straight to his suite from the project room. He'd started kissing her long before the doors opened, and she'd done her share of kissing back. Alex shrugged out of his shirt, urging her to do the same. He didn't say a word, just ran his hands and lips over each expanse of skin she revealed.

Their breathing was ragged, Merrily's as well as Alex's. It seemed she lost her mind every single time he touched her. Part of her said it was too fast, that he was too good to be true, but her heart recognized him as the man she'd forever want above all others. His body told her he felt the same, but Merrily tried not to read too much into it. It might be the truth, but she was intelligent enough to know that Alex was a worldly man. Even if his body said one thing, his mind might resist. Didn't mean she wasn't giving him every opportunity to come to his senses if the need arose.

Right now, however, she just wanted to take comfort in his touch. She wanted him working her body with that magnificent body of his. The hold he had on her, both his brawny arms wrapped tightly around her body, was possessive. The stubble of his face scraped over the tender skin of her breasts, and she cried out. All of it was so wonderful, so erotic and beautiful she knew she'd found heaven. However long it lasted, Merrily would take it.

Alex seemed to love handling her, placing her exactly where he wanted her whether it was above him, facing away, or securely under him. She knew she loved that he could. He was so strong and powerful, his muscles heavy and large, she never failed to feel tiny next to him. That blatant show of strength was a mighty turn-on for her. In her mind, it meant he was powerful enough to protect what he claimed as his own. For whatever reason, he'd claimed her and Rose. Merrily was certain of it.

She was on the verge of a momentous discovery about herself and her predicament, but the pleasure soon rose above everything else. Reflection could wait. What she was experiencing currently was mind-scrambling. Her body was on fire! All of it, every single ounce of pleasure, was all because of Alex.

"God, Merrily," he panted as he rose above her. "Need you so fucking much!"

"Then take me," she whispered. "Anything you need is yours." She wrapped her arms around his neck, meaning what she said. If he needed, she'd provide. Just as he was providing for her.

With a ragged groan, Alex sank into her, his cock a hot, pulsing, living thing inside her. The heat threatened to sear her to the bone. It had been like this the other times as well, but this seemed more... intimate? Something she couldn't name. Nearly like it was their first time together, though, by now, they knew each other's bodies well. He gazed into her eyes, his blue ones piercing and intense and so lovely she was mesmerized, unable to pull her gaze away even if she'd wanted to. He was telling her something. With his eyes. With his body. Something he didn't seem to be able to voice. His brows were drawn together almost in confusion, as if he couldn't quite grasp the situation.

"I..." He swallowed. "Merrily..."

She threaded her fingers through the hair at his nape and pulled him to her for a kiss. She tried to pour all her gratitude and budding feelings for him into her kiss. Merrily absolutely wanted him to know she didn't consider this payment for him protecting her and Rose. Even if he saw it as such, she didn't. She'd give herself to him over and over, as often and as much as he needed, simply because *he needed*. If he got to the point he no longer wanted her... Well. She'd figure that out when the time came.

Once he took over the kiss, he thrust his tongue deep, licking over and over. He tasted like mint and musk and man. Though he pinned her tightly to the bed with his big body, his arms didn't loosen their hold. He still had them wound around her like he was afraid she'd escape. Not that she minded. It was just one more thing she loved, one more thing to make her feel safe and cherished.

The driving rhythm Alex set was jarring. Hard and rough. Merrily found she needed rough. The more he kissed her, the harder he fucked her. The harder he fucked her, the more Merrily found herself responding. Her fingers dug into the muscles of his back, clawing with each jolt of pleasure she got. It wasn't long before her climax approached, and it promised to be nothing short of explosive, unlike anything she'd experienced thus far.

Her breaths shallowed. Her body tensed.

"Now," he growled. "Come on my cock, my Merrily."

With a shriek, she did. Her body spasmed out of control. She thrashed in his arms so hard he seemed to have trouble containing her. Likely he was afraid of squeezing her too tightly. Instead of reprimanding her, however, Alex praised her. She wasn't exactly sure what he said because of the intense roaring in her ears, but his tone was clear. At the peak of her orgasm, she clamped down on him so that he threw he head back and yelled to the ceiling. Merrily felt his cock jerk inside her as he held himself buried deeply inside her. At once, she felt the hot jolt of his seed hitting her inside, the thought so erotic it triggered another orgasm for her, though not as powerful as the one she'd just experienced. It was as if her body wanted more of him. Wanted his entire essence.

When he collapsed atop her, his breathing as ragged as hers, he finally loosened his hold on her but didn't let her go completely. Instead, he rolled them so that she lay sprawled over him, then pulled the duvet over them. They lay in silence for a long while. So long, Merrily had started to drift.

"My Merrily," he murmured. "What am I going to do with you?"

She wasn't sure if she was supposed to answer. Normally, she'd figure it was a rhetorical question. Now, she had a pressing need to convey to him.

"You never answered my question the other day," she said, not meeting his gaze. He stilled beneath her, cupping her face in both of his hands so she had to look at him.

"What's that, baby?"

"I asked you if you'd break my heart." She met his gaze steadily, though inside she knew she would shatter if he answered wrongly. "When a powerful man such as yourself takes a woman not his equal, he tends to use her and throw her away because he's either looking for a woman more suited for a wife, or because he's already got a wife. If that's the case, he just needs a woman to do things his wife won't. Is that what you intend? To use me and throw me away?" When his expression flared to anger, she hastily continued. "Because, if that's your plan, I'm okay with it, but I want to know up front. I'll be perfectly honest with you -- and this is only because you promised to be honest with me, not any attempt to guilt you into any kind of relationship -- I'm growing to care for you very much. If it's not reciprocated --"

He cut her off with a kiss that started out rough, but quickly turned tender. Languid sweeps of his tongue coaxed her to kiss him back. She was helpless not to. Alex's hands threaded through her hair once again. He seemed to have this need to dominate her, even when he was being gentle. Always, he seemed to control her movements. Which, Merrily admitted to herself, she found hot as hell. There was never a time he pressed her to do something her body wasn't completely ready for, even if her mind was a little hesitant. Even then, he managed to get her so crazy for him she just let her body take over.

When she relaxed once more, Alex ended the kiss gently before holding her gaze with his. "I'm not using you, Merrily. I won't lie and tell you I've never used a woman for my own pleasure before, but they always knew the score."

"Why me? I'm nothing but baggage to you." Saying it out loud hurt her, but Merrily plowed on. "I'm not in any way your equal in life. Your circle of friends will always see me like Victoria did."

Now, he just looked pissed off. "Oh, come on, Merrily. You know better than that." He swatted her ass for good measure, which made her yelp. His lips quirked before he resumed his scowl. "The only reason Victoria treated you the way she did was because you were playing the part of a servant. I'm one of the richest men in the world. All of us are. Some of them, like Giovanni, don't venture into the public, but those of us who do are so far above everyone else we could give a shit what they think. Everyone wants our favor. To do that, they can't earn our displeasure. No matter what they think of you, they will never disrespect you where I will ever learn of it."

"Look, it's not so much about me. I just..." She took a deep breath, again fighting back tears. "I don't want to embarrass you."

He looked at her like she'd grown two heads. Then chuckled.

"What? It's not funny!" Once she voiced her outrage, Alexei gave in to a full-bodied laugh until tears streamed from his eyes down his temples. "Let me up. Now!" Merrily tried to push off him, but Alex was having none of it. He simply rolled them until he pinned her beneath him once more. Despite her irritation, Merrily couldn't help but feel a thrill at being helplessly trapped.

"Okay, okay! I'm sorry," he soothed. Then he ruined it by burying his face in her neck and continuing to laugh.

"I'm less than amused," she groused. "I don't see anything so damned funny!"

"You? Embarrass me?" Another snort of laughter. "Baby, I'll be the one embarrassing you because I'll be glued to your side, never letting another man so much as glance your way without me giving him killing looks." He wiped his eyes with the back of his hand, then grinned down at her. Then his gaze drifted lower to her jutting breasts. They were small but proud, the nipples puckering as if to tempt him.

"How would that embarrass me?"

Alex seemed distracted by her chest, turning his head from side to side as he viewed her, as if considering which peak he wanted to devour first. Merrily wanted to be outraged, but instead, she subtly arched her back. Just to see what would happen.

With a growl, Alex dove for her right breast even as he held the left one in a firm grip. He found the nipple of that one and pinched firmly until she cried out from the conflicting sensations. He flicked her other nipple with his tongue before biting gently at the same time he pinched the other.

"Ahh!" Merrily nearly screamed. She wasn't sure if it was pleasure or pain, but she knew she'd just grown wet for him in a rush. "Sweet God! Alex!"

He said nothing, merely wrapped his free arm around her like a vise while he continued to suck one breast and knead the other. There was nothing gentle about it either. Surprisingly, Merrily found she loved this side of him. Loved riding the edge of pleasure and pain.

When he lifted his head, there was intensity and lust like Merrily had never witnessed in him or any other man. No one had ever looked at her like he did. He pushed himself up so that he knelt in the V between her legs, her thighs draped over his.

"So, what *are* you going to do to me?" The question came out throaty. More of an invitation than a demand to know.

"Fuck you," he said without hesitation. "Hard."

Lust hit her hard and she cried out, her hands going to her own breasts. She pinched them like he had even as she spread her legs wider, inviting him to take what he wanted.

"Fuck!" The expletive was whispered as he watched her manipulate her nipples. "That's it, my Merrily. Pinch them. Pull on those needy little buds."

She did, following his instructions as he watched.

"Have you ever made yourself come in front of someone?" God, he was dirty! And she was following him into a pit of lust so deep she'd never dig her way out.

Merrily shook her head. "I have a feeling I'm about to."

The cocky grin he threw her was almost more than she could take. The man was seriously sexy. And wicked. Deliciously wicked.

"Keep working your tits," he said, his hand dropping to his cock. That big fist curled around his impressive shaft, stroking lazily. "Keep your legs spread wide. I want to see how wet you get."

Merrily obeyed, tugging and rolling her nipples with increasing roughness. She loved his gaze on her while she touched herself. The harder she pinched, the heaver his eyes became. She got the feeling he needed to do this to her himself but was unwilling to mistakenly hurt her. After several minutes, Merrily was unable to keep her hips still and didn't try. She thrust her pelvis at him, lifting herself off the bed as she continued to play with her nipples.

Her cries mingled with his rough growls as they moved together. She, thrusting her chest and hips at him; he, working his cock over her. His cock was hard and angry, the tip a deep purple as he stroked himself. Merrily wondered if he'd come on her or simply thrust inside her and empty himself there. She honestly didn't care which as long as she got to watch his face as he released. She loved the way his neck muscles corded and the veins stood out starkly as he strained to hold himself back. When he came, it was even better. The look of ecstasy on his face was enough to turn her on all over again.

She spread her legs wider, pulling her knees up to leave her pussy completely vulnerable to him. He could see everything. Could see how wet she was for him.

"Look at you," he whispered, his eyes glued to her quivering sex. "My innocent little wanton."

"Not so innocent." She cupped her breasts tightly, lifting them to drag her tongue over one nipple. "I have a kid."

He chuckled. "Just because you have a child doesn't mean you're not a sexual innocent. I'm willing to bet every single thing I've done with you -- other than penetrative sex -- is a first for you." His cock pulsed in his fist. A pearly drop of pre-cum beaded the tip. "There are so many things I'm going to show you. So many things I'm going to do to your little body."

"I'm on fire, Alex," she whispered. She slid her hands down her body to her sex, parting the bare folds so he could see her entrance. Trailing one finger around and around, gathering moisture, she moaned, rubbing her clit in a slow circle. Heart pounding, hands shaking, she lifted her finger to his mouth.

"Vixen," he hissed before engulfing her finger in his mouth, sucking hard and swirling his tongue around the tip. "Mmmm." He thrust his hips, his cock fisted tightly in his hand. "When I fuck you, my Merrily, it's going to be hard and fast. You ready for that?"

In answer, she dipped two fingers inside her. Then three. "Give me everything you've got, Alex. Fuck me hard and make me come."

"Not until you make yourself come. I want to watch you rub your little clit. Want to see you fucking yourself with your fingers."

"What if I wanted to rub my clit with your cock? Would you let me touch you, too?"

He growled, scooting closer to her. His cock was long and thick. When he let go of it, his dick lay on her belly, nearly reaching her belly button. Pearly drops painted her skin with each pulse of his member. Merrily couldn't help herself. She dragged her fingertip through those drops and stuck her finger in her mouth, tasting his very essence.

"Fuck!" he bit out. "So fucking hot!" He put his hands on her hips, holding her gaze as she played with herself.

With shaking hands, she used one to rub her clit while reaching for his cock with the other. Could she really do this? More than anything, in that moment, she wanted this act. She wanted to be the girl who did things like this with her man. And Alexei Petrov was definitely her man. She gripped his cock, trapping it between her palm and belly. She moved her body so she jerked him off like that, reveling in the leaking pre-come with each stroke.

"You're going to be the death of me, woman. Get on with it!"

Sweat broke out over his body, his breathing coming in ragged pants. Beads of sweat dripped from his brow to her belly and breasts, yet he still let her play. Rigid muscles stood out over his torso and arms, veins growing with every second his body was tense.

He pulled back, urging her to do as she'd suggested earlier. When he nodded, she eased back until the head of his cock tucked against her clit. At the first touch against her swollen clit, Merrily trembled. A gasp escaped her as she continued to move and rub, masturbating herself with his dick. Up and down she let it slip, letting it glide with a mixture of her moisture and his. The sight of them together, of his cock and her bare pussy together, was erotic as hell. She looked up at him helplessly, not understanding her body's reaction. All she knew was that it felt too good to stop.

Over and over she rubbed, her heart pounding, her body out of control. Cries came from her lips as the pleasure and pressure inside her increased. An orgasm was just out of her reach, so close yet she was unable to catch it. She rocked her hips, tossing her head from side to side as she masturbated on his cock head until the slit in the center engulfed her swollen clit. The pleasure was instantaneous. And explosive.

Merrily screamed, a long, loud wail. Her body wasn't her own, but a writhing mass of nerves that only wanted Alex's cock. Wanted his body inside hers, mastering her, taking everything she had to give him and returning it tenfold.

The second the pressure started waning, the contractions in her lower body easing, Alex gave a brutal yell, gripping her hips and flipping her over. He pressed his hand across her upper back, forcing her upper body down even as he pulled her hips up so she was on her knees, her ass in the air. In one swift, brutal thrust, he entered her, his cock forced inside her body past the muscle inside her pussy until he was buried deep, his body flush against her. One arm slid around her waist as he clamped her to him in a brutal hold. Then he began to fuck her.

Short, sharp snaps of his hips plunged his cock deep. That didn't seem to be enough for him. He bent one leg, gripping her ass with both hands, his fingers digging into her flesh as he continued to fuck her. He pounded out a hard, staccato rhythm, sweat landing on her back with every smack of her ass against his belly.

"Fuck!" He threw back his head even as he pulled her against him harder and harder, meeting each pull of her hips backward with a surge of his hips forward. They slammed together almost violently. Merrily was along for the ride. She knew she'd feel this later, but right now, it was more pleasure than she'd ever dreamed of.

Finally, Alex must have taken all he could stand. He pulled her legs back so she fell to her belly. Without ever leaving her body, he lay on top of her, pumping into her with a furious frenzy. He yelled as he humped her, fucking her harder than she'd ever dreamed. Then he froze just before slamming into her one last time, his cock pumping seed deep into her. Alex bellowed to the ceiling, a brutal, primal sound that hurt her ears. But she found herself responding in kind, their yells mingling in the vast room.

The second Alex collapsed on top of her, Merrily whimpered, her orgasm still making her pussy tingle. She still pushed her hips at him, even pinned as she was, needing that last little bit. Alex reached around, finding her clit with his fingers, and tugged as he thrust inside her again. This time, when Merrily came, her vision blurred, and she was dizzy. With one last, ragged scream, she went limp beneath Alex, knowing she'd never been so completely sated in her entire life.

And... she was completely, totally, head-over-heels in love with Alexei Petrov.

Chapter Eight

"So nice of you to invite us to your lovely home."

Sharon Maddison was every bit as elegant and regal as Merrily remembered. Hiding inside that classy lady, however, was a waspish, judgmental woman who couldn't see past her own self-importance.

"Daniel has told me about the merger of your two companies. I'm so happy you worked things out."

Alex took Sharon's hand when she extended it in greeting. Merrily wanted to scratch the woman's eyes out for no other reason than she touched what Merrily considered hers. "Bitch," she muttered. Giovanni snorted before coughing to cover his indiscretion. She blushed. "Sorry."

"No apology necessary. I think the same thing myself from time to time."

Giovanni had the whole room rigged with cameras and sound. Alex had an earpiece so he could hear when Giovanni gave instructions or warnings. Merrily was learning how they worked and was helping from time to time, but mainly she was waiting her turn to enter the room. Her snarkiness came mostly from a healthy dose of nerves.

"You, uh --" he cleared his throat "-- like Alex. Yes?"

Merrily closed her eyes, mortification stealing over her. "Yeah. I guess you could say that."

"I only ask because I think he's kinda serious about you." Giovanni looked uncomfortable, his fair skin pink with his own embarrassment. "Alex hasn't ever been serious about a woman, but he likes you. And Rose."

Her heart pounded. As encouraging as this was, Giovanni didn't know Alex's mind. Or his heart. "He probably has White Knight Syndrome. Once Rose and I are safe and all the dragons slain, the novelty will wear off."

"You keep telling yourself that, girl."

"Please have a seat." Alex had finished greeting Dan Maddison, Sharon, and Danny and was getting to the "settle in" part meant to put them at ease before they got down to business.

"Though I'm thrilled to meet you," Sharon said, "I'm confused as to the nature of this visit. I'm not a part of Dan's business."

"On the contrary, Mrs. Maddison, I find family is an important part of any successful business. Family is how I've managed to build what I have. My brothers. My household. Now, my own family. You'll meet my wife soon."

Dan Maddison sat up straighter. "*Wife*? I had no idea you were married, Alex."

Alex smiled. Merrily could see the smugness on Alex's face through the monitor. Alex was as aloof as he had been the night of the gala. The plan was for her to pose as his wife when she entered. This was the setup.

"Well, I may have misspoken. She *will* be my wife, but it's as good as done." He gave a mysterious smile. "Even though we've yet to make it official, she's already privy to company business and she'll help me with this merger."

"Stay with the script, Alex." Giovanni was all business now. And more than a little pissed.

"Well then," Dan said. "I can hardly wait to meet her."

Again, Alex gave a mysterious smile. "I guarantee you'll love her."

"Asshole," Merrily muttered. "They're going to lose their ever-loving shit when I walk in."

"He knows that," Giovanni said, his eyes glued to the monitors. "Azriel. Any movement outside?"

"Only Benedict and Sebastian." Merrily's gaze went to the monitors where the two men were undercover. Benedict was at the gate while Sebastian manned the pool house, which incidentally, held an arsenal. Both men saluted the camera easily when their names were mentioned. From what Merrily understood, Benedict and Sebastian were two of their outside "brothers" who'd come to help in case the Brotherhood proved too much for them to handle alone.

"Nothing so far," Sebastian said. Both men wore night vision goggles and continually scanned the area for the uninvited company they were expecting. "But I seriously doubt we'll see them before they want us to."

Azriel had given them all a rundown on the Brotherhood. No one was taking them lightly.

"Copy that," Azriel confirmed. "I have our first guest in the wings waiting for our grand entrance."

"Danny." Alex turned to the younger man. Merrily wanted to cringe. Danny had always been able to make her doubt herself. Even now, not even in the same room with him, those old insecurities came rushing back. Just like they had the night of the gala. "Thanks for accompanying your parents."

"I'm not sure I can do this," she whispered, her voice wavering. "They'll see right through me and call Alex's bluff. He told them I know about their business deal. What if they try to blame all this on me? It was my father who scammed them, after all."

"Calm down," Giovanni said, resting his hand on her arm. "Take a deep breath and don't freak out on me. Alex will handle everything. You just play the part he taught you. We've *all* got your back on this, no matter what anyone says to or about you."

Merrily felt like a band was tightening around her chest, threatening to explode her heart. She could barely catch her breath. "I'm scared."

"That's okay." Giovanni didn't look at her but had his attention glued to the monitors. "You just have to work through it. Follow Alex's lead and don't freeze. Everything will be fine."

She smoothed the black sheath dress over her body, trying to let the silky material soothe her frayed nerves. Alex had presented her with the dress and accessories almost formally, helping her dress and placing a gold, braided necklace and matching bracelet with diamonds interspersed throughout around her neck and wrist. He'd also placed a gold band with an array of colorless diamonds on her finger, kissing her palm afterwards while holding her gaze. In the center was what she'd thought was a ruby, but had, in fact, been a diamond. She had no idea how much the jewelry had cost, but she knew the pieces were beautiful. Especially her "engagement ring." At the time, she'd wondered if he could really mean the smoldering, possessive look he'd given her. Now, she wasn't so sure.

"Since I'll one day take over Maddison Robotics, I thought it prudent I be involved in this merger. I was eager to accept the invitation."

The elder Maddison gave his son a sidelong glance, and irritation flashed over his face, but he said nothing.

"Oh? Really, now." Alex raised an eyebrow. "My team was prepared for you to be at the helm, Dan. If Danny here is taking over before our agreed-upon time for us to dissolve our partnership, I'll have to rethink the merger."

"Why would you do that?" Danny stepped between Alex and Dan. He was so close he had to be nearly touching Alex. Unfortunately for Danny, Alex was a large man, tall and muscular, and not easily intimidated. "I'm just as good at running the company as my father. I don't need him."

Alex gave him an "embarrassed for you" grin. "Honestly, Danny. Do you really believe what you're saying? Because I can show you line for line exactly what part of Maddison Robotics' books you've been toying with and which ones your father's accountants have fixed."

There was silence for a long time. None of the three Maddisons said anything. Even Sharon looked wary. Danny turned red in the face. Alex had just dropped two bombshells. They had to be wondering what he was going to do with them.

"Good job," Giovanni murmured. "Now ease the tension. Dinner is served."

Alex threw all three a grin. Merrily could see just how much it didn't reach his eyes. Their vivid, beautiful color was cold and flat now. This was the killer he'd named himself. Surely he wasn't going to hurt the Maddisons. Not really. "You must forgive me. I invited you all here for dinner, and here we are talking business." He made a sweeping gesture toward the formal dining room. "This is supposed to be an opportunity for all of us to get to know each other."

Alex led them into the spacious room with a long table set formally. Everyone had a placard at their place. Alex sat at the head with the place at his right marked "Mrs. Petrov." Four spots to Alex's left were marked for the three Maddisons and one more simply marked "Guest."

"You're expecting someone else?" Dan queried.

"Yes," Alex said simply, not elaborating. He sat and snapped his fingers. Instantly, several servants appeared, serving the wine and appetizers before disappearing into a side room. It was time for Merrily to make her entrance.

"Go now," Giovanni told her, not taking his eyes off the monitors. "You've got five minutes. Is your earpiece in?"

"Yes." Merrily checked the placement once more before stepping into the elevator. "Mic check," she said once the doors slid shut behind her.

"Loud and clear," Giovanni replied. "Volume comfortable for you?"

"Yes. Exiting elevator." This was it. She'd face her nemesis and establish her place with Alex -- assuming nothing went sideways. Once that was done, she could leave with the pretext of checking on Rose. Especially if the Brotherhood was spotted. She would evacuate with the rest of the staff to the sublevels of the manor and wait until Giovanni gave them instructions. If there was a danger of being overrun, they had fast transportation away, while the men fought to buy them time.

She couldn't think about that. One thing at a time. Get to Alex without embarrassing him or herself. After that, she'd move on to the next task.

With a deep breath, she took one step into the foyer leading to the dining room. Then another. Her heels clicked on the marble floor with each step, echoing in the silence around the talk at the table. As she approached, Alex stood, reaching out a hand to her. Merrily was terrified. She was about to face the family who'd changed the very course of her life. For better or worse, they were responsible for so many things in her life, both good and bad. They didn't care, but it was their decisions, in one way or another, that had led her to this point.

"My Merrily." Alex reached for here, steadying her with the genuine affection in his voice. She took his hand and let him pull her into his arms. He cupped her face before kissing her lips gently. "You're so beautiful," he murmured. "So very beautiful, my Merrily."

She smoothed the lapel of his suit jacket just to feel how the expensive material molded over his broad chest. She could easily forget anyone else was around if the stakes here weren't so high. These people were wrapped up in something sinister and had set demons on her to cover their own greed. Well, she'd found her own demon in the form of Alexei Petrov. Looking into his eyes now, she knew he was the real demon in the room. Her demon protector.

"Alex. I'm sorry I'm late."

"You're not late, love. You're exactly on time." He kissed her gently once more before turning to acknowledge the others again. "You'll forgive me, of course." He again looked at Merrily, a soft smile on his lips. "I'm sure you understand how captivated I am by my Merrily. She's become very important to me. With rumors of the Shadow Demons in the city, I'm always anxious when she's away from me, which makes me that much happier when she brightens my day with her appearance."

As he spoke, smiling at her with such affection, Merrily could believe he was falling in love with her.

She had to remind herself this was a fiction. A way to keep the Maddisons off balance so he could get the information he sought.

"Merrily... *Dane*?" Sharon Maddison looked like she'd seen a ghost. "Merrily Dane is your *wife*?"

"Ah! I see you remember her," Alex commented brightly, as if the whole thing were one big happy reunion. "She told me you had met."

"Indeed," Dan muttered.

"Then there's no need for introductions." Alex helped Merrily into her seat before taking his own again. "I believe Gregory -- my chef -- has outdone himself this time." His small talk did nothing to ease the tension in the air. It was all Merrily could do to eat her Lobster Thermidor. Her stomach was in knots and her hands shook.

"It's delicious, Alex," she finally managed, doing her best to keep a serene expression on her face. She took a sip of wine, careful to appear to drink without taking too much. She knew she'd need her wits about her tonight.

"I beg your pardon," Dan began. "How do you know this girl?"

"Merrily?" Alex looked up from his meal. "I met her through a mutual friend. Once I realized how truly brilliant she is, I snapped her up. She's been working with me on the merger of our companies. Working out all the angles with the handling of company secrets."

"She's what?" Danny's face was red, his anger rising with every second. "You let that b --"

"I caution you to be very careful here, Danny." Alex's voice was soft, almost serene, but the warning was delivered all the same. "You're talking about the woman I intend to make my wife. And I have my pick of any woman on the planet. Think about the fact that I chose... *Merrily*."

"Do you have any idea what she is?" Sharon protested right alongside her son. "I'm not certain what she's done to deceive you, Mr. Petrov, but I assure you that girl is nothing but trouble. You talk about Demons in the city. That girl is just as evil as they are."

"Oh?" Alex turned his head to wink at Merrily. He grasped her hand firmly in his, bringing her fingers to his mouth to kiss the backs. "Why would you say that?"

"Look, she tried to get involved with my son when they were in high school. Chased after him mercilessly. She even tried to ruin his good reputation by insisting she was pregnant by Danny."

"So, you tried to entrap a wealthy young man, did you, my Merrily?" He grinned at Merrily, kissing her fingers again. It probably looked like he was sharing his mirth with her in a private exchange.

"Hardly," Merrily muttered. This could get dicey. The only thing she really had to offer Alex was her word. Was she intelligent enough to concoct a plot to blackmail someone? Certainly. But she didn't steal from innocent people, and she certainly didn't need to use a child for that kind of game. She could just take what she wanted, and no one would ever find her electronic footprint. She just hoped Alex saw it that way, because when it came right down to it, it was her word against Danny's.

"Tell me, Danny." Alex looked amused, but, again, his eyes gave him away. There was a dangerous glimmer there. Merrily shivered, wondering just how ruthless Alex would be with the Maddisons. "What did you do when Merrily told you she was pregnant?"

For a moment, Danny just blinked at Alex, like he knew something was expected of him but didn't know the right answer. Then he just shrugged. "I didn't believe her. I figured if she was pregnant, it wasn't by me."

"Why?"

"Because she told me she was on birth control. And she could have been fucking any number of guys." The smug look on Danny's face made Merrily want to claw his eyes out. This was a man who considered her to be nothing. He considered himself Alex's equal and fully expected Alex to see his reasoning and agree with him.

"Were you guys in an exclusive relationship?"

"She said she was. Me?" He shrugged. "I've always had my share of women. You're not the only one who has his pick." Again, there was that superior look. Merrily was so angry she was shaking. "Besides, women trying to land a rich man are *never* sleeping around." He chuckled like it was all a joke.

"You said you loved me," Merrily whispered, unable to stop herself. She'd never once considered Danny had been with others. Now, the way some of the more popular girls treated her at school made sense. He was probably making fun of her the entire time. Bragging about his conquest of the class geek. Alex squeezed her hand again.

"And you believed one thing but not the other two?" Alex didn't sound angry or impatient, just curious.

"Women lie all the time."

"Again -- to be clear -- you believed her *so much* when she told you she was on birth control that you -- the son of a very wealthy man, heir to his fortune --

came inside her when you fucked her, but you didn't believe her when she told you she was pregnant?"

The crude description made Merrily's face flame, but Alex again gripped her hand tight, warning her not to say a word. His words were harsh, but his tone was casual.

In her ear, she heard, "Steady, Merrily. Eyes on Alex." Giovanni's effort to keep her calm worked enough for her to focus on Alex and not look at the Maddisons. She was mortified. But this had to be done. Whatever Alex had planned, he'd assured her it was important and necessary for everyone concerned. If she and Rose were to ever be safe, they had to get the Maddisons to either call off the hit on her and Rose, or confess to their bosses what had really happened to their money and face the music. Not for one moment did Merrily believe the latter would happen, but she was willing to follow Alex's lead.

Sharon gasped. Though Merrily was focused on Alex, she couldn't miss the older woman snapping her head to the left to look at her husband. Taking a deep breath, she glanced slowly at the three people sitting across the table from her. Of the three, Dan Maddison was the only one holding his poker face. Sharon's mouth was agape, and she looked like she might pass out. Danny was red-faced with anger. He looked like he was about to explode.

When no one said anything, Alex sat back with a smile. "What? Don't look so shocked and angry. It's a valid question."

"That girl is nothing but trouble," Sharon said. "Always was."

"We'll get to you in a minute, Sharon," Alex said, waving her comment away. "I need Danny's answer."

"Fine," the other man spat. "I didn't care if she was pregnant or not. Why should I? It's not like my life was affected. There was no way Dad was going to let a skanky bimbo have any part of our fortune or business." The second the words were out of Danny's mouth, Merrily knew he'd made a mistake.

"I see," Alex said. He let go of Merrily's hand and picked up the napkin from his lap to blot his mouth. When he raised his gaze back to Danny, there was death in his eyes. "Remind me to come back to you in a few minutes." Alex spoke softly, his tone even, though not quite as controlled. "Dan, how well do you know what your family does in private?"

"More than they'd like," was his clipped answer.

"I'm going to need you to elaborate." The smile Alex gave him was shark-like.

For long, long moments the two men stared at each other, a contest of wills. Merrily could hardly breathe for the tension in the air.

In her ear, Giovanni murmured, "Not a word..." while the silence stretched on and on.

Finally, Dan sat back from the table. "What do you want to know?"

"I want the answer to my question, Dan. How well do you know what your family does in private?"

"We don't have to sit here and take this," Sharon snapped. She started to rise from her chair, but Dan stopped her with a hand on her arm. Danny bared his teeth at Alex.

"You're on questionable ground as it is, Danny." Alex pointed at him. "Your best play is to stay seated and keep your mouth shut."

Dan finally spoke. "Is this about the merger?"

Alex smiled brightly. "Of course! What else would it be about?"

"It just seems that you're trying to pry into our personal lives. Our past relationship with your fiancée is just that. Past."

"True, of course. I just need to know that you are aware of what your family does in private. I mentioned before that we detected Danny's hand in your company's books. I want to know if you're aware of what he's done, and how you plan to rectify that particular situation."

Looking as if he finally understood what Alex was getting at, Dan's face relaxed slightly. "I know everything. He embezzled a few hundred thousand from the company and tried to cover it up with a little creative accounting. I knew it and stopped him before he could do more. He's paying back what he siphoned."

"A few hundred *thousand*?" Alex laughed. "Are you sure about that figure?"

Dan grew still before sighing. "Fine. He stole twenty-six million, two hundred thirty-three thousand dollars before I stopped him. But I'm serious when I said he was paying the company back."

"I doubt Danny Boy over there could pay for a candy bar without you helping him. You're wealthy, but I doubt even you have that kind of money."

"Believe what you want, Petrov," Dan bit out.

"Honestly, Dan, you can't blame me for needing some answers. If I'm supposed to just turn over my robotics program over to you, I need reassurance it will be safe. I told you. I protect the greater company."

"Fine. I know everything. I know my wife is having an affair with one of my vice presidents." Sharon gasped but wisely kept quiet otherwise. "I know they embezzled ten point four million from the company she helped me build, not because she knew the money wasn't all mine but because she felt it was part hers even if she left me. I know my son was aware of exactly who he was taking from -- he just never thought he'd get caught. And I know --" Dan finally ran out of steam, slumping back in the chair as if defeated "-- I know there will be hell to pay if I don't make up what they stole before my... investors... find out."

Alex gave a sympathetic nod. "Good, Dan. That's good. I appreciate you trusting *us* with that." The praise made it seem like it had come from a priest after a confession. Or maybe like an errant child confessing something to long-suffering parents. "It seems as if you truly know your family and their... skeletons."

"What do you want, Petrov? There's nothing you can do to us worse than what my investors will do to us if I don't replace the money Danny and Sharon took."

"Again, we'll get back to that." Alex focused his gaze on Sharon next. Merrily was more confident now, seeing Alex work and how he obviously knew the answers to the questions he asked before he voiced them. If she was petty for enjoying watching Alex take down the Maddisons, then she'd own it proudly. They'd cost her everything. Though, looking back, if they hadn't insisted she get an abortion, hadn't bribed her mother with enough money to support her drug habit for a long while, she wouldn't have met Alex, and Rose might not be as well off as she was today. Merrily's mother kicking her out of the house was probably the best thing that could have happened to her.

"Sharon," he said, sounding greatly disappointed. "You don't like Merrily, do you." It was a statement. Not a question.

"Little whore. She tried to ruin my son. My *family*. You heard Danny. She probably had no idea who the father of her little whelp was. I was protecting my family." Sharon managed to sound regal, justified in whatever actions Alex was about to make her own up to.

"I see." Alex sounded mild enough, but Merrily saw the tension running through him with every word out of the woman's mouth. This time, it was Merrily reaching for Alex, laying a hand on his arm and gripping gently. Alex gave her a tight smile. "I know, love. I'll be good." Again, he focused on Sharon. "Was it you who approached Merrily? Or Daniel?"

"I approached Merrily," Dan said. "I told her it would be better for all concerned for her to get rid of the pregnancy. She wasn't getting a single dime of money from me or my son."

"And when she refused?"

"I gave her mother the money for an abortion. Paid her twice what one would cost so she could take care of Merrily afterward."

"And by 'take care of,' you meant..."

Dan opened his mouth to answer, not looking at Merrily, but not meeting Alex's gaze either. Before he could, however, Sharon gave an exasperated huff. "I told her mother to have her fixed while they were getting rid of the baby."

Merrily gasped, unable to hide her shock and outrage. She snatched her hand away from Alex and stood abruptly, not sure exactly what she was going to do, but knowing she was about to unleash hell on someone.

"Not now, Merrily," Giovanni commanded in her ear. "Excuse yourself and go to Rose if you can't stay silent. This is critical."

With great effort, Merrily smoothed her dress and faced Alex. "I apologize, Alex." She took a deep breath and sat once more, reaching for her wineglass and taking a hefty pull with a small gasp. Alex took her other hand and, once again, brought her fingers to his lips to place several gentle kisses there.

"Well, it's not like she'd be a fit mother for any child," Sharon continued. "It was a sound choice. Though, perhaps knowing she's unable to have children you're rethinking your offer of marriage?" Sharon looked nearly triumphant. "You can do so much better than a girl like that."

Alex took a sip of his own wine. He didn't let go of her hand. Instead, he regarded Sharon over his glass. "Why would I rethink our engagement? Even if she were unable to give me an heir, I'd never leave her. The fact is, I'm almost hesitant about trying to get her pregnant just now. We've had such a short time together I find I want to enjoy her for a while and get to know her better. Merrily is an angel to my devil."

He winked at Merrily, though she knew he was anything but lighthearted at the moment. She got the feeling it was meant only to reassure her, not to convey any kind of private joke.

"Okay, that's not entirely true. I look forward to seeing her grow big with my child. However soon or distant that time may be." He gave her a look so full of feeling Merrily would have blushed if her stomach hadn't been so tied into knots. She was certain she was pale as a ghost. "Since you've proven you know everything your family does in private," he addressed Dan, "I'm going to assume you knew about this, or at least a version of it."

Dan scrubbed a hand over his face wearily. "I did, though I never intended for the extra money to be used to sterilize Merrily. Only for her mother to make sure she was comfortable."

"Too bad *you* won't be able to knock her up," Danny sneered at Alex. "Apparently, I'm the only one man enough for that, and I made her get rid of it. Do you want to know why?" He leaned forward, pointing at Merrily in a stabbing gesture. "Because she's nothing but trash. And garbage should never reproduce." He finally took a breath, sitting back in his chair with a gloating smile.

Silence.

"And, that's the cue to send in Mr. Black," Giovanni said.

Chapter Nine

Merrily jumped at the sound of Giovanni's voice in her ear. She'd forgotten he was listening to everything. She was so embarrassed her face should have been flaming. She couldn't look at any of them. She didn't think Alex saw her the way Danny described, but what did she know? He'd made promises, told her he meant to make a place for her in his home, but no matter what he said just before they had sex, there was always the specter in her head that he was only giving her a place in his life in return for sex.

At least, that's what her brain said. Her heart said he was growing to care for her as much as she was him. Now, she had to face her father as well as Danny's accusations and assertions. "Just hang in there a little longer, Merrily," Giovanni encouraged.

"Just get this over with," she hissed, beyond caring if anyone heard her. If she made it through this, she'd never complain about anything as long as she lived.

A door slid open to their right, behind the Maddisons. Steve Black, Merrily's father, walked in with Azriel urging him forward. Though dressed in a suit and tie, the older man looked worse for wear. Merrily might have had a pang that her father had been hurt, but it was quickly doused when she remembered that he had probably had at least a part in putting her and Rose in danger in the first place.

"Merrily!" Her father started to veer off, but Azriel steered him on to his seat across the table, clamping a hand on her father's shoulder and forced him back to the chair beside Danny. "Let me go! I need to go to my daughter."

"Not now, buddy," Azriel said, forcing him into a chair and pouring him a glass of wine. "Sit. Eat. Enjoy the company." Azriel grinned, looking over their guests. "We're all just one big happy family here, aren't we, Dan?"

Dan obviously knew when to keep his mouth shut. He just sat there, looking angry and more than a little defeated.

"My Merrily," Alex said, stroking her hand gently. It wasn't until that moment Merrily realized a tear had slid from her eyelashes to her cheek. Angrily, she brushed it away. Before she could set her hand back on the table, however, Alex snagged it. He kissed the tip of the finger with the offending moisture, a tender, intimate gesture Merrily appreciated more than she ever thought she could. "It's nearly Rose's bedtime. Do you want to go to her? You know she likes you there when she goes to bed. I can finish this ugly business if you want me to."

Merrily stilled. He'd given her a way out, but he'd also mentioned Rose to everyone around them. Her father knew, but the other three obviously thought she'd aborted her daughter and was unable to have more children.

"Wait." Sharon lifted a hand. "Who's Rose?"

"Bellarose," Alex said mildly. "Her daughter. Soon to be *my* daughter."

Danny perked up, his eyes sparkling, smelling blood in the water.

In that moment, Merrily realized three things. First, Alex had purposely told them about Rose with the idea that Danny would seize on the fact that Rose would be Alex's heir. Second, Alex fully intended on marrying her and adopting Rose as his daughter because... Thirdly, he was about to get every single person on Rose's paternal side to sign away their rights to Rose, effectively cutting them out of Alex's fortune.

Her heart pounded and she was sure she was going to pass out. "I'm good," she managed to say. "I'll see this through. I just have one question for you, Alex."

"Anything, my Merrily."

"When this is over, how many of these signatures are going to be strictly necessary? Because I know there are consequences coming."

"Oh!" Giovanni sounded like he was doing everything he could not to cackle with glee. "Good one, Merrily. Alex, remind me never to piss your woman off!"

"Girl's got a point, Alex," Azriel said. He didn't bother to hide his mirth.

Alex merely shrugged. "That's hard to say. Which is why I'm not taking any chances."

She put her shoulders back and sat up straighter. "I suppose that's fair enough. This is important. Rose will be fine without me one night. You know how much she loves Mrs. McDonald and Gloria."

"I do indeed." He smiled as if remembering something amusing. Attention back on the four people at the table, Alex's expression hardened. "So." He raised a hand to Azriel, who placed blue-backed legal documents in front of each guest. "As you have probably figured out, Rose is the child of the pregnancy all of you agreed should be terminated."

"I didn't --" Steve, her father, tried to argue, but Alex cut him off.

"Steve, you may not have actively sought to force Merrily into that course of action, but you didn't prevent it."

"Was this the whole reason for the meeting tonight?" Dan was angry, no question. "Is it why you humiliated me tonight?" He bit out his question sharply. "Not because you were worried about your company. You never intended for this merger to happen, did you?"

"Not in the least." Alex's tone was abrupt and completely unapologetic. "You're right. The merger was never going to happen. I needed to get your books legally so I could see what kind of situation Merrily and Rose were in." His grin was completely at odds with how Merrily knew he felt. "We've been watching you and your company for several months now. We weren't quite ready to move on you because we hadn't figured out who you were laundering for, but the threat to my Merrily and little Rose escalated things a bit. By gaining access to your books, I could at least see the amount of money involved and get an idea of what I needed to do next. As to the rest... I merely wanted to make the point that none of you deserve to ever meet Rose. If you do, however, it will be with no rights to her. Period."

"Rose is my granddaughter," her father said, tears in his voice, his face lined with worry. "I warned Merrily they would be coming for them so she could run before they were caught."

Alex stilled. Then, slowly, he turned to face her father. "Be very sure you want to do this, Steve."

"I admit, I've not been the best father over the years, but I love my daughter. I risked my life to tell her about the danger headed her way."

"Dad," Merrily's voice was soft. "He's giving you a way to keep this to yourself. He already knows what your true intentions were so just let it go. If you try to gloss it over, he's going to call your bluff."

Steve looked as if he couldn't believe Merrily was taking Alex's side over his. "Has he poisoned you against me, then? I love you, Merrily. I stayed away to protect you from the realities of my life." He wiped a hand over his face. "I've always loved you."

"Dad..."

"Tell me about your employers, Mr. Black." Merrily knew Alex would be as merciless with her father as he'd been with the Maddisons. She wasn't sure she wanted that, but knew it was unavoidable.

"This isn't your business," Steve snapped. "This is between me and my daughter!"

"Answer him, Dad," Merrily said, her voice unsteady.

"They're bad people. Which is why I kept my distance from you."

"If that's true, how did they find out about us?" Merrily asked quietly. She knew Alex would drag it out of Steve if she didn't. He'd done all the heavy lifting until now. This was her responsibility.

"You can leave this to Alex, Merrily." Giovanni was a soft voice in her ear, but she ignored him.

Steve hesitated. "Your mom knew. She probably told them when they were torturing her."

"Mom kicked me out of the house when I refused to get the abortion. She had no idea where I was or if I'd actually had a child. The only way they could have found us is if you told them."

"I didn't tell them *anything*!"

Merrily's heart was breaking. Of the people in this room, the only one who had any kind of blood tie with her cared nothing for her. She was a pawn in his life. A means to an end. Alex and his band of Demons, however, truly valued her. She knew that in the way they all treated her. With respect and dignity. Like she was a valued member of their team. Of their family. She had a choice now. She'd choose to believe.

"When you came to warn me, you knew they were watching you. You didn't have to tell them anything. My guess is, you knew I could make a good showing of falling off the grid. Probably expected me to do more than I did since I'd told you some of the things I could do with computers. You figured they'd spend time and resources chasing me and give you time to figure something out." She held her father's gaze. "Is that about right?" To his credit, he didn't refute her. "Sign the document, Dad. Just… sign it."

"I'm not fucking signing anything!" Danny smirked, thinking he'd won something. Merrily knew better.

"That's not a good idea," she responded quietly. "Alex and I haven't known each other long, but one thing I know with absolute certainty is that he's just looking for a reason to make the remainder of your life a living hell, Danny. Signing that paper and leaving us alone will give him a reason to… maybe not see you harmed."

"Are you threatening me?" The longer this went on, the more hostile Danny was going to get. She knew this from the time they were together in high school. "Because I'm sure I can sue your ass for that."

"You're not going to sue anyone, Danny Boy." Alex chuckled. "In fact, there is a very good chance you won't live to see tomorrow, whether or not you sign that document."

Dan reached for the document in front of him. Scanned it. Then signed in his bold, flourishing script. "Sign it, Sharon. Danny."

Sharon threw Merrily a malicious glance. "Looks like you landed the big fish, honey. I may sign this under duress, but that kid of yours is still my flesh and blood. I'll figure out a way around this and sue you for all the pain and suffering you're putting me through by not letting me see my granddaughter. When I'm in front of a judge, I'll be appropriately distraught. I guarantee you, I'll get my rights to Rose." She glanced at Alex. "And my share of Rose's inheritance."

When Sharon reached for her document, something inside Merrily snapped. She grabbed her crab fork and lunged, planting the two-pronged utensil between Sharon's thumb and forefinger. Sharon shrieked, snatching back her hand. Merrily laid her palms flat on the table, still standing.

"Sign the fucking paper, Sharon." Merrily bit out the words between clenched teeth. "You try to work your way out of that document, I swear by God and sunny Jesus I will be the one you answer to. You won't have to worry about Alex, or whoever Dan's in bed with. When you threaten my daughter in any way, implied or otherwise, I'm the *demon* you should fear."

* * *

If it was possible for Alex to be more turned on by a woman, he couldn't imagine how. When Merrily stabbed Sharon, he could only watch in fascination as events unfolded. No one else seemed to be able to function, either.

Finally, Azriel managed to find his voice. "If you decide she's not the one for you, Alex, please tell me first. Because I'm sure she's the one for me." The bastard sounded awestruck.

"You keep your fucking hands to yourself, Azriel. That's *my* woman, and I will fight you to the death for her." Alex was serious -- which Azriel knew -- but he tried to keep his tone light. No sense muddying the waters. There was a goal and, if Azriel was right, a finite time to reach it. They expected the Brotherhood to show up soon, and he wanted the business of Rose out of the way before they did.

"You're all crazy," Sharon spat. "Every single one of you!"

"Probably." Alex didn't care what the woman thought. Hell, she was probably right. "Please sign the document."

She did. Danny, however, still sat back in his chair, arms crossed over his chest defiantly. An evil sneer spread across his face, and Alex knew there was no way he was lifting a finger to save him from whatever fate the Brotherhood had in store for him.

"Last chance, Danny," he said, all traces of amusement gone. "Once this starts, it's out of my hands."

"There is nothing you can say or do that would make me sign away rights to my own child."

Alex could almost pity the man. Rose was his daughter, a child he truly hadn't known existed until a few minutes ago.

"That girl is my key to Easy Street, and I won't give her up willingly."

And just like that, all sympathy evaporated. The man was truly a monster. "So be it."

"Perfect timing." Giovanni's voice was quiet but insistent in his ear. "Ben's reporting a car coming to the gate. I've instructed them to let it pass without confrontation. Sebastian says there are several armed men at the border wall of the property settling in to wait. Says the only mistake they've made so far was shooting one of his drones out of the sky -- otherwise he might not have even noticed them."

"So." Alex looked at Merrily. "They're on their way. Go to Rose."

"What about you?"

Bless the woman. He could see the anxiety in her face. For *him*. He smiled at her, rising and urging her to do the same. "I'll be fine. I've done this a few times, you know."

She seemed to flow into him, wrapping her arms around him and burying her face in his chest. Alex clung to her tightly, loving that she didn't hesitate to show affection in front of the others. This had been hard for her. He wasn't going to pretend otherwise. Far harder than she wanted anyone to know.

Alex knew. She'd been stripped bare, her past laid out for everyone to judge. He was sure she fully expected everyone to side with the Maddisons. "Baby, you know everyone here believes you. Right?"

She looked up at him, a small, sad smile on her face. "It doesn't matter, Alex. I realize now that it never did. All that matters is that Rose and I are safe. Thanks to you, that's possible now." She laid her hand on his cheek. "Whatever happens next, know that I'm proud -- so very proud -- to know you, Alex. Rose was right. You and your brothers are truly Angels."

"You might rethink that after tonight, love." He cupped her face in his hands before taking a tender kiss from her sweet lips. "You know where the safe room is. Rose is waiting there with Ruth and Gloria. Go take care of them for me."

"Promise you'll come get us when this is over. Promise you'll be the one to come to us."

God, he loved this woman! "I promise, my Merrily."

She kissed him this time. In the background, Alex heard Danny laying down a disgusted commentary. One he would pay for soon, likely with his life. Then she walked to the back, to the elevator that would take her to her daughter and safety.

Alex watched every step she made away from him. She took his heart with her, which made his job that much easier. When he turned back to face the group at the table, he knew death shone in his eyes.

"Sign, Danny," he snapped. "Now!"

Danny was the only holdout. Even Merrily's dad had signed with little protest after Merrily called him out. Danny hadn't moved from where he sat with an arrogant smirk on his face, arms crossed over his chest. "Go fuck yourself, Petrov."

Alex glanced up. He knew where the representatives from the Brotherhood would enter. Giovanni was guiding them through the manor much the way he had Merrily and Rose.

"They're following my lead willingly, Alex. Just outside the dining room now." Giovanni, ever the eyes and ears of the team, had this covered.

The door opened. In walked five intimidating-looking men. Four of them were covered head to toe in black. The fifth was in the middle, dressed in black except for a yellow sash around his middle, and no head or face covering.

"The guy in the middle isn't the leader. He's the decoy. The leader will be to his right, slightly behind him. The first guy. He's the most dangerous of the group. Keep on him at all times."

Azriel glanced at Alex and nodded his agreement. This could go bad fast.

"Gentlemen," Alex greeted, making a sweeping gesture at the table. "Please join us."

The "decoy" waved him off. "We're here for your guests." He indicated the Maddisons and Steve. "Don't interfere, and no one gets hurt."

"While I have no problem in you taking the four of them, this is my home. I can't simply let you do whatever you want."

"I respect that." The man looked to Azriel. "Good to see you again, Brother."

"Malcolm." Azriel was tense but congenial.

"Your guests took something that didn't belong to them."

"I'm fully aware of the extent of the damage." Alex hadn't expected things to be this... non-violent. Oh, well. It would probably go south in a few minutes. He was sure he'd get to punch someone before it was over. "My only question is in regard to Merrily Dane."

Malcolm shrugged. "The woman and her daughter are no concern of ours unless Mr. Black proves uncooperative."

"What do you need from him? This ends now. I want the threat to Merrily and Rose gone tonight."

"It's quite simple. I want the money he stole from our employer."

"I didn't take anything," Steve said instantly.

"Do you have the total missing? Because Danny took quite a chunk."

"We are fully aware of the amount stolen by both Daniel and Sharon Maddison. The rest we tracked to Mr. Black."

Alex looked to Azriel, who shrugged. "The Brotherhood has nearly as many resources as we have, and highly intelligent people doing their forensic accounting. It's possible they missed something, but I wouldn't bet on it."

"Mr. Black." Alex turned back to the other man. "I can't help you. Your only hope now is to turn over the money and pray for mercy."

"That's a lie!" Steve insisted. "I didn't steal anything."

"If not you, then who?" Alex didn't really care, but he wanted the threat to Merrily and Rose gone. Tonight.

"How should I know? I just delivered the load I was given to the appointed drop off. No questions asked. I turned it over to my contacts and left. Follow the trail. I'm sure those two guys know something."

"We did." Malcolm didn't take his eyes from Alex. "His contact was two of the Brotherhood. They counted the money before Mr. Black left as instructed. Mr. Black signed for the drop off the same as he did for pickup. He has copies of both documents. The numbers are there."

Instantly, Steve's face drained of blood and Alex knew he was caught. Waving his hand, he said, "You can't fix stupid. He's all yours."

"And the Maddisons," Malcolm was insistent. "They have a considerable debt that has yet to be paid."

"What will you do with them? Steve included."

Malcolm's face turned hard. "Exact payment."

"You can't let them take us!" Sharon clearly looked terrified. "If you do, you're just at much to blame for whatever they do to us as they are!"

Alex smiled at the older woman. "Sharon, my dear, you can't begin to imagine how much I really don't give a fuck."

Then the Brotherhood took possession of the four of them. Alex meant what he'd said. He really didn't give a shit what happened to them. Danny fought hard, as did Sharon. All it got them was a beating. Fortunately, it only took one blow to the face to knock Sharon out. Alex got the feeling that was as merciful as the men would be with the woman. Malcolm's face screwed up with distaste, as if he didn't like striking a woman any more than Alex would in similar circumstances. Except, with this particular woman, knowing all she'd done -- or tried to do to Merrily -- he would be able to get past the fact she was a woman with ease. Danny, however, didn't receive such gentle handling. By the time they dragged his limp and bleeding body out of the manor, Alex was certain Danny fully comprehended what he was facing.

"Malcolm," he called to the other man. "What about Merrily and Rose?"

He faced Alex, his face expressionless. "We know Mr. Black has little love for his daughter. His reason for keeping contact with her was his contingency plan, keep everyone looking for her while he ran. I'll tell our employer she is of no use to us, but he'll likely still insist we go after her."

"How much would it take for your employer to forget about the girls?"

"Mr. Black's debt is close to fifteen million. The usual interest rate is three hundred percent."

"Forty-five million, and your boss leaves Merrily alone. You can guarantee that."

"You have my word."

Alex looked to Azriel. If Malcolm's word was questionable, he'd know.

Azriel only nodded.

"Then tell your boss I'll make it an even fifty. He can do whatever he feels appropriate with Mr. Black, but Merrily and Rose are both off limits. Forever." He took a step toward Malcolm. "Or I find him."

Malcolm gave a slight smile. "If Azriel follows you, I know the threat is not idle. I'll accept your offer on his behalf. I'll contact Azriel with delivery instructions. Consider the matter closed."

"Good. Get your trash off my lawn."

Malcolm barked a laugh. "As you wish." Then the Brotherhood was gone.

* * *

When Alex opened the door to the sub-level-three safe room, Merrily's heart leapt. Everyone had gathered there, protecting the children while making it seem as non-threatening as possible. It struck Merrily that they apparently did this often, given the order with which everything proceeded. At no time had Rose been frightened, and she kept Snowball and Smokey with her with no problem. Alex had a grin on his face and swung Merrily around when she jumped into his arms. Rose had danced around them, unsure why her mother was so happy, but willing to play. Smokey and Snowball had meowed in protest at Rose dumping them out of her lap but remained where she'd left them. It was late, and most of the children were asleep. Rose probably would have been too, but she was very attuned to Merrily.

Alex had suggested they all go back to Merrily's suite and get Rose settled, Ruth and Gloria included. Which meant Alex intended for her to go with him to his suite the minute the little girl was asleep. Which was fine with her.

Sure enough, an hour later, Merrily found herself naked in Alex's bed. The man was insatiable. But then, so was she when it came to Alex.

Once they'd spent themselves, they lay in a sweaty heap on the bed, Alex solidly on top of Merrily. She loved his weight pressing her into the bed. Loved how he was so dominant during sex. Merrily still had the beautiful ring he'd given her before the confrontation with the Maddisons snugly on her finger. She didn't want to remove it though she knew she needed to. It had to be worth a fortune.

"I suppose you'll be wanting your ring back," she said, stroking her hand down the side of his face. "It's so lovely I didn't want to take it off, but it's not mine."

He raised his head, giving her an impatient look. "Why would you ever take it off? You better *not* take it off!"

"Alex, it's an engagement ring. Not only are we not engaged, we barely know each other."

"And you knew when I got every single person related to Rose other than you to sign over their rights to her I intended on marrying you and adopting her."

She blinked. "Well, yes. But…"

Alex cut her off with a hard kiss. Which led to another. Which led to more sex. Which led to more pleasure. By the time he'd finished with her a second time, Merrily was too worn out to protest.

"Consider that my official proposal," Alex murmured. "We'll be married as soon as I can arrange it. Adopting Rose should go rather quickly as well."

"You're something else, Alexei Petrov." Merrily snuggled closer to him. "I don't think I could love you more if I had known you for years."

"I guess that's something we'll find out. Because I plan on being with you for many, many years."

"I thought my life was good. It was good." She smiled at Alex. "Then, along came a demon and everything changed."

"For the good, I hope."

"Now my life is better than good. It's complete."

"My Merrily."

"My Alex." She drifted off, happier than she could ever remember being.

Who said demons were bad?

Marteeka Karland

Erotic romance author by night, emergency room tech/clerk by day, Marteeka Karland works hard to drive everyone in her life completely and totally nuts. She has been creating stories from her warped imagination since she was in the third grade. Her love of writing blossomed throughout her teenage years until it developed into the totally unorthodox and irreverent style her English teachers tried so hard to rid her of.

Marteeka on Changeling: changelingpress.com/marteeka-karland-a-39

Changeling Press E-Books

More Sci-Fi, Fantasy, Paranormal, and BDSM adventures available in e-book format for immediate download at ChangelingPress.com -- Werewolves, Vampires, Dragons, Shapeshifters and more -- Erotic Tales from the edge of your imagination.

What are E-Books?

E-books, or electronic books, are books designed to be read in digital format -- on your desktop or laptop computer, notebook, tablet, Smart Phone, or any electronic e-book reader.

Where can I get Changeling Press E-Books?

Changeling Press e-books are available at ChangelingPress.com, Amazon, Apple Books, Barnes & Noble, and Kobo/Walmart.

ChangelingPress.com

Printed in Great Britain
by Amazon